BODY

ON THE

ISLAND

A gripping murder mystery packed with twists

VICTORIA DOWD

Smart Woman's Mystery Book 2

JOFFE BOOKS

Joffe Books, London
www.joffebooks.com

First published in Great Britain in 2021

© Victoria Dowd

ISBN: 978-1-78931-663-6

For Kev, Delilah, James, Sarah & Catherine

CHAPTER 1: SHIPWRECKED

As I'm drowning, I see my dad's murdered eyes below me. They are wide in warning. I hear his voice below the waves. *'Do not come over to this side. There is nothing good here, Ursula. Stay. Stay alive.'*

'Stay alive,' I call back. 'Stay alive.'

'I'm trying!' It's not Dad who answers but Mother's voice shouting back at me, her mouth filling with icy saltwater, before she is thrown out from me on another high wave.

'Don't die!' I shout.

'That had occurred to me.' Her eyes are wide like Dad's. She spins out from me as if she's been carelessly thrown away.

'Mother!' I scream. 'Hold my hand.'

She reaches and grabs me. We are so small among this broken sea. The freezing spray pits my skin.

'Ursula,' Mother shouts. 'Stay with me!' Always a command. She scans the mineral black waters quickly. 'Charlotte?' Her mouth is wide but the sound is washed away in another wave.

I see a hand rise up across the bow of the listing boat. Aunt Charlotte's fist, strong and capable above the waves.

'Mirabelle?' Mother calls.

No response.

'Mirabelle?'

There are heads floating all around, rising high on the waves before plunging down fast, roller-coastered against the wet shale sky. The water is bitter, and I'm pushed under again. The cold shocks my head as if I'm being baptized in ice water. I can't feel or move my limbs, yet I'm moving so fast that my eyes, raw with burning salt, are unable to process the changing snapshots of sky and water. I catch a glimpse of Mother's face again, her eyes are ripe with fear.

Somewhere in another great swell, I lose Mother's hand.

'Mother? *Mother*? Mother!'

I am that lost child in a crowd again, feeling her hand slip from mine.

I'm falling.

I hear screams and see the faces of my other travelling companions full of panic. They don't seem to see me. I lock with a pair of bewildered eyes for a moment. A woman's, sea-green and two perfect mirrors of the water. Her head turns before I can make out the face. Then the hands grab her.

I'm thrown high again by another wave.

The hands are on Green Eyes's shoulders, making their way spider-fast to the crown of her head. Her eyes are wide and pleading now. Fear, desperation reflect on their surface. Then the thin-boned hands push down on her delicate head and the green eyes disappear beneath a spume of white water. Her small hands reach up and twist with tiny dancer's fingers.

Whoever reaches out and pushes the woman down again has their back to me.

She struggles free for a moment, her mouth gasping above the water, her head tilted back against the waves. The mouth lingers open as if caught on a word that is instantly swept away. Her head is forced below once more.

In that moment, it's as if I'm looking at them from the other side of a window. I see the final push below the waves. Those perfect stained-glass eyes linger on the surface of my thoughts before dissolving into the sea. She is gone.

2

Another swathe of water covers me. I'm washed below the waves and carried. I claw to the surface and scream out, 'Stop!' There's no one there.

Green Eyes has gone, eaten by the sea. Was there even a man there at all or something else that's in these angry waves? I look down. I'm being crazy. I try to calm my fast breaths. There were hands that pushed her down, I know there were. But whoever it was has collapsed into nothing but foam.

I can't find the light of the green eyes anymore either. They linger in my imagination, thick with a film of watery fear, pleading for help. I was the last thing she saw before the sea took her. What can I do?

I feel the panic rise. I swing my head from left to right. Nothing. I try to shout but another great slope of water collapses on me, forcing me down. This time, I don't surface.

I dream of Dad's open arms beneath the waves. They are balm to me, weaving effortlessly through the fierce currents. I close my eyes so I can't see the body falling lifelessly towards the sea's deep floor.

I can't see Mother or Aunt Charlotte anymore. I even look for Mirabelle. But they are all gone. I look into the dark green forest below. Such tiny, clean white bones we'll make one day on this ocean floor's abyss — then we shall form small fields of fragile coral. It is a calming thought as I drift down.

But not yet. There is more life to contend with. Death will have to wait. Death is always waiting.

CHAPTER 2: TWENTY-FOUR DAYS BEFORE THE SHIPWRECK

'I'm not going. I'm not doing it. I never will. Does that answer your question thoroughly enough?'

It was one of Mother's negative days. She attempted to raise her eyebrows but was cosmetically challenged. She'd paid a recent visit to Brighter You in a hope that they could make her look less disappointed with life. Mother likes to visit salons that would sound more at home in a sci-fi novel. Whatever they'd done, it hadn't worked. It would be better if they were called *Tighter You*, although a name like that could give the wrong impression, I suppose. But it would be more accurate given the only effect they'd managed to achieve was that her face looked as shrink-wrapped as a Sainsbury's chicken breast.

'All I'm saying, Mother, is that we need to be tougher. We need to get out there and be strong and learn how to—'

'What, gut a fish? Piss on our hands?'

'Piss on our hands?' I frowned. 'What the hell have you been watching?'

'You know, all that Bear Grilling nonsense.'

'It's not cooking endangered species — you know that don't you? He's *called* Bear Grylls.' I watched her confusion

4

unfold slowly like a used paper napkin. 'That's his name, Mother.'

'Of course I know that! I don't care what he does or how naked he is when he does it, I'm not going to put myself in harm's way. And I'm certainly not stepping away from mobile phone signal or Wi-Fi ever in my life again. You have no idea the therapy bills I still struggle to meet.' She folded her arms, caught sight of a bobble on the cashmere and, with the concentration of a cat, instantly became distracted.

'He's still charging you? I mean, I thought, what with you two, you know . . .'

'What?'

'Well, does he charge all his girlfriends?'

The Look. Mother's principal weapon of minor destruction, issued randomly yet effectively, is *The Look*. It creates that deathly moment filmmakers employ when the bomb drops and there's a silence, a pause where everyone braces for the destruction about to unfold.

'I'm not his *girlfriend*.'

'I don't know what else you want me to call someone your age who sleeps with their therapist. Desperate? Pathetic? Needy?'

She tried to look shocked, but Mother's skin didn't have room for extra emotions. Recently, it had begun to take on the look of a death mask.

I'm not sure what Bob the Therapist would make of me imagining such things. I don't share my real thoughts with him since he's Mother's therapist too. He did her a two-for-one deal. That was before Bob and my mother started *seeing* each other. He just feeds back everything I tell him to Mother. Basically, he's like Mother's paid spy inside my head. He thinks I don't know what he's up to. My best lie so far has been that I've won the lottery but I'm not telling Mother because I don't want it to *change* us. Obviously, he told her immediately and within a week she was doing the 'big shop' at Fortnum & Mason and giving me knowing little smiles.

'All I know is that you're sleeping with a guy who is then telling you how you should feel. Doesn't it seem remarkably . . .'

She waited.

'. . . *impolite* of him to then send a bill? Isn't that a little bit like a surgeon shooting you and then asking for payment when he's removed the bullet?'

'He's fulfilling a need.'

'How many needs have you got now, Mother?'

She looked somewhere beyond the window, as if she was being wistful, although I knew she was watching the neighbour and checking the number of bottles the woman was putting in the recycling. Mother takes ours out in the dead of night to avoid any judgement. One of her greatest life skills, which she has honed over many years of practice, is being able to stack bottles absolutely silently.

'Mother, I'm asking what you're going to do with the rest of this life you've been gifted?'

'*I* haven't been gifted anything. I survived *That House* by virtue of my stealth, grit, determination and—'

'You're not talking to the papers now, Mother. I was there, remember? "Blind luck" and "chance" don't sound quite as catchy though, do they? Words like that don't sell as many papers.'

She watched me as closely as a hypnotist. I know this because she sent me to one of those as well. When it didn't work, she blamed my 'obstructive brain.' It was exactly the same as when she sent me to someone to 'read my colours.' Mine came back as black, and she said I'd done it on purpose.

'Oh, and what a marvellously heroic sidekick you made!' she sneered.

'Sidekick?'

'Listen to me, Little Miss No-Money-or-Pennies, the cash from those stories is what keeps a roof over your head. Don't forget that. If I have a loose grip on the truth, it's for your benefit.'

6

Bob the Therapist has recommended that I should pause sometimes with Mother and just let the silence flow. It's one of the few useful things he's ever said. But Mother doesn't do meaningful silences.

'We survived being murdered, so why not make a little money out of it? God knows, there's no other pot of gold waiting for us. Your angst poetry isn't going to keep us. And don't go thinking we were left anything by your father.'

The word landed like a grenade between us. We both looked down to the floor as if he was still lying there. The fact that he was taken from us is a daily ache — our mutual scar that binds and numbs us. There's always a lingering voice wondering how long he'd have lived if he hadn't been killed. It's the black noise behind every day.

I often imagine a parallel world exists where he hasn't been murdered and I'm living with him, completely oblivious to this post-death world I exist in now. I watch that other self from the shadows like a spurned lover, hiding, spying on life — the life I could have had. And I loathe it.

I'm fascinated by other people's happiness now. It's a new hobby — watching happy people. I watch the children go to school, screaming, running, unaware their parent could casually fall under the wheels of that passing car. I watch the parent taking their teen shopping — the parent who could fold in on themselves, an undetected illness, an unseen killer who strikes without thought and suddenly they just blow away like ash. When Dad died, I googled how much cremated people weigh. I did Troubled Teen very well. Two kilograms, if you were wondering. It didn't matter anyway. They buried him — until they dug him up again. Technically, they *exhumed* him. There's no special occasion for that though. No standing round reminiscing with people you barely know.

All I have now are fragile images that actually weigh nothing at all. They're useless really — remnants of a life I barely remember, heavily embroidered to make them seem real and, let's be honest, mostly made up. Memories can be so delicate and easy to manipulate.

I just thank God I have Mother to correct my recollections and make them much less fanciful.

'Anyway, Mother, why are you watching something you think is a cookery show? You can't cook.' It's very important for both of us that we pull the conversation back round to something trivial.

'I *don't* cook. That is not the same as *can't*.' She tilted her head as if she'd said something important. It was a little seagull-esque — the bird, not the play. Mother doesn't do profound. She hates the theatre and says it's full of people trying to look intelligent. Which is not something that has ever troubled her.

'I suppose it's similar to shooting someone,' she continued, 'just because I don't, doesn't mean I can't.' Somehow, our conversations always seem to come back round to death.

'You can't. You haven't got a gun.'

'How do you know?'

'I go through your stuff.'

She looked shocked for my benefit. I'm well aware of the fact that she audits my belongings as well. It's a level of mistrust that keeps us on an even keel.

'How very—'

'Dare I? Because I've lost one parent to their secretive ways, I don't intend to lose another. That would be careless, wouldn't it? And if I'm not here, then who would be?'

'"Secretive?" That's certainly one word for your father.' She watched me, carefully deciding whether she should be flattered that I'd shown a glimmer of concern for her or annoyed that I was going through her stuff.

'And anyway, you can't cook. I know you can't.'

'Really? Just look around you.' She waved a casual hand across the vast cavern of our kitchen as if she was an estate agent in someone else's house. It was so white and gleaming that it was like sitting inside a giant igloo. 'Look at all the cookbooks.'

'They can't cook either. You just have them there to remind you it's a kitchen.'

8

Mother colour-codes our freezer — brown food, grey food, beige food, green food, greige food. Ingredients are irrelevant. She never eats it so she doesn't know it's inedible. Mother doesn't do food. Sometimes she heats things up, then Nutribullets them so they don't resemble food anymore. She hasn't Nutribulleted pizza yet, but that's down to a lack of imagination.

Unlike so many people who survive a near-death experience, Mother hasn't felt the need to reassess her life. She's just continued in the same mediocre vein as before, warming up ready meals that she never eats. The only difference is that now she can fund her lifestyle by selling ludicrous stories to newspapers greedy for as much death as possible.

But as Mother so often says, you can't live on the truth. And she's right. The simple truth was that last year we stayed in a house and four people were murdered while we were there. Mother and I, along with my Aunt Charlotte and Mirabelle, lived to tell our tales of the Slaughter House. Bridget and her dog, Mr Bojangles, also made it out alive and it really was a miracle that no one murdered them. The house was actually called Ambergris Towers but that didn't sound quite as salacious to the press. And that's all there is to it, really. An everyday story of death. Some people find it shocking, others just look the other way when they see us in the street, as if we might in some way be dangerous or bad luck. Perhaps we are.

Those of us who survived have had to find a new way of living. When you emerge from a life-threatening event, be it a train crash or a serial killer, it's like bursting from a chrysalis. You are changed irreparably. But then, who wants to be the same person all their life? I'm many people. Ursula Smart, survivor of the Slaughter House, is just one of them. I go by many names. All I can tell you is that we were a book club who went on an ill-conceived weekend away, where people died in a variety of gruesome ways. Book club stopped after that, but then most book clubs have a shelf-life. Perhaps ours ended in a more dramatic fashion than most but you'd be surprised the tales people now tell me about their book clubs.

You might think that I have now experienced my full quotient of dramatic horror. My dad died thirteen years ago and then there was the whole business of the Slaughter House last year. But people who live through a disaster somehow seem to attract even more tragedy, as if fate has found a new lightning rod. Calamity and chaos seem to gravitate towards certain individuals. I decided we should be ready for it next time.

And that is why I signed us up for a survival course.

CHAPTER 3: TWENTY-FOUR HOURS
BEFORE THE SHIPWRECK

I woke in the night to the sound of my own screaming. I was
in a strange place I didn't recognize. That's never good for me.

It was bone cold and the damp soaked through me. The
blankets were mildewed and worn thin with the rub of too
many strangers. When I opened my eyes, it had no effect at
all. It was still a dead black. This was not a living world. This
was a world for ghosts.

'*I know this place*,' my thoughts whispered.

'You know this place,' I answered out loud.

I was back in the Slaughter House with its rusty smell of
blood, an old sour taint that would never leave my memories.
It hung in the back cabinet of my mind, like a meat locker,
waiting for me to open the door and look inside again. The
ghosts wandered around the dark corridors in my head waiting for me to fall asleep, only to wake up with the bodies all
around me, frantically trying to find a way out.

'I know this place,' I shouted.

A thud. The fast scurry of rat-like feet on bare boards. In
an instant, I was blinded by the acid-yellow light.

'For Christ's sake, Ursula! I agreed to share a room with
you on the basis that you wouldn't be doing the whole "*I see dead*

people" routine again.' Mother was standing by the door, cross in cashmere — a signature look. Her finger hovered over the light switch as though she was about to ask if I had any last words.

'I was back there at Ambergris Towers. You remember, Mother, the Slaughter House where your friend proved what I'd always said about her? *She was not a good friend,*' I whispered.

'Ursula!'

'Christ, you can't still be protecting her. Don't "*Ursula*" me!'

'She's dead, *Ursula*!'

'Good.'

Mother gasped as if she thought she should sound shocked. Mother is never shocked.

'All I've done is have a few nightmares.'

'Yes, yes,' Mother sighed, as if sympathy might burn her tongue. 'Just a few *nightmares.*' She rolled her eyes. 'Bob's filled me in on all that *business.*' She sat down reluctantly on the end of my bed but kept her distance. She tried to soften her voice. 'I was there too, *remember*. But let's also remember that I warned you against coming on *this* trip *this* time. It was never going to quieten the demons, dragging us out here to a godforsaken motel in this Tartan Horror Story, was it dear?'

'Tartan Horror Story? You mean like the coat you bought me for Christmas?'

'Oh my God, that was Burberry!'

I shrugged, which is always unwise with Mother.

'Just look at the place! Even the décor is channelling *The Exorcist*. I've not seen this much brown furniture since we went to your Aunt Charlotte's filthy burrow.'

'We haven't been to Aunt Charlotte's since I was three!'

'She never changes the furniture.'

We paused for a moment to look across the faded room. Mother and I spend a lot of time like this, trying to make moments look meaningful.

'Well, at least Aunt Charlotte might like it here then.'

Mother shook her head. 'I doubt it. She's sharing with Mirabelle. I should imagine they'll be seeing who loses the will to live first.' She made a sound like laughter. As with all dictators, Mother doesn't like her friends and relatives to get on too well. It makes her feel redundant.

'I'm going to make some cocoa,' I said wearily.

'Good God, what century are you from? No one's said, "I'm going to make some cocoa" for fifty years!' she scoffed. 'Down the corridor on the right, there's a kitchenette next to the lavatory. Be careful, the rooms look interchangeable. I've brought some of my first-blush Darjeeling—'

'Flush, Mother. It's not embarrassed tea.'

She stared at me. 'Never, ever use the word "flush" in my presence again. Do you understand? I've spoken to Bob about it and he just thinks I'm sensitive to room temperature. I'm still very young! Now let me sleep. You can use the out-of-date chamomile and goji berry.'

'Generous.'

'Drink it there and *don't* put the light on when you come back.'

'How will I—'

'Use your mobile phone like everyone else from the twenty-first century.' She flicked off the light and I could have sworn the line of her white teeth lingered just a second longer in the darkness, like the Cheshire Cat.

The kitchenette was a mean little space, all defiant sparseness and, Mother was right, with its algae-green tiles, it did look very similar to the bathroom next door. A kettle, powdered milk and one mug had been lined up on the side. The single light bulb gave off a dingy, jaundiced light as if I really had stepped into a 1970s horror film.

Mother's luxury hamper sat incongruously on the peeling Formica. I flipped it open. Nothing really bore any resemblance to the kit list we had been provided with. Certainly, Sir Nigel Havers's vodka-soaked plums were not something anyone had specified — although it's hard to imagine a place where they would be a requirement. As with all the expensive foodstuffs Mother purchases, none of it had any nutritional value whatsoever. Mother's reaction to the kit list had been the same as everything else prior to the trip. 'I don't want to see it because I'm not going.'

* * *

I'd finally got her to look at it by telling her the new John Lewis Christmas ad was streaming on my laptop. When we saw the kit list though, I think it would be fair to say we were both quite surprised.

- Sleeping bag (I didn't admit to Mother that this was the first moment I'd realized it was a camping trip, but I did begin to wonder what else I might have overlooked when I'd booked it so impulsively. I decided not to share my misgivings with Mother.)
- Sleeping mat (It definitely did look like we were camping.)
- Bivvy bag (A bivouac bag, which, when I googled this, seemed to bear more than a passing resemblance to a body bag.)
- Basha (I googled *What is a basha?* and we watched a YouTube video showing an army guardsman stringing a piece of material between two trees with the constant sound of gunfire in the background. This did not calm Mother down about the forthcoming trip.)
- Waterproof clothing (Mother refuses to wear anything that looks flammable. I assume this is out of a fear that someone might try to set her on fire. I've told her a thousand times that I'm sorry and the incident with the Christmas pudding was an accident, but she doesn't believe me.)
- Torch (Mother said her phone light would be perfectly adequate. I didn't tell her there wouldn't be any electricity on the island to charge it. She hated the trip enough already.)
- Toothbrush (They recommended that we '*put the toothpaste on at home and wrap it in cling film*'. Given the

14

amount of money Mother's spent on cosmetic den-
tistry, comments like this certainly would not encourage her so I scrolled through them at speed.)

- Toilet paper and a mess tin (Listing these items
together was a bad idea and gave entirely the wrong
impression to Mother. We learned very quickly that
outdoorsy people do seem to be fascinated with all
things toilet-based. This extended to the next item.)
- Toilet trowel (I said it was a typo and should have been
towel. Mother has the John Lewis, or 'Mothership',
as she calls it, app on her phone for emergencies, so
she clicked it immediately and ordered three luxury
cotton John Lewis bath sheets in white. Later on, I
made sure I got her a little Cath Kidston gardening
set with mini spade, rake, gloves and seeds. She didn't
question why we'd be gardening on a survival trip.)
- Small penknife (Given that on our last retreat there
were a lot of murders, Mother did express a little concern that we were embarking on an expedition where
everyone would be armed.)
- No alcohol (Mother edited this with the simple word
'*bollox*', which she spelled with an 'x' in the same
manner as Botox. To be fair, I do still carry my dad's
old hollowed-out Bible everywhere with its flask of
brandy in it, so I shouldn't judge.)
- Personal items (Mother hasn't needed these for years.)

At the bottom of this list of requirements in bold letters
was the excruciating statement:

AND THE WILL TO SURVIVE!
Play It Simple & Survive

Survivalists and outdoors people seem to like nothing
better than an acronym.

All of this carefully bought and packed equipment
would be at the bottom of the sea within twenty-four hours
of our arrival.

The list neglected to mention a few other things that I always try to take with me on a trip with Mother — patience, self-belief, forgiveness and sustenance that isn't just bottle-shaped.

I downloaded the brochure and there were lots of pictures of people looking dirty and depressed. It probably wasn't a coincidence that this literature had only been disclosed after payment.

'I'm not going.' Mother was in defiant mode.

I'd thought it would be a good idea to show her the brochure. Which reminded me not to have good ideas around Mother.

I don't think it helped that the brochure began with the words:

THE BROWN WATCH
TAKE IT TO THE LIMIT . . .
ONE MORE TIME

It did admittedly seem ill-advised that they'd named themselves *The Brown Watch* given the focus on toilet matters in their kit list but, as I explained to Mother, it all had something to do with Scotland and being courageous.

'I'm not going.'

'Mother, how hard can it be?' I gave her my most appealing face. 'It says it's a family survival course.'

'A course in how to survive your family? I should be bloody running it—'

'Don't be disingenuous, Mother.' Though I'll be honest, Mother is rarely anything she can't spell. 'It's *for* the family. Look, it says we'll learn about human nature and basic survival.'

'I think we've learned enough about that, don't you?'

I sighed. 'But we didn't, that's just it. Back at the Slaughter House, we were a shambles. We need to be better at this.'

'At what?'

'Staying alive! Knowing what to do in the worst of times.' I put my hand on her arm. She stared at it until I removed it, then brushed down the sleeve. 'I've already lost one parent and you've lost a . . . a friend. The point is, we need to be tougher than this. We need to be ready.'

'Ready for what?' She shook her head. 'You make it sound like we're at war.'

'That's how it *feels* sometimes, Mother.' She paused and I assumed she was thinking, although you never can tell. She's refined the art of making distraction look like thought.

'Ursula.' She tilted her head and pointed to the laptop screen. 'This is all a pile of horse shit.'

'I've booked it.'

'What?'

'And paid for it. You've got to go now.'

Her face seemed to deflate. Her mouth hung slack like an old puppet. No voice came out.

'I've booked all three of us on it.'

'Three?'

'Me, you and Aunt Charlotte. It says it's a *family* survival course. She's the only surviving family we've got now.'

'And what about Aunt Mirabelle?' Mother widened her eyes as far as she could.

'What about her? She's not family. She's not my real aunt. That's it. No more. No discussion.' I realized I sounded churlish but Mirabelle had to be involved in everything and was in some way meant to be my godmother. God had nothing to do with her. Mother had attempted to draw her into our lives even more after we all survived the Slaughter House together, which had cast our survival in a more bittersweet light. Mother somehow seemed to have this idea of us playing happy families just because we weren't dead.

'How can you say that about Mirabelle after all we went through together?'

'Avoiding being murdered is no reason to band together. "*We're Not Dead*" is not a good name for a club.'

Mother tried to purse her lips. 'Well, I'm not bloody going. Unless Mirabelle does.'

'Really?'

She issued *The Look*.

'I just thought we could . . .' I watched her unmoving face. It was pointless trying to sway Mother when her mind was made up. I sighed dramatically. 'All right, she can come.'

A smile lifted her lips. 'What's that, dear?'

'She can come. She can come. She can come. Bloody buggering Mirabelle can come on our bloody holiday *again*.'

'What a lovely idea, darling. And stop calling it a holiday. It's hateful.'

* * *

So here I was on the first night of our survival course, standing in the green tinged kitchenette, freezing cold and staring at Mother's basket and Sir Nigel Havers's plums. I had no idea that Mirabelle would never thank me again for letting her come on one of our trips, or that most of our group would die. But I was already beginning to think Mother may have had a point. I should stop calling it a holiday.

CHAPTER 4: LANDING IN ANOTHER WORLD

I should have known from that first moment that it wasn't a holiday. The journey here had been far from the voyage of discovery I'd been hoping for.

I'd imagined my eyes opening to the isolated beauty of it all, finding myself as a woman in the wilderness. But from the outset it had looked a lot more like *Women on the Verge of a Nervous Breakdown*.

When we arrived on the Isle of Harris, we decided to get some food in Stornoway airport, which is not something I'll repeat.

Aunt Charlotte and Mirabelle had flown out with us. Our little group seemed to fill the small airport, particularly Aunt Charlotte, who was dressed entirely in Harris tweed. She had the distinct look of Agatha Christie about to embark on an expedition, and that was before we even discovered anyone was dead.

'Excellent!' Aunt Charlotte announced staring into a plate of liquid egg and burnt toast. 'Stornoway black pudding too.' She held up what looked like a tarmacked hamster and inspected it. 'How the devil are you, dear?' It was hard to tell if she was talking to me or the black pudding. 'Pandora, you look like you need to eat.'

Mother has cultivated a starved look over many years which makes her look so ravenous that she might eat you at any moment. She hasn't, however, eaten a full meal since she was twelve, a fact she reminded me of repeatedly after Dad died and I tried my best to look after my one remaining parent. Mother didn't settle well to grief. I often had to prepare a quick breakfast for her before I went to school that would soak up excess alcohol but would also be easy to clean up from the carpet and bedclothes.

The airport terminal bore a remarkable resemblance to a 1980s TV set. Mother adopted her appalled look, the one she uses when faced with someone wearing jogging bottoms. I've explained numerous times that I find them comfortable, but she still sees them as an insult.

'I'm not eating that.' She was using her Harrods voice to remind everyone she was better than this.

Mirabelle, of course, joined in immediately. 'Me neither. Whose idea was all this?'

'Darling, it's a nightmare. Whose idea do you think it was?'

They both looked at me as if I was something they might regret stepping on. But it didn't stop them.

'Another needy attempt to draw attention to herself. I know how hard it is for you, Pandora.' Mirabelle moved closer towards Mother and shook her head.

'Stornoway? Where the hell is that anyway, Ursula? Isn't it somewhere there have been, you know, *troubles*?' Mother mouthed it in a way that suggested incontinence. She leaned in but strangely raised her voice at the same time. Mother doesn't do quiet, unfortunately. 'Terrorists!'

Stornoway airport paused to acknowledge the unmistakably shrill use of the unforgivable word in a room the size of a small church. The middle-aged woman serving coffee to no one stared as if someone had just announced *Shetland* was being cancelled.

'No, Mother, you are referring to Stormont in Ireland. There are no political upheavals occurring in the Hebrides

20

currently so you can come down from amber alert. According to the guidebook, Stornoway boasts black pudding and Donald Trump's mother as its output. Even if those two things ever did converge it would not pose any form of risk to you.'

'How can you be so sure of that?' Aunt Charlotte said with that intense, serious look she calls her Paxman face.

'I don't believe you.' Mother held out her hand. 'Let me see that guidebook.'

'I forgot to pack it.'

'What? The guidebook?'

Now they were all staring.

'Yes, *the guidebook*!' I reached for an excuse. 'I was reading it in bed last night.' I looked between them. 'I must have left it on the bedside table.'

'So, what you're saying is that you have no idea where we're going, as usual.' Mirabelle sat back victoriously.

'Yes, *Mirabelle*, of course I have! Anyway, did anyone else think to bring one?'

They all looked away. Except for Mother, with her resting disappointed face. 'Christ.'

* * *

We left the airport under a lingering cloud of irritation and annoyance, a familiar state of affairs for my family. No one spoke as we boarded the small, antique bus.

The journey across Lewis and down into Harris towards Leverburgh was like sinking through time. As we left Stornoway we could see the shadow of the mainland, its high peaks clear against the dull granite sky. The driver, who was possibly as old as the mountains himself, told us there were signs bad weather was imminent. We would learn very quickly that everything on Harris was a sign. There were signs everywhere, even in the smallest thing. With hindsight, perhaps we should have paid more attention to them.

I stared out the window at the stark tranquillity. The bus rattled on through Stornoway as if it was the only remaining escape route. The small, clean houses were lined in neat candy colours, perfectly reflected in the pewter waters of the harbour.

'Looks like bloody Balamory,' Mother announced.

'Where?' Sometimes it's just easier to ignore Aunt Charlotte.

We hurried past an armada of fishing boats crouched against the harbour walls as if they were readied for the next brutal onslaught of the sea. So far, our experience of the airport and the suburbs of Stornoway had been of a land that was constantly braced for severe times. It had a stoic nature that made our bewildered faces look even more incongruous.

'This cold, I swear it's like needles all over my face.' Mother huddled into her cashmere scarf.

'Should be familiar, then.'

'Leave her alone!' Mirabelle always does this. 'Your mother can't help her dysmorphia.'

'My what?' Mother looked genuinely confused.

'It's OK, Pandora. Some of us are sympathetic to your . . . your *needs*.'

'My needs?'

'Last bus to Grosebay,' the driver called down the bus when we were well past the outskirts of town and Stornoway had trailed into dark clouds behind us.

'Grosebay?' I said. 'We're heading to Leverburgh.'

'Apparently not.' Mother turned away.

'I thought you knew exactly where we were going,' Mirabelle sneered.

'I'll sort it out.' I swayed down the bus towards the driver, looking out the windows either side as if I might recognize something. Lines of condensation rolled down the fogged-up glass, leaving a dampness lingering in the air. Outside, the leaden sky was heavy with great dark clouds that threatened to break at any moment.

We were beyond the main port, past the edges of town, where derelict houses looked out to sea as if they were searching for their owners. But they'd long been abandoned. Grey remnants of curtains fluttered like ghosts at the windows, their thin, gauzy fingers reaching out through the broken glass as we drove by.

I explained to the driver our misunderstanding and he entirely misunderstood. He just continued driving and whistling some unrecognizable sea shanty through his wide teeth. The landscape rolled out in moss-coloured swathes. There were no stops and no other passengers. I finally persuaded the bus driver to take us on to Leverburgh. He seemed quite ambivalent about where he was going and shrugged as if it was all the same to him.

We travelled on through the harsh wilderness. It was a desolate land, barren with wear from long winters and the sea's constant rough wind. I watched redundantly as this new world rolled by. It was relentlessly bleak but there was something captivating about it all. Part derelict, part timeless, it was as if it had been paused in its last moments. It was all just waiting for something to return. There was that unmistakable sadness of somewhere that had been left to fall into decay.

We passed an old van that had been turned into a mobile shop. It didn't look like it had moved in decades. The back was open, revealing a sparsely stocked array of basic supplies and some tattered posters for digestives, Ovaltine and PG Tips. One old man was sitting in the driver's seat smoking a cigarette, his eyes closed. Utterly unmoving, the only sign he was still alive was the end of the stub intermittently glowing amber.

We drove on past other abandoned vehicles. The carcasses of decaying cars and the occasional tractor littered the landscape, some so old that they had become part of the scenery, with shrubs and weeds winding through their broken windows and empty engines. Solitary tin huts were rust-red against the evening light. The bus driver had called this the Golden Road, but we were looking at a tarnished wasteland. We passed an abandoned phone box with a bird's nest on the receiver. There were no houses anywhere near. And no more people.

But perhaps it wasn't neglect I was looking at. Perhaps this place was just as the brochure had said: "untouched". Wars and famines had raged through the rest of the world — some had even flared momentarily on these islands — but they stood unchanged, a hard, grey stone world.

We didn't see anyone else until we surfaced on the other side of Harris. If there were any people living out there, they were so much a part of the landscape that they had become indistinguishable from it.

The light trailed away across the charcoal sky. Our bus was the only movement in those dwindling remains of dusk. Mists began to settle into the valleys and out towards the water we watched the shells of broken boats swaying on the tide. Only small apricot streaks of sunlight lined the grim horizon now.

We followed the road, a long black ribbon pulling into the land. There was an overwhelming feeling that the island was somehow watching us, its new intruders. We fell silent. We seemed so exposed out here. Countless pin-holes of light began to appear in the black sky like spy holes through from another world.

When we finally surfaced in Leverburgh, it was an empty place, stark with only a smattering of buildings. The driver pointed to an underwhelming Portakabin before leaving us standing in the cold road. It was a lightless place and there wasn't much more than the dark silhouette of a large shed cut from the surrounding hills. The building's flimsy walls didn't look like they could withstand this landscape.

A lone night porter greeted us and informed us we'd arrived too late for introductions or any food. There was something morbid about this man who showed us to our rooms. The dirty brown carpet tiles curled at the edges and the floor seemed to move a little as we followed him down the long dark corridor. When we arrived at the battered door to our room, I couldn't shake the overriding impression that it had been hurriedly cleared of the previous occupants — dead or otherwise.

* * *

After that first sleepless night in our bunks and only Mother's out-of-date tea and Sir Nigel Havers's plums for sustenance, we found ourselves standing among the cold remains of breakfast time. And we were confronted with a new horror.

'Well, well, well, if it isn't my little old book club.' Bridget Gutteridge, the only other survivor of the Slaughter House — unfortunately.

'Old?' Mother was clearly in no mood for reminiscing this morning.

'Oh, it all makes more sense now!' Aunt Charlotte smiled. 'Bridget was a member of the book club. I had wondered why she was with us in the Slaughter House.'

Bridget looked at her, dumbfounded.

Yap. A tiny dog quivered intensely at Bridget's feet as its beady eyes zeroed in on Aunt Charlotte.

'Oh, Jesus.'

'No, he's called Mr Bojingles.' Bridget lifted her chin haughtily.

'Bojangles,' I corrected.

'Bojingles.'

'It's Mr Bojangles. I distinctly remember that part of the Slaughter House.'

'Mr Bojangles is dead.'

We paused.

Aunt Charlotte leaned forward, conspiratorially. 'Murdered?'

Bridget and the dog stared, maliciously, I'd say. For a moment it even crossed my mind that Mr *Bojingles* might have had more than a hand or paw in the demise of the previous occupant of that tartan dog coat.

Mirabelle sighed. 'Why are you here, Bridget?'

'Other than to annoy the hell out of everyone.' Mother was beginning to sound quite frustrated now. She doesn't like surprises, not since Dad bought her a Segway for her fiftieth instead of a Steinway. She doesn't play the piano but an interior designer friend had said they were that season's must-have photo shelf. Mother doesn't have any photos either and didn't warm to my suggestion that she could maybe take a few shots while she was touring around on her Segway.

Bridget gave us her battle-line smile. One thing I will say for Bridget is that she has the kind of face that clearly sets out from the very beginning just how much she dislikes you. 'I'm still on the book club WhatsApp group.'

'Is she?' I looked around at the others, who all shrugged.

'It's my duty to be here. You can't have a book club holiday without its key member.'

I frowned. 'Key member? Really?'

'You're not even a member at all of the book club.' Bridget stared at me.

'This is not a book club holiday. There is no book club.'

'Don't say that!' She looked genuinely distressed. 'This holiday was clearly on the group chat.'

'Who put that on there?' I looked around them all. My eyes finally landed on Aunt Charlotte who was shifting her feet uneasily. 'Are you still using that group?'

Aunt Charlotte took a deep breath. 'I like to put little things on there. It's just a bit of nostalgia, really.'

'For a book club that ended with five deaths?'

'Well, now you put it like that . . .' Aunt Charlotte looked at the floor.

'Dear, dear, did you not read your *in–for–ma–tion* booklets?' Bridget dragged out each syllable of the word until I could feel myself twitch. 'This is a survival course. So of course I should be here. Remember, survival? Something I ensured for all of you. Yet you repaid me with abandonment and silence.' Her sour little smile remained in place.

'I don't remember you being the architect of *my* survival or indeed anyone else's.' Mother turned away.

When Bridget Gutteridge laughed, it was steely, unnerving and invariably accompanied by dead, staring eyes, so that she was remarkably reminiscent of an end-of-the-pier clown. I watched her rocking to and fro with her murderous little dog. Bob the Therapist says it's these kind of ideas that might lead people, and by people he means Mother, to the conclusion that I need help. That's why I mostly keep my imaginings to myself these days.

'Oh, Pandora.' There it was again, Bridget's sideshow laugh. 'Contrary to your little newspaper articles and television interviews, I seem to remember that it was me who solved the murders at the Slaughter House after you were purposefully leading us up blind alleys and throwing in red herrings.'

'Oh no, no, no, no!' Aunt Charlotte wagged her finger in Bridget's face. 'We're not doing all the herrings and fish thing again. Not this time. No.'

'Aunt Charlotte, it's just a figure of—'

'Leave it, Ursula. Just shut up, Charlotte.' Someone once suggested that if we invented a drinking game where we had to drink every time Mother said 'shut up', we'd spend most of our time semi-inebriated. We don't need a game for that. It was definitely a tempting thought right then, though.

Mother stepped closer and looked down at Bridget. 'You can remember whatever you like from that house.'

Bridget shook her head slowly, her smile growing wider as if she was remembering it all with such fondness. 'Ah, nothing changes. I see you and your dear family are still the emotionally disturbed, seething little rat's nest you always were. I suppose I should be grateful you ruthlessly cut me out of your lives.'

'I'm sorry, Bridget—' I looked at her with fake confusion — 'help me out here, but when were you ever *in* our lives?'

She watched me through her small, thick glasses, her eyes strangely wide as if she were looking through a magnifying glass analyzing a new specimen for her collection. 'Oh, so you've grown a little braver, have you? What happened to Mummy's little mouse?'

'What is it with the rodent theme?' Aunt Charlotte looked irritated. 'Fish? Rats? Mice?'

'Right, you crazy dogs!' a voice called. The door swung open. 'Who's ready to get *extreme*?'

'Dogs as well now! I'm so confused.'

'Shut up, Charlotte.' I imagined taking a drink. Mother had an increasingly disturbed look about her now. But then no one wants to go on holiday and discover there's an ex-member of their book club there, especially not one who had been so ruthlessly cut off. Mother leaned over to me and whispered through pursed lips, 'You will pay for this, Ursula.' Somehow, I had a feeling she was right.

CHAPTER 5: THE LESSONS WE DIDN'T LEARN

We'd only just settled into the front row seats of the conference room when the man at the door suddenly shouted, 'Alexa, play *Brown Winner* playlist!' He had a melodic Scottish accent that seemed to lift each word up at the end like a smile. Sadly, that would not last.

Loud music filled the room. The theme tune to *Game of Thrones* accompanied the procession of this man to the front of the room. He was in full combat gear, which did seem a little unnecessary for a Portakabin. I resolutely stared ahead, careful not to catch anyone else's eye, especially Mother's.

The conference room was a small section of the Portakabin that swayed with the insistent wind. It had been set out with a mismatched selection of broken chairs: the carpet a sort of mid-brown that had soaked up every stain and smell for the past twenty years. It looked out on an unforgiving landscape. The silent hills were still netted with a mist that hadn't lifted since we'd arrived. A flat belt of grey sea lay beyond the small port, surrounded by grassland. Even though there was only a small scattering of houses, the constant rush of the wind seemed to drown out any idea that this could be a calm world.

'Look fear in the face,' the man shouted over the raucous music. It seemed to take him a lot less time than he'd anticipated to stride to the front. It was a small room with only five rows of chairs and, besides our group, only six other people. Undeterred, he continued. 'Take time to embrace.' He held his arms around the large dome of his belly, making great gaps appear between the straining buttons of his shirt. Then he leaned towards us and whispered, '*Leave no trace.*' He stared round the room, his eyes set wide. The soft sound of the last word lingered in the air.

Game of Thrones continued to rise and fall in great waves of emotion as the man's eyes remained round and unblinking. He stood with his legs just a little too far apart to look comfortable. I could clearly see a hint of charcoal eyeliner round his eyes and some form of camouflage make-up smeared across his head as if he'd used it to fill the gaps in his sparse hair. He looked remarkably similar to how a Playmobil figure of Ross Kemp might look, if Playmobil ever decided to diversify their range into a 'Dangerous Gangs' set.

He waited in silence until it was obvious there'd been some miscalculation about when the music would end. At last, it quietened and trailed away. But just as he began to relax, another song started. He frowned as the unmistakable sound of Justin Timberlake's *Sexy Back* flooded the Portakabin. His shoulders fell and he closed his eyes before holding up his hands. 'Sorry, sorry,' he murmured. 'Workout playlist.'

This seemed extraordinary given the figure of the man standing in front of us.

'Alexa, stop,' he commanded. The music continued and was now at maximum volume. 'Alexa, stop!' he said more forcefully. 'Alexa, stop!' he shouted. 'Please, just stop!' He stared at us and we stared back.

The dog began barking.

'You're scaring Mr Bojingles,' Bridget said.

Kempmobil looked around in confusion at the silent faces. Finally, there was a click and then silence. Mother stood, looking fierce, with the plug dangling from her hand.

She marched back to her seat. Kempmobil waited, nodded once, and saluted her. I don't think anyone has ever saluted Mother before.

'Not exactly Lewis Collins, is he?' Mirabelle murmured.

'Who?'

'Shut up, Charlotte,' Mother hissed. I took another virtual drink.

'Right, so why are we here?' Kempmobil began, a keen smile on his face. He attempted to put a foot up onto a chair but couldn't seem to raise his leg high enough. He put the leg down and smoothed his hand down his trousers.

'Why indeed.' Mother crossed her arms across her chest. I could feel her anger settling on me like a mosquito, ready. I didn't look at her.

'Someone else, please. I like this to be a joint experience.' His smile remained fixed in place. 'Why are we *here*?'

I looked at the other captives. A couple of rows back, four weighty mid-ranking, middle-aged executives sat in a line of fresh new combat trousers. Somewhere in the City, a bank or finance house was lacking a substantial proportion of people who wear Tough Mudder T-shirts to the gym. Every ounce of them screamed, 'Team builders who'd rather be anywhere else — except work, of course.'

On the row near the back of the room, there were two serious-faced women with exceptionally tight ponytails that gave them a severe, almost pained expression. They'd clearly perfected a look of complete focus over many years of dull boardrooms and conferences. In the hours of boredom that rolled on, they informed us that they were 'influencers'. Although, they didn't seem to have any influence whatsoever on our party.

Kempmobil looked at the room with tired, slightly jaded eyes and I wondered how many times he'd delivered this lacklustre introduction. 'This course is designed to heighten your connection with nature, to make you mindfully aware of the world around you—'

'Sorry, can I just have my light on for a moment?' Bridget had a distinct talent for making her voice so acerbic that it cut through any room. 'When you say "mindfully aware", I was just wondering if there is another way of being cognitively aware of something rather than through your mind or brain?' Bridget unleashed the vicious smile which, in conjunction with the voice, was a truly toxic combination. 'What I mean is, whether you're suggesting you can be mentally aware of something without it being processed in your brain? I'm fairly sure all such functions *are* performed in the brain anyway so, if you're aware, you are, by definition, using your mind — you are being mindful.'

He looked at her blankly.

'It's a tautology, you see.' The sharp smile persisted.

'Been reading the dictionary again have you, Bridget?' Mirabelle muttered.

'You would have no idea what I've been reading as you failed to invite me to any book club meetings since the Slaughter House holiday.'

A distinct look of concern flashed across Kemp's face.

'Bridget,' I said slowly, 'do you think book club continued after the weekend away became known as "the Slaughter House book club holiday"?'

She looked away.

'Book club is dead!' I said. Firmly, yet compassionately, I thought.

She gasped and recoiled before covering her dog's ears. 'Don't say such things.'

'Wait, so *that's* shocking to you and Mr Bojingles, but staying in a house where four people were brutally killed is not a genuine reason for ending book club?' I shook my head and slumped back in my chair. 'And anyway, that dog wasn't even there so I don't know why you're covering his ears.'

Kemp, who'd been keenly following our conversation, looked a bit shocked. He cleared his throat and began again. 'Ladies, ladies, this little escape pod we've got here is all about mindfully listening to one another—'

Bridget shifted her gun sights. 'I'm sorry to be pedantic—'

'She's not,' I couldn't help myself.

Bridget continued with strained patience. 'Again, I would like to clarify whether you think you can listen to something and interpret the sounds without the use of your mind? If, as I suspect is the case, you do need to use your mind to perform that cognitive function, then I'm afraid you may have inadvertently committed another tautology.'

Kemp sighed. 'Apologies for the . . . the ology thing. But we're not going down the astrology route on this particular tour of duty. Don't get me wrong, I think there is scope to include it. I am naturally a very inclusive person, but at the moment we're just going to be focusing on getting off-grid, washing away those stresses and dialling out.'

'My own experience has been that any form of dialling out is completely detrimental to survival,' Mother said.

He ignored her, presumably in a mindful way. 'We are going to set some intentions and recapture our own flow by some Blue Mind meditation—'

'Disgusting.'

He paused for a moment and looked at Aunt Charlotte.

'We've got mindfu . . . we've got some yoga, sensory walks, foraging, some meditation sessions and immersive experiences designed to create a positive ripple effect through your lives. Because after all, how can we survive the world if we can't *understand* the world?' He nodded slowly in response to his own question.

'Just one thing—'

'Oh, for God's sake, Bridget,' Mirabelle shifted forward and stared at her.

The smile melted from Kemp. 'Why is there always one?' He shook his head. 'Listen, we're going to do a little mindfu . . . a little walk and then do some sensory awareness through paddle-boarding.'

'No, we're not.' Mother straightened up. 'Absolutely not.'

'No?'

'No.'

Kemp moved awkwardly from foot to foot as if he was trying to end this as quickly as possible. 'Well then, we can start with the survival element. *Everyone* enjoys that bit! We can have a little look at some of the kit and talk through a few strategies for ultimate survival in the wild. It's camping but *for the brave*!' He gave a little forced laugh, followed by an ill-advised wink.

No one winks at Mother. Mother doesn't do friendly. His smile fell away quickly.

'So—' he rubbed his hands together — 'what do you say we get *survivaltastic*?'

'I say fu—'

'Mother dear,' I said quickly, 'have you taken your meds today?'

Kemp's face fell into the large folds of his chin, which seemed to create a collar of pleated skin all round his neck. As he turned away, I could see there were three large rolls of flesh resting under his skull as if propping up his head. He had the obligatory pseudo-military tattoo on his neck, which from a distance looked like a spider's web but was in fact a compass. I couldn't stop looking at it and only realized why it held my attention for so long when I noticed that the compass points were in the wrong places.

Underneath all the positive words, he had that thinly disguised haunted look men in the pub have when they've spent too much time contemplating how they came to this. His voice had the dry rasp of a man thinking about his next drink. I tried to imagine him as the younger, motivational man he was trying to present but the image was too distant. Whatever disappointments and sorrows he'd walked through, they had left their mark. Every part of him seemed hollow as if the threadbare outfit might just crumple to the floor at any moment and leave nothing more than an empty pile of clothes.

'Now, what are our priorities when we're faced with a survival situation? Anyone?'

'Not to die,' Aunt Charlotte offered confidently.

He readjusted his trousers and stood with his hands on his hips and legs spread. He shoved his thumbs under the utility belt and thrust the buckle forward. This was a man proud of his utility belt. And so he should be. Batman would have been proud of it. It seemed to have everything for every conceivable situation, except perhaps those involving Mother. There was obviously his mobile phone, which had to be stored on his belt in a pouch to enhance survival safety rather than in a pocket like everyone else. There was a torch, pocketknife, another bigger, serrated knife and a roll of gaffer tape. It was quite disturbing just how much his survival equipment bore a striking similarity to the equipment a psychopathic killer might take on a night out.

The heavy belt seemed to be dragging his gut down, as if he was being pulled towards the floor.

'See you looking at my belt there, missy.' He'd suddenly adopted the persona of a Scottish cowboy.

My mouth fell open and he nodded with mistaken pride. 'This ain't just any belt. Say hello to my little *friend*.' He slapped his sweaty fingers into the belt and left a dull, wet mark.

Aunt Charlotte leaned very close towards his middle and smiled. 'Hello.' She wriggled her fingers as if she was staring at a newborn baby rather than Kemp's belt struggling for survival under his stomach. She was now inches from Kemp's buckle.

Kemp paused to look down at her.

'Does he or *she* have a name?' Aunt Charlotte leaned further forward and there was the rising thought that she might actually reach out and touch the belt.

'No.'

Her smile faded and she looked cautiously around us in that way she has when she's not sure if this is acceptable or not.

'Right,' Kemp took a step back and shuffled into his wide-legged stance a little more as if he was settling himself in. He patted the belt but then gave a swift look at Aunt

Charlotte. He took another step back. 'So, yes, right here you've got everything you could need to survive. Swiss army knife, hunter's knife, compass, torch, mirror, rope — all top-of-the-range. What you've got here with this little baby, the Beaver Special, is your ticket to survival.' He flicked the buckle and, as it released, his trousers slipped two inches further down. He held up the belt, gripping his trousers with the other hand and gave Aunt Charlotte another quick nervous look. 'With this little friend, you can drag a body to safety.' He mimed dragging a body with his belt. 'It can pull your food behind you.' This looked remarkably the same. 'It can bind two things together.' He acted out, in careful and precise detail, binding someone's hands together.

We watched, mesmerized and more than a little concerned.

'It can haul you to safety or be an improvised weapon — a whip, perhaps.' He whipped the ground with his fully loaded belt. Everyone stared. 'Use the buckle end—' He took the other end of the belt and began whipping the floor with the buckle — 'and you got yourself a flail.' The only noise in the room now was his belt buckle thrashing the floor. Finally, his phone fell to the ground with a crack and the torch flew backwards and landed in Mirabelle's lap.

'God damn it, that's the second time this month,' he murmured as he picked up the phone to inspect its newly cracked screen.

Mirabelle didn't flinch but merely stared down at the torch in her lap. We sat in silence as he gingerly walked over, belt in hand, and reached into her lap to retrieve the torch. She didn't look down, her eyes remaining in a fixed stare straight ahead.

All eyes followed his slow walk back to the front of the room. The City boys now had puzzled looks on their faces as if they were beginning to doubt the fully fledged Tough Mudder credentials of this particular course. The thought was spreading across each face in turn — was this really a life-changing experience or was it possible that this man might just be an utter clown?

36

'Integrity!' Kemp jerked suddenly. The syllables came out fast, in a sound similar to a child imitating gunfire. Everyone jolted in their seats.

Aunt Charlotte leaned over to me. 'Is he all right do you think, dear?'

I shrugged.

'What's the most important part of that word? Come on! Think! You have to think to live.'

'Not necessarily, Mr Wild Geese.' Mirabelle let her eyes travel over the dome of his camouflaged belly.

'Wild what?'

'Shut up, Charlotte.' I'd given up on the 'shut up' drinking game. It was too exhausting, especially since I was the only player.

'Grit!' he shouted. It was as if the words were surprising his own mouth. He waited for some sort of understanding to arrive in the room. It didn't.

'Grit,' he repeated, still energetically keen.

'Filthy bugger,' Aunt Charlotte muttered and closed her legs.

I frowned at her but she just shook her head slowly as if I knew what she meant.

'You see? Grit is the most important part of in–te–*grit*–y.' Kemp waited, smiling into the silence. 'InteGRITy.' A fine seam of spit had gathered on his lower lip.

The room shuddered to another gust of the brutal wind. The windows chattered in the loose frames. It dislodged a cup from the side table which fell onto the Alexa, letting a slow stream of cold tea run silently into the holes.

'God damn it!' Kemp waddled over to the machine, still holding his trousers up with one hand and the belt in the other.

We watched in silence as he tried to organize his trousers before finally letting go. Mercifully, they stayed up but slipped just enough to create an uncomfortable moment for us all.

'Technology, eh?' He shook his head and hoisted his trousers back up. 'Who needs it?'

'Hospitals, schools, financial institutions,' Bridget began, 'law enforcement, government, the—'

'OK.' He held both his hands up as if they were a large pause symbol. He took a breath, then continued carefully as though he thought every word he said was under scrutiny. It was. 'What I meant was that we all need to unplug, get off-grid, reconnect.' He held his hands up again in defence. 'Occasionally! And I guess that's why you're all here, right?'

'Wrong.'

He looked at Mother for a moment with a sort of desperation, as if he could see every single hour of the next few days stretching out ahead of him.

'So, when do we start, I hear you cry.'

Silence.

'Right here, right now.' He attempted to point to a spot in front of him but the trousers slipped again and he was forced to make a quick grab for the waistband.

'We don't mind if you want to take a minute to put the belt back on,' one of the City boys offered tentatively.

'Thank you,' Kemp said in a low voice. He began to grapple the belt around himself, sweating and panting. The belt was squeezed so tight that he bore a remarkable resemblance to a camouflaged balloon tied at the bottom. Finally, he let out a great exhausted breath. 'OK, let's go survive!'

'Yeah!' One of the bankers shouted and punched the air. The word lingered in the room on its own.

We slowly filed out in a single line, heads bowed in an awkward monastic silence. None of us was really sure what had happened in the last half an hour but it certainly wasn't what we'd expected.

'This is not how it looked on the website,' one of the tight-haired women commented to him as we were leaving.

'Ah,' Kemp said, 'life never is!' His warm voice almost sounded hopeful. He looked round for acknowledgement but no one could meet his eye. There was a strange sense of embarrassment among us that we just wanted to leave behind in that room. Sadly, it followed us for the rest of the day.

We broke into groups and the remainder of the morning was spent learning how to light some damp kindling while being buffeted by the wind. When the answer came to us, it was in the form of some lighter fluid and matches.

Kemp spoke a little about Taransay, the island that would be our home for the next week. There'd been a TV series set there years ago which had sparked a lot of interest in off-grid living and inspired hordes of ill-equipped urbanites to spend a week being hungry and cold before going home to tell people they'd found themselves. Kemp proceeded to talk us through his three 'Shhhs' — shelter, sheffing and shit-ting. Which, judging by the schoolboy grin he'd adopted, he thought was amusing. It might have been previously to some other group. But not this group. Not this time.

The shelter element of the course he described seemed to involve finding what the TV crew had left behind on the island and making use of that. No one could fault Kemp for seeing a cheap business opportunity. Toilet facilities involved a lot of sphagnum moss, which Kemp demonstrated in detail for us. As for 'sheffing', the food was foraged.

'The answer to poverty and hunger is that we all need to slow down and look at Nature's supermarket.' He smiled in a distant way as if he was remembering some old grocery store from long ago.

'No way. I'm not getting involved in that again,' Mother said. 'It's all poisonous black magic.'

I was watching Mother closely for signs of a relapse.

'Food foraging is for privileged, middle-class people, not the genuine poor and hungry,' I began.

'And what exactly do you know about it?' Bridget watched me with her unblinking, doll-like eyes. 'Other than the "privileged" part, of course.'

'I do know that people without money don't head out into the wilderness and rummage around for various morsels of possibly edible foliage. They are hungry and desperate, not on a wild food retreat. They couldn't give a stuff about Nature's supermarket. That's for people who feel the need to invent a new life.'

Bridget inclined her head. 'Which is why *you're* here, isn't it?' She gave me another sharp smile and carried on stroking her dog.

'It's why we're all here.' Kemp tried to sound reassuring, then pulled out one of his large knives. He spent the rest of the morning showing us that there really is only one way to skin a rabbit and, frankly, it's brutal.

I could smell the coppery, stale blood the minute he slit along the skin. The sound was just as if he was pulling out a piece of tape in stuttered sections. The slow trail of guts slopped out from the wound. My blood seemed to pool in my feet and ankles, and a sparkle of black stars clouded my eyes.

I'm no stranger to this sensation. Ever since I can remember, I've had a tendency to faint. Bob the Therapist says it could be a heightened sense of anxiety. Such magnificent displays of intricate diagnostics are why I call him *House*, but he doesn't get the reference. I stopped using it when I saw him write on my notes, 'Strange obsession with Bingo.' Mother just blames it all on Dad for dying.

The sweat had gone cold on my face. The world dimmed and I felt the floor rushing up towards me.

CHAPTER 6: TITANIC DECISIONS

'We saddle up at daybreak!' Kemp announced dramatically to a Portakabin of dejected faces. The rest of the day had been as desperate as first impressions had suggested and after my small fainting incident, I'd spent most of it hiding in bed with the brandy flask that I keep inside a cut-out section of Dad's old Bible. The others had attempted to follow a training exercise but Mother had retired early when the mindful role-playing started.

The day had never really broken through the thick layers of cloud and now there was only a dusting of light left on the edge of the hills. Dinner had been the butchered rabbit so we were all going to bed hungry.

'Well, I'm not saddling up anything, even you, Bravo Two Zero! I hate riding.'

'No, Aunt Charlotte. He means—'

'OK. We set sail at first light!' Kemp called as he tried to edge his way out of the room.

'No one mentioned sailing. I hate sailing.'

'We're going to be staying on an island, Pandora dear. How else did you think we'd get there?'

'Shut up, Charlotte. I'm not getting in a boat with all these fat men in technical clothing.'

They all looked around for who she might be talking about.

Kemp was at the door looking concerned, bemused and possibly even a little bit less enthusiastic than this morning. It seemed to suit him more than the forced-fun version of himself he'd been selling us. 'OK, what I meant was that we board the RIB at zero nine forty-five hours.' The keenness was definitely fading and I wondered what he'd be like at the end of all this. My family sometimes have this draining effect on people.

'So, to confirm, it's not "first light" or "daybreak", and we're not riding anywhere,' Mirabelle folded her arms. 'I mean, you did originally say "first light", but I suspect that's quite a lot earlier than you intended, isn't it?'

'Sunrise is zero seven nineteen hours. Breakfast at zero eight forty-five hours and off—'

'Zero eight forty-five hours? Off?' Aunt Charlotte said. 'Can you speak normally, please?'

'We'd be setting off then usually, but I'm out tonight with someone who's coming in and I need to feel *fresh* tomorrow, if you know what I mean.' He winked again but this time did it twice so it looked more like a twitch. The fact that someone was 'coming in' seemed to be something he thought we should be impressed by. He bent his head into his underarm and sniffed deeply. 'So, no, ladies. It probably won't be first light.' He gave us all a smile before letting out a long, satisfied breath.

I looked out of the dark window. Granite hills lifted through the low rain clouds and fields stretched out into nothing. The sea tremored in the wind, iridescent colours flashing across its black surface like light off a rook's wing. The water stretched round every border I could see. It was hard to imagine where he would be going out to. I could just make out the sign of a small bar swinging in the wind a little further down from us, by the harbour front, but it didn't look like the sort of place you'd linger in. It was a place to wait for something else to happen — a boat to come

42

in, a boat to go out. It wasn't a place to stay after that had happened.

Kemp was still standing in front of us gently sweating in polyester. He frowned at me as if he'd noticed my look of distaste. 'We might need to get you up to speed. You've missed a lot of training today. Are you sure you're going to be OK? You gave us all a little scare back there, missy, you know, with Mr Flopsy.'

'Mr Flopsy?'

'My rabbit. Well, he *was* my rabbit.'

'He means the bunny-skinning exercise where you fainted,' Aunt Charlotte clarified. 'You know, Mr Flopsy — or dinner, as he became known.'

'Yes, thank you, Aunt Charlotte,' I sighed, 'I realized that. I'll be fine, thank you.'

'She's always doing it. Favourite little attention hook,' Mirabelle said.

'My daughter has a few *problems*.' Mother made it sound like I had an unpleasant infection.

'Right.' He was watching me with increasing concern. 'Well, perhaps you should have mentioned them on the forms.'

'They're not those kind of problems.'

'Right.'

'She's just . . . sensitive.'

'Mother, stop! Please.'

'I'm not going to say any more.'

Mirabelle tutted. 'What more would you say? There's nothing bloody wrong with her, unless you count being self-indulgent and spoiled.'

'Spoiled?' I stared at her.

Kemp stood awkwardly at the door, unsure if he should enquire further or just make a run for it. The exit seemed much more attractive. 'Right, well, ladies and gents. I'll see you all in the morning.'

He edged out of the door as if we were dangerous animals that he should maintain eye contact with and not turn his back on at any point.

'By the way,' I asked as he was about to leave. He flinched. 'What's your real name?'

'Real name?'

'You know . . . We can't go on calling you K—' I paused. 'What would you like us to call you?'

'My name is Brendan. Brendan Brown. The Brown Watch?' He waited.

'Oh, oh yes. Now I understand!' I laughed in what I thought was a friendly manner. 'I thought . . . Well, you know, Brown Watch . . . I thought given all the references to toilets . . .'

His eyebrows raised.

'Never mind,' I said quietly.

He left, looking confused and worried.

* * *

The next morning, we were lousy with exhaustion. Mother blamed my screaming in the night but I think the crippling cold of our dank tomb and the wind howling at the window like some sort of loosed beast may have had something to do with it. I'd spent most of the night sipping on the hip flask of brandy before finally putting it back inside my hollowed-out Bible. I held it tight until dawn.

It had been one of Dad's few possessions that Mother hadn't sent to a charity shop or landfill after he died. I closed my eyes and smelled the familiar memory of his whiskey-tinged breath. He somehow converted cigarettes and the stale remains of a night's drinking into a cosy perfume, a safe cloud. I held the worn black leather Bible as tight as a wayward preacher desperate for some salvation. It was still warm with the memory of him. He'd never needed salvation. There'd been no sin, no impurity — until the end of course. Perhaps if I reached out my arms now into the darkness he'd be there, a solid body, not just smoke and memories.

'Go to sleep, Ursula.' The only voice in the darkness was Mother's, thin with suspicion. She knew. She could

44

smell the sour trail of brandy soaking through the darkness. Perhaps it reminded her of Dad. Perhaps that's why she sounded irritated. For a man who did no wrong, ambling through memories of him is still like walking through nettles to Mother. I don't ask. Some things have to be unspoken between us.

* * *

Breakfast was dry bread and instant coffee with UHT. I could feel the acid rising in my stomach almost as soon as we stood on the pier at Leverburgh, looking down at our backpacks piled between us as if we were on a cheap dance floor. The pontoon cut a single line through the rippling black waters. The quick wind dragged at an old flag strung from a pole, its colours faded. Only a flimsy light hung on the edges of the low mist. Heavy clouds threatened to keep it this dark all day, their reflections barely moving across the water's surface.

'What the hell are we doing here?' Mother shot me a murderous look.

'Waiting for the zero eight forty-five RIB, remember, Mother.'

'Don't start with me. I'm cold. I'm tired. I'm not in Fulham.'

'We need to do this. It will—'

'Will what? Exhaust us? Kill us?' She turned away. 'We could have found better ways to die at home and at least we'd have been warm there.'

'Not if you were dead.' Aunt Charlotte pulled up the collar of her thick tweed jacket.

I didn't respond to Mother but adopted a look that suggested I was considering what she'd said. This was another one of Bob the Therapist's tricks that actually worked. When I began to speak, I used a quiet, slow voice to keep her calm. 'It will hone our survival skills.'

'Skills? Trailing around after old Bravefart wiping his backside on moss? I think not.'

'Well, we're here now, so we might as well make the best of it. You never know, you might like it, Mother.'

'Like it in the same way as last time? You know, when we stayed somewhere that ended up being renamed the Slaughter House.' Mirabelle was always quick to see an opportunity to cast me in a bad light.

'Mirabelle, I did not arrange that. It was your—'

'Look out,' Aunt Charlotte said, 'action stations! Wicked Witch of the West and Tonto are here.'

'Toto,' I corrected. 'The other one's the Lone Ranger.'

Aunt Charlotte looked confused.

Bridget and the dog trotted in tandem down the pontoon, legs perfectly synchronized. As she drew closer, I could hear the rhythmic rustle of her polyester waterproofs.

'Good morning!' she called. 'You weren't trying to leave us behind now, were you?' She grinned with her scalpel smile.

'No,' Mother turned away. 'We'd actually forgotten all about you.'

'Even if you have started calling yourself "The Lone Ranger",' Aunt Charlotte added. I stared at her for a moment but decided any attempt at explanation would be far too long and painful.

Pulling in at the end of the pontoon was a small red boat with a large angry man dressed in army combat uniform leaping from the back unnecessarily early. I know nothing about sailing but clipping the end of the pontoon with the boat probably wasn't an indication of advanced-level steering. The unmoving man at the wheel could easily have been dead judging by his *Old Man and the Sea* look, and the fact that his eyes were completely shut. There were two or three other people wedged in the boat, but their hooded heads were bowed in what looked like solemn penance.

Angry Army Man was running towards us and shouting. We looked behind us. There was no one there. He was shouting at *us*. His words sailed away on the wind but it was fairly obvious he was not a happy angry army man. Strangely, none of us moved. We were like rabbits in the headlights and we'd all seen what they did to rabbits here.

'We're late. Come on, move it. Move it. Move it.' His combat waistcoat flew behind him in slow motion, his giant boots reverberated on the pontoon and the weak sun repeatedly sparked like a flashlight off the hilt of his extraordinarily serrated knife. 'Come on. Packs on backs.'

We didn't move, even though it was becoming increasingly obvious that Angry Army Man wasn't going to be able to stop in time.

He slipped on a pile of bird mess which seemed to slow him down a bit. When he came to a standstill in front of us, his chest was heaving and droplets of sweat were running down his temples, framing his furious face. His hair was short in a way that suggested he disliked hair intensely. Everything about him was clean and scrubbed with anger.

'Survivalists?' He shot. His voice had traces of a Scottish accent but, unlike Kemp, there was none of the soft edge to it. Every syllable came with an aggressive little stab.

I nodded, although it somehow felt like I was sealing our fate.

'We got zero eight fifty on the clock and no disembarkation. Let's saddle up.'

'We were told there would be no riding of horses.'

'Shut up, Charlotte.' Mother stepped forward. 'Now, you listen to me Steven Siegel—'

'Who?'

Mother continued, ignoring Aunt Charlotte. 'I believe you'll find we were here on time. *You* are the late one.'

He looked at her as if he'd just been stung. 'My captain had a few morning issues to deal with.'

Our eyes travelled down the pontoon to Captain Birdseye retching over the side of the boat.

'Bit too much grog?' Aunt Charlotte laughed.

'He was out last night. Now, come on, grab your stuff and let's get tough.'

'May I just ask something?' I attempted a smile. 'Does all survival speak rhyme?'

He watched me closely for a moment as if he was considering the best way to skin me. 'Right ladies, I'm Spear.'

'Of course you are.'

'And I'm going to be leading this tour of duty. You need to listen hard, dig hard and stay hard.' We watched in appalled silence as he clenched both fists. He seemed quite pleased with himself, albeit still in an angry way. 'That's my personal motto.'

'Stay hard?' Aunt Charlotte frowned. 'Your personal motto is "stay hard"?'

He leaned closer towards Aunt Charlotte and narrowed his eyes. Everything about this man was as sharp as his name. Even his beard had been meticulously clipped and shaped to look perfectly rugged — 'artfully army' would be a perfect name for this kind of look. It could be the name of his aftershave. '*Artfully Army* . . . *by Spear.*' He glanced over at me and saw me smiling. I let my face drop quickly.

Spear didn't wait for us and was striding down the pontoon as if he was heading into battle. We grabbed our bags and walked quickly behind, Mother swearing spitefully all the way. Mr Bojingles trotted along looking fretfully between us all like a child watching the grown-ups argue.

We stood by the side of the boat and watched it nudge repeatedly into the pontoon.

'Well, hello there, ladies.' The old captain coughed and wiped away something from his beard with the back of his hand. He held out the offending hand and we watched the lingering piece of food dangling from his fingers. When it became obvious we weren't going to touch him, he saluted and the small foodstuff shot from his finger onto the floor. Mr Bojingles immediately busied himself with eating it. 'Welcome aboard *The Terror*. Captain Bottlenose reporting and ready for duty.'

'Bottlenose,' Aunt Charlotte leaned her head to one side, curiously, 'like the dolphin?'

'Nope, he's called Bottlenose because he's always got his nose in a bottle,' Spear said. 'And if he doesn't smarten up a bit, we might need to find ourselves a new captain.'

'Yes, sir.'

'Oh, leave him alone,' a woman's voice called from the cabin. 'Old Bo-No just likes a little drink sometimes. Who doesn't?'

'Meet Nell,' Spear announced as the woman climbed up on deck, 'our foraging expert, shelter organizer and my *wife*.'

We watched her surface, her skin the colour of smooth sand. Her pale hair was roughly tied back, her sea-green eyes a perfect mirror of the water. She moved like someone who was very aware of just how attractive they were. She didn't take any of it for granted. On the contrary. Every movement looked carefully manipulated to create exactly the desired effect.

'Nice to meet you all.' The blue-grey sunlight lit her face as though it had been designed to frame her. When she spoke, there was a timeless sound to her voice, traces of Celtic rippling under each word as if she was about to deliver an old folk tale, not the introduction to a boat trip. My eyes were drawn to a dark pendant artfully hanging low on her chest. It caught the faint light and moved like liquid silver. In fact, all of her moved as effortlessly as the water around us. She held out her hand and a vast number of leather bracelets and friendship bands slid down her arm. She was the very essence of annoying festival chic.

'Bo-No,' Aunt Charlotte said, 'as in the millionaire rock star who tells us how we can help the poor?'

'No. As in Bottle — Bo. Nose — No.' The woman's smile didn't shift. 'Sounds like Boho but not quite as Mossy, hey?' She laughed and nodded towards the staggering captain.

'Mossy?' Aunt Charlotte said.

'Kate?' The woman's smile was fading now. 'Kate Moss?'

Aunt Charlotte shrugged in bemusement. We stood for a moment in an awkward silence.

'Anyway, welcome aboard and you're going to have to excuse me looking a little worse for wear.' She curved her mouth down in mock sadness as if she knew very well she didn't look anywhere near as disastrous as the rest of us. She gave a finely tuned laugh. 'Huge night last night, if you know what I mean.' She tilted her head coquettishly.

Mother, Aunt Charlotte, Mirabelle and Bridget just looked at her blankly. They clearly didn't know what she meant.

I glanced back at Leverburgh. There was the closed café on the front, and a sparse collection of houses. That was it. Where was everyone going out to?

Mother smiled and said, 'Charmed,' in that voice she reserves for people she has taken an instant dislike to.

We looked around for somewhere to sit. On the opposite bench, there were two miserable-looking people, a man and a woman, dressed in outdoor trekking gear. So far, we hadn't seen anyone who looked happy in technical clothing. The couple's clothing was entirely matching, as were their stern expressions.

'They're Tecnica CAS, if you were wondering,' Technical Man said, following my gaze down to his shoes. He had a severe face and dark-rimmed spectacles in the manner of an architect who was into weekend trekking but really wanted to be taken a lot more seriously than just a *weekend* trekker. High-end technical clothing was definitely a necessity. Everything about him was serious — hair, coat, trousers, kit bag and shoes, of course. 'The Tecnica CAS are the best money can buy.' This was clearly very important to him. 'CAS — Custom Adaptive Shape?' He looked at us as if this should be familiar. 'Heat-formed custom mouldable hiking boots with a Vibram sole?' He held his foot up for inspection.

'Very nice,' I nodded. Somehow my reaction didn't seem quite enough. His face grew even more severe. He lifted the leg a little higher until it looked extremely uncomfortable.

Technical Woman held hers up for inspection too as if that might push my decision over the line. She had the raw-edged intensity of an estate agent driven to seal the deal. I nodded profusely. 'They're great,' I said with a look of encouragement that didn't impress either of them.

'Hardly Louboutins, dear,' Mother had settled herself in and taken up a large proportion of the bench. With Aunt Charlotte and Mirabelle occupying the entirety of the other bench, and Bridget and Mr Bojingles viciously guarding another corner, there was little room left for much more than the technical couple's matching rucksacks.

'You're gonna need a bigger boat,' I laughed.

No one else did.

'It's a quote. Where do we meet—

'Sit down, girl,' Bottlenose shouted. He spoke with a coarse voice, that made every word seem like a struggle. Unlike Spear and Nell, his Scottish accent was very concentrated as if he'd never stepped foot anywhere else in his life. 'You've already walked across a parcel o'ropes and fishing gear before we was 'bout to set out to sea! Don't you be bringing no more bad luck down on us.' He turned back, shaking his head. 'Women on board, always bad luck.'

'Any views on drunk and incapable captains being on board?' Mirabelle called. 'How lucky is that?'

'Sit down, Ursula,' Mother said impatiently.

I turned and saw a thin section of unoccupied bench at the back next to the remaining member of the group. He hadn't spoken to anyone but simply maintained the long smile of a man who had a lurid secret. He was the one notable exception to the full-combat look. He was dressed in a way that wasn't ageing well, his black leather jacket and low-cut V-neck already offering a glimpse of the sad middle-aged man he would become. A large number of chains and pendants dangled from his neck and round his wrists. His boots had small Cuban heels on them. In spite of it all, there was something about the total disregard for any practicality that I admired, but he clearly wasn't going to survive.

'I see you eyeing my style there, lady,' he sneered and winked.

'I'm sorry, young man, but you need to move,' Mother cast her disapproving eye over him.

He laughed at Mother, which is never a wise move.

'I'm Ursula.' I stepped forward quickly in an attempt to defuse the Motherbomb.

He hesitated before smiling. 'Angel.'

I looked quickly towards Mother.

'Angel?' Aunt Charlotte whispered.

'Yes, as in wings and God and all of that.' He frowned. 'It's Puerto Rican, like my mother.' His accent was pure Hackney. 'So if—'

'No, no, it's not that,' I stammered, 'it's just—'

'We knew some people called Angel,' Bridget interrupted. 'They're dead now, though.' She was distractedly stroking her dog in the manner of a crazed Bond villain.

Angel's mouth cracked open a little. I was growing increasingly aware of the rest of the boat's attention.

'Can we carry this on later, ladies?' Spear stood with his hands on his hips and a particularly keen expression settling on his face. He had the look of a determined PE teacher who's seen the calibre of his students but still refuses to accept defeat. 'It's time to start surviving!' This last comment didn't seem to create the buzz of confidence he'd been hoping for.

CHAPTER 7: COFFIN BOY

I wedged myself into the bench seat. Somehow, after Bridget's comment, the technical couple had seemed happier to make more room for me, shuffling down the benches as far as they could. We're used to this reaction now. As soon as anyone knows anything about us, or remembers why we've been in the papers, they back away as if we're some kind of bad omen. Maybe we are. What happened in the next few hours certainly seemed to indicate that that might be a possibility.

Given how small the boat was, we were still squashed together pretty tight.

'Hi.' Technical Woman next to me spoke in a clipped, efficient way.

'Hi,' I smiled, 'I've only been introduced to your shoes so far.'

She looked quizzically at me as if she was trying to work out if it was a joke or not. 'I'm Jess.'

'Ursula.'

Up close, she was softer, as if the severe outfit might just be a costume. The sharp edge of her seemed to blur. She had clear, pearl skin, and falling from her black beanie was a mass of rust curls. She'd enhanced the colour, making it just a shade too vibrant for the insipid pallor of the rest of her as if she knew she had to in some way compensate for everything else. It was as if she thought she could distract everyone from her shy, introverted nature simply by issuing one great big loud scream of colour. She was young, mid-twenties, but had such fragile, translucent skin that the area under her eyes was already a thin, bruise-like purple. There was a tiredness, almost an anxiety that hung about her like a new mother. This didn't in any way seem like the kind of trip she was used to.

'This is my partner, Ryan.' She put her arm around the serious man next to her. The thick, dark-rimmed glasses dominated his face in a way that announced his specs before him. He nodded as if words were too much, his face already troubled, drained, with a sickly sheen to the skin.

'Don't mind him,' she smiled. 'Landlubber! We run a lifestyle blog.' She said it as if that was all we needed to know about them. I gave her my look of intense interest, the one I reserve for Mother's chats about her barre class.

'We're vloggers,' Ryan added.

'Oh dear.' Aunt Charlotte looked concerned. 'I suspect they'll be able to cook you something though, if you've warned them in advance.'

Jess looked confused. 'And you?' She nodded towards me.

I pushed my hair back from the wind. 'Oh, I've just finished university and I'm exploring a few different options.'

'She finished five years ago. She's unemployed and still living with her mother because of her *issues*,' Mirabelle leaned back in her seat, her eyes fixed on me.

We banked sharply over another wave and Ryan the Vlogger's face took on a deeply sour look. Jess didn't acknowledge Mirabelle's comment, or at least chose not to focus on it. 'This is our engagement present to ourselves — this trip.' She looked nervous, her eyes flicking from one of us to the next.

'That's nice,' I said unconvincingly. I looked out at the morbid sky. 'An interesting choice.' The waves were becoming more insistent and I wondered just what exactly these two imagined they'd need to be prepared for in married life. I'm sure Mother would agree with the 'nerves of steel' approach, but then she always saw married life as a long campaign. When Dad was gone, there was only me to battle. It's been a long war.

The boat was reeling more now. I looked back and the landing stage was far behind us. We were heading towards that distant part of the sky that seemed to be no more than a black stain. It was then that I felt the first spots of rain on my face.

Bottlenose cleared his throat over the side of the boat and began whistling a kind of tuneless sea shanty as he steered. We all sat on our rocking benches in silence watching the early light move across the distant iron hills. I looked out to the point where the horizon fell into the sea and felt my stomach lurch with the waves again.

'Storm rising.' Bottlenose nodded towards the thickening sky. The clouds hung low in a great wash of tin-grey that settled above us. 'Grab my supplies, boy.' He turned to a waif of a boy, huddled deep into the corner, on the floor. I hadn't seen him until now. He couldn't have been much more than sixteen and the nervous shadow that crossed his face suggested this was not the best career choice for him. There was already a livid bruise under his left eye and the rest of him looked frail, his hair an unkempt mess, his skin gaunt and knuckles raw from the seawater. He looked exhausted, afraid even.

'Come on, lad, snap to! No use regretting all that ale last night.' Bottlenose laughed as if he might lose part of his lung in the process.

'There's no storm predicted. Don't be ridiculous,' Spear called over the wind. 'I've checked the long-range weather forecast. No storms.'

'All I know is that when them there geese are flying inland like that to the hills, 'tis a sure sign of snow and storm.'

We all looked towards the great millstone hills and sure enough, there was a cloud of birds rising over them.

'Snow? I can't be in the snow again,' Mirabelle said.

'Who's got *issues* now?' I looked at her and she watched me with her venomous little eyes.

Bottlenose emptied his throat over the side again. 'The birds' feathers be needed for snowflakes, you see.'

'What?'

'You should talk to Ursula about that,' Mirabelle sneered. 'She knows all about snowflakes.'

'You can mock, missy.'

Mirabelle looked confused. She wasn't accustomed to being called 'missy'.

'But there's a truth in the old ways. When you've seen the sun turn backwards in the sky and faeries leap across the hill lights, when you've heard the kelpies dancing at dawn and the mermaids crying their salt tears, then you can tell me there's no truth in my world.'

I think it was around about then that we first began to doubt the sanity of our captain and, to a large extent, the concept of the whole expedition. He steered round and a great wash of briny water, thick with seaweed, doused one side of the deck. My face was thrown to one side and as I opened my eyes and looked back round, a silver spark glinted above the ship. It was sitting on the top of the mast.

'There's something up there.' I tried to sound calm. 'It's moving around! Look. On the top of the mast.'

The captain started with his full-throated laughter again, which inevitably ended in him emptying another mouthful over the side and wiping the back of his hand across his face. Everyone looked up to the sky, the mast reeling around like an old branch against the cold metal of that sky.

'See!' I pointed. 'It's glinting.'

'I can see it,' Aunt Charlotte said. 'Perhaps it's one of your wee sprites or faeries, Captain.'

His smile fell. 'Course it ain't, stupid witch-woman.'

'I beg your pardon?'

''Tis a horseshoe from another witch who weren't so lucky. Guards against evil agencies — witches, petrels, faeries and evil eyes. You know the sort of thing.'

'No,' Mother said, 'I'm afraid I don't.'

He turned his eye on her. 'You will, missy. You will before this is all done. I'll tell you of a man who didn't believe and he ain't breathing no more.'

'Really?' Mother said. 'Are you attempting to frighten me? I warn you, Worzel, the last man who did that ended up dead.' She looked around the rest of us and saw our troubled faces looking back. 'I meant the butler! Angel.'

'Wait.' Angel frowned. 'You killed this man called Angel?'

'No, no. I *didn't* kill him. That's why I said "ended up dead".'

'What you said was very misleading.'

'At no point did I say *I* killed him.'

'But I invite you to consider that you did encourage us to think you'd had a hand in his death in order to frighten this tramp captain into believing you might in some way endanger his life if he attempted to frighten you.'

Mother stared at Angel. 'You have a very interesting turn of phrase for a . . . what exactly did you say you do?'

Angel shrugged. 'I run a *botánica*. Health and well-being products for the spiritually inclined.' He winked, which didn't seem wise. 'Anyway, all I'm saying is we need to be specific about our words if someone is going to get killed.' Angel shook his head and the chains and bracelets jangled around him.

'No one is going to get killed.' Mother sighed. 'I was simply saying . . .'

Another wave broke heavily into the side of the boat and again we plunged down into the sea. Spume rose up around us and fell, washing over the deck with the rain.

Bottlenose laughed. 'Don't you be worrying, now. The sea can get more evil than this.' His voice had a vulgar sound to it. 'Years back when men went on great voyages to new worlds, one ship was leaving for distant lands — Australia, if my old memory serves me.' He paused to drink from a bottle and staggered as the boat mounted the sharp edge of another

57

wave. He struggled to control the wheel with his one free hand. 'Just as the anchor was lifting, a man, not much more than a boy, comes running and leaps right onto that ship. "*Room for one more?*" he says. Well, there was always room for more hands back then. So, they sets sail with him. Not long after, as they delve into deep waters and the waves rise up like Titans round the ship, up comes one mighty tower of water and spills its guts on the deck. What it leaves behind mystifies the crew.' Bottlenose leaned closer to us and whispered, his mouth full of spit and liquor, 'A coffin.'

'Shit,' I heard Jess say next to me.

I leaned closer to hear above the waves.

'Well, those boys, they didn't know what to do with that. It was so smooth and new and when they opens it up, they see it all lined with rich man's velvet. But it was small, see. So small that it intrigued those men. And they gets to trying it out. One after another, laughing and joking, egging one another on. But no one can fit in it. Almost as though it was built for a child.'

Aunt Charlotte shifted in her seat.

'Well, now they've all tried it. All except the young lad who almost missed the boat. He goes last and as he lays in it, the men sees he fits it as perfectly as if it was made for him and they all laughed, they did. He's smiling away lying there until with a great *smash*—' Bottlenose stamped his foot suddenly on the deck — 'that coffin lid comes down and before anyone can move, another great wave covers the deck. And when it's cleared, the coffin is gone, snatched back by the sea with the lad still inside it.' Bottlenose paused to swig from his bottle. He staggered into the wind, watching our faces as if he was enjoying our fear. 'Well, they searched those wild waves as much as they could but there was no trace of either the boy or the coffin.

'When they gets to their port, the captain has to report the loss but he doesn't want them thinking he's gone stark raving mad so he makes no mention of that coffin. He just tells them this lad ran on and asked for work. Poor lad was washed overboard. The harbour master waits a moment and writes up the loss. Then he says, *"Well, there be no loss there. That young lad who boarded your ship had murdered some poor gal in Liverpool. Happen he got his just deserts."'*

We stared in silence as the rain lashed our wide-eyed faces.

'Devil took him, they do say.' Bottlenose staggered again. 'Got his special coffin all ready he did and sent it for the lad. Fit that murderer proper grand and—'

A wave rose and smashed over the deck. More than one of us screamed out. There was no coffin but Bottlenose laughed his thick laugh and turned the wheel hard into the rising storm.

CHAPTER 8: DON'T GO OVERBOARD

Lightning splintered out and left behind a black, stark sky as though it had been charred. A spent-match smell lingered in the briny air. Waves reached up to the sky with desperate hands and the white light fractured out across the sea again. The waves thundered down and battered us relentlessly. We were thrown as if we were already driftwood. Jess leaned over the side, her red hair fighting against the wind. She was quickly sick, closely followed by the young lad, his face sallow and drawn. Bottlenose just gave his thick, guttural laugh before swigging from his bottle wrapped in wet paper.

'This be the Sound of Harris, girl,' he called to Mother who looked confused. It had been a long time since she'd been called a girl.

'A local band?' Aunt Charlotte fell back into the bench.

'Best be careful those mermen don't rise up from their sunken world and drag you down to their kingdom with all the other girlies they've snatched.' Bottlenose turned and grinned to show his chessboard teeth. 'There be monsters here.' He winked.

'I can see that,' Mother shouted.

Another flare of lightning cut the sky into fragments and clouds swirled above us in dark mussel-shell colours. The reflection flashed in long shards across the black sea. We rose up on a wave and tilted into the water before being cast down again. Our eyes were raw with salt spray as the wind gathered and rolled over us. Each wave rumbled towards us, building in noise like a great rolling boulder before collapsing onto us again.

'Ship disappeared back there in the Little Minch and never was found,' Bottlenose called over the voice of the wind. 'The *Duffac*.'

'Enough now, Bottlenose.' Spear waded through the buffeting wind and stood alongside him. He'd been sitting silently all this time, with a brooding look. 'Enough of your tales. That was just a whale or some basking shark.'

'Shark?' Aunt Charlotte cried over the wind.

'Or a mermaid,' Bottlenose added.

'That's right, Bottlenose. *Or a mermaid*. Or a princess on a unicorn.' Spear shook his head.

'No unicorns in the sea, missy. Seahorse, more likely.'

Spear looked confused for a moment. He wasn't used to being called 'missy' either.

The boat suddenly tilted, the wind spraying hard salt water into our faces. It was Ryan's turn to hang precariously over the edge. Bridget was clinging to her dog and seemed for all the world like she was praying. She looked older, frightened. I looked around our group and it suddenly occurred to me that Mother, Mirabelle and Aunt Charlotte might not be suited to this either. This might actually be too much for them. It had all seemed so anodyne in the literature, a fun camping trip with a bit of camouflage and fire-making then home for some mindful tea. Certainly, that's how it had seemed in the briefing. I looked around again. We'd not seen any sign of the boat with the others. Where were the fat City boys? In fact, where was Kemp? What had Spear said when we were on the pier? I couldn't remember, but it had definitely seemed like we should be going with him. There hadn't been any reason to question it — not then. We'd been where we should be, waiting for a boat. But this was a whole different league of technical clothing — more SAS than H&M, or, in Aunt Charlotte's case, C&A circa 1982. We certainly didn't fit here.

'We shouldn't be here,' I said, dazed.

'Too bloody late for that.' Mother drew her hair back from her face. 'This was your—'

'No, Mother, listen. Look.'

'Which one?'

'Look around.'

Mirabelle and Aunt Charlotte leaned towards us. The wind buffeted so heavily that it was hard to open our eyes beyond a squint.

'Remember the briefing.'

'The what, Ursula?

'The briefing, Aunt Charlotte. The introduction. *Game of Thrones* and *Sexy Back*?'

'He wasn't called that, I don't think, dear.'

'Never mind what he was called. Take a look around.'

She scanned the weary, seasick faces.

'What do you see?'

'Very little really, dear.'

Mother was growing impatient. 'Just tell us, Ursula, without the dramatics. What are we supposed to be seeing?'

'We're on the wrong boat,' Bridget said.

There was a pause. No one moved, as if staying still might in some way help. Slowly, we looked from person to person. Not one of them had been in the briefing. There were no fat City boys, or Tough Mudder T-shirts, no tight-haired influencers and definitely no Kemp. We were on the wrong boat. And it was a boat being steered by a crazed drunk chasing Moby Dick and mermaids into the full force of a rising storm.

'Excuse me,' I shouted, 'but where is Kemp?'

'Who?' Spear shielded his face from the spray.

'Kemp?' I saw Mother narrowing her eyes at me. 'Sorry, I mean Mr Brown. Brendan Brown.'

Spear's face gathered into confusion. 'What's that clown got to do with anything?'

'Are you taking us out there to meet him or does he come along later?'

He was frowning at me. 'I'm not going anywhere near the man.'

I paused and Nell staggered to her feet as the deck rolled to the side. 'Brendan Brown?' she said. A look of realization seemed to spread across her face. 'Bo-No, have you got that register up front? Did you check it this time?'

Bottlenose laughed manically.

Nell looked back to me, her face slick with seawater and rain. 'Are you supposed to be with Brendan Brown?'

I nodded. 'We thought . . . Well, we were told . . .'

'We need to turn about.' Spear drew up his shoulders and sighed. 'You ladies have got on the wrong boat.' He turned to Nell and lowered his voice a little. 'How did this happen?'

Nell looked suddenly angry. 'Oh come on, we were picking up at Leverburgh. How is it always my fault?'

Spear looked away. 'Somehow it always is. Got a bloody talent for it.' He turned to Bottlenose. 'Turn her around.'

'Aye, Captain.' Bottlenose laughed and drank from the bottle as he fell across the wheel. The boat lurched into the fierce waves. The lightning sparked against the flint sky.

'What the hell are we going to do?' Mirabelle shouted. 'How have you only worked this out now, Ursula?'

'Oh, and what about you, genius? The boat was there to pick us up. I'd no idea if Kemp was meant to be there too. He could have just been for the introduction. These guys look more serious. We could have been meeting him at the camp. I tried to ask when we were meeting them, but as usual I was ignored and told to sit down.' I pulled myself up straight. 'You've got eyes in your bloody head as well.'

Aunt Charlotte leaned towards me. 'Can I just ask who this Kemp person is? And also, are we being kidnapped? I've always wanted to be kidnapped.'

'Don't start, Aunt Charlotte. I've just about—'

The rain drowned out our voices, drumming on the deck as loud as falling stones. The boat tilted so hard we grabbed for the sides. Waves smashed high and over us, soaking our skin and clothes.

'Pandora, Ursula, what can we do?' Aunt Charlotte's eyes were wide and frantic. I could see the salt crystals crusted on the ends of her eyelashes, the raindrops falling across her raw face like tears. She was so desperate. And in that single moment I saw it. Aunt Charlotte, *my* Aunt Charlotte was in grave danger. We all were, and I had put us there. The wind was filled with such a fine grit of sand and salt that the air itself felt like it was scouring me, as if it was trying to wear me down.

'It'll be OK,' I shouted over the squall, but I couldn't tell if she could hear me.

Nell stumbled in front of me and before she could steady herself, she was quickly thrown onto the bench next to Angel. He didn't flinch. In fact, he didn't move at all. I watched the young man as he looked into her face and gave an unnervingly calm, long, slow smile. It was just a moment, but she seemed to linger in it. So did he. I watched his fingers slowly slip through hers. She noticed his vast array of bracelets and Angel seemed all too ready to start talking her through them. She looked genuinely engaged by him.

We were hit by another wave and a slash of lightning opened the sky. A sulphurous smell clung to the damp, salt air. Nell and Angel still didn't move.

Then everything seemed to move in a strange shift. Spear started shouting angry words above the top note of the storm. 'Right, ladies and gents, time to get serious.' He seemed almost disorientated by his own temper and pivoted onto his back foot as another wave took us. He grabbed the first rucksack — Mother's unfortunately — and hurled it over the side. He managed to throw out three more packs before we could process what he was doing. It was all happening before we could move or scream.

'What the hell do you think you're doing?' Mirabelle dragged herself to her feet, staggering from side to side.

'No gear, no fear!' Spear shouted and flung another rucksack overboard. Aunt Charlotte made a lunge for her bag and lay spreadeagle across the deck.

'There's no way. No way.' She was shaking her head wildly.

'That was bloody Hermès!' Mother's mouth hung open. The boat rolled hard to the left and Mother was thrown back into her seat.

'We're heroes of pain!' Spear roared above the noise of the engine and the baying wind. He was utterly manic. He hurled another rucksack, then spun round, crazed and wild.

'Have you lost your mind?' Mother stared at him, seawater pouring down from her hair. 'What the hell is going on?'

Jess and Ryan, both looking disorientated and angry, began to stand, but as they rose, the boat listed again and the deck was almost vertical. A long line of lightning fell out of the dark clouds and filigreed across the sky. It lingered in the darkness for a moment like the white roots of a tree spreading out. Bottlenose was leaning hard on the wheel and as we rounded another wave, noise filled the air as if we were being shelled. A great split of wood was the last thing we heard before we hit the water. As the mast keeled over towards the sea, I saw the distinct shape of the horseshoe fly through the air and strike Bottlenose squarely on the back of the head.

White, foam water filled up my mouth and my nose. I was blind. My ears surged with pain from the pressure of the water and a great tide of blood rushed through my head. My legs were being pulled towards the seabed. My breath was so loud in my head that the outside world faded into a dull pulse. My clothes circled my waist, twisting around me, my hair wound round my face like weeds. I was being gathered in by the sea, swallowed. I could hear voices, distant screaming but it was a muted noise. Then I was rising, fast through the waves. And I could see hands pushing down on a head . . . and those green eyes were staring back at me in desperate horror.

And then they were gone.

CHAPTER 9: AN ANCIENT WORLD

Coarse waves, thick with salt, washed over my legs. Cloying sand sucked me down, rough pools of water gathered beneath my face, grinding grit into my cheek. I was in that weightless moment on the cusp of waking where nowhere seems familiar, when no memories will settle or form into a recognizable pattern. My eyes were raw, stinging with seawater. Salt crusted my skin with crystals and stuck to my lashes like barbs.

A view formed through the letterbox slit of my lids. A bruised sky. A world grey with rain. It was an insipid mist that hung over the land, the sky still heavy and the air dank with briny water. It was dusk. I had no idea how long I'd been there. Fragments of memory washed in like wreckage. They bore no resemblance to anything I remembered. My recollection was just remnants of what I'd seen, driftwood that no longer fit together.

I could see Dad lying in my young arms, the breath so desperate to escape quickly from him, to leave the body of a dying man.

Now I saw Mother sending me off on my first day at boarding school. She didn't wait for me to disappear before she turned away back to her life.

Then Mother was there, in front of me, her arms slick with water as she held them up.

'Christ!' Clumps of wet sand fell into my mouth. 'Mother!' I sat up and the full picture of our vast new prison opened out. An abandoned wilderness, bleak beneath a dead sky. The sand was dark with rain. I could taste the salt on the air, hardening everything. The contours of the hills merged with the layers of cloud into one lost landscape, thick mist stealing their edges and smudging their form. Distant islands were no more than dark silhouettes, shadows on the horizon. When I stared long enough, strange forms seemed to move through the mist.

I took one long breath of silty air then pushed it out. 'Mother!'

'Don't shout, Ursula!' Mother stood over me, her shape flat against the stone sky.

'You're alive!' I breathed. A great flood of relief surprised me.

'I'm yet to be convinced.'

Another groan and a body rolled over on the dark sand.

'Am I alive too?' Aunt Charlotte moaned.

'No,' Mother answered. 'This is hell.'

The wind and rain all seemed to be advancing over the sand, bombarding us.

My clothes hung heavy around me, bloated with seawater. They rubbed against my bruised arms and shins. My hair fell limp across my face and my eyes bulged with wet, salty grime. I felt sick, as if I'd been pumped full of brine.

I looked around. There was a small amount of wreckage but no big pieces of debris and crucially, no other bodies. Mother and I had washed ashore together, spat out by the sea in an unceremonious heap. Aunt Charlotte was sprawled out on the sand a few feet away, her face half-buried in the sand. She was moaning like a snared animal but making very little attempt to move. There was no one else on the beach — no Captain Bottlenose, no Spear, nor his wife, no Jess and her partner, no Bridget, not even Mr Bojingles.

'Where's Mirabelle?' Mother was nothing if not predictable.

Sadly, I hadn't forgotten Mirabelle either. I'd just hoped Mother had.

'Mirabelle?' Mother scanned the beach as if she had in-built Mirabelle radar. I can't be sure she hasn't been fitted with something like that.

In some ways, I hoped Mirabelle was alive because if she was actually dead then Mother would never let her go. She might as well move Bob the Therapist in at that point.

We began to peel ourselves off the sand.

'Is everyone OK? No broken bones, no—'

'No, everyone isn't bloody OK, Ursula.' Mother was smoothing down her hair manically. 'Where the hell is Mirabelle?'

I shrugged. That was unwise. It did look a bit flippant.

'For God's sake, Ursula. Show a little compassion!'

'For Mirabelle?'

She sighed and walked towards the shore, looking out at the fierce waves. There was little chance of anyone coming out of that alive now but I decided it probably wasn't the time to say that to Mother.

I tried to envisage myself being whirled by the force of the sea, the waves churning around me. My mind tumbled. I couldn't settle on one face, they just melted into the surf. It was all confusion. Then I saw them again. They shone out at me from the waves of memory. Green eyes. That's all I could see. Why green eyes? What had I seen?

Yap.

The image was gone.

'We're alive!' Bridget's voice carried along the full length of the beach. There was no sadness or shock on her features, just joy for her own survival. 'We're alive!'

'Oh, joy,' I called.

'It's Bridget, darling,' Aunt Charlotte murmured. 'Joy's gone, remember?'

Yap.

'Mr Bojingles is so *wet* though.' Bridget shook her head in dismay.

'That's because he's been in the sea, Bridget.' Mother doesn't do sympathy.

'We're all wet!' Aunt Charlotte was flicking sand out from her hands. 'We've been bloody shipwrecked, Bridget. What did you expect? I nearly drowned!'

'Well, I'm sure you'd float, dear.' Bridget picked up the wet dog and stroked slowly down his back. 'So, who's left alive this time?'

We stared at her silently.

'You do have a nasty habit of going on trips where people die, don't you?' Her teeth closed into a grin, like a bone-white cage. The dog yapped again in agreement.

'And yet, *you* always seem to survive, Bridget?' Mother was in no mood for Bridget or the dog.

In the distance, I saw a lone dark figure trudging across the sand. The rolled shoulders and disgruntled stomp were unmistakably Mirabelle. She filled my view like a great storm cloud.

'Oh, thank God!' Mother ran towards her as if war had just ended. I couldn't bear to watch. I gathered myself and scraped back my hair. My throat was raw with salt, my fingers brittle with cold.

I stood and scanned the shoreline. Debris littered the waves: unfathomable and disjointed pieces of a boat, some luggage, bottles and tins. Then, among the wreckage, I spotted a bundle that seemed to turn against the foam with a strength of its own. A long, white hand reached through the thick sand and clawed its way up. There was a sudden glimpse of a face before the body collapsed into the water again.

'Someone's alive!' I said, almost to myself. Then louder. 'Someone's alive!' I ran to the edge of the water. The body, face down, tried to move. It struggled to raise its head with the helpless motions of a newborn. I crouched down and rolled it over. The black hood fell back.

'Angel.'

He coughed and salt water slipped down his chin in a silvery, thin trail. 'I'm dying,' he breathed.

'No, you're alive,' I said. His hair clung to his head in slick, black curls. His face was haggard and drawn.

'My . . . my boots.'

We looked down his legs to the bare feet. He'd been in the sea so long the skin was puckered into colourless ripples of skin. Violet veins traced below his pale flesh.

'They were . . . *everything*.' He shook his head.

'Is this one alive or not?' Bridget shouted over.

'Yes.'

'Well, which one is it?' She was faultlessly callous, and I found myself imagining her rolling around like a dead fish in the surf.

'Shut your mouth, you dirty old bag,' Angel shouted. 'Don't even speak to me.' His reaction was bizarrely sudden and vicious. It was so incongruous that it seemed a little crazed.

Bridget drew her head back as if she was offended. But then we all knew that nothing offended Bridget. She covered the dog's ears. 'I'll thank you not to speak to me like that in front of Mr Bojingles.'

'The dog can't bloody understand.' Angel began rearranging his various bracelets and chains.

I looked down to the rolling water's edge. Among the debris, there was another bundle of filled-out clothes turning over in the waves, but this one did not struggle against the sea. It followed the water's flow like the rest of the wreckage. It was face down in the water. I ran towards the floating dark mass. 'Someone's out there!' I waded into the waves.

'Wait, Ursula!'

Aunt Charlotte was beside me. The water pulled round our legs as if it was dragging us back under. We strode further out, each step pulling through the heavy waves.

'Hello! Hi there!' I shouted into the sharp-edged wind, my voice drowned by the rush of the sea. I glanced at Aunt Charlotte, but she didn't speak.

'Hey!'

The body wheeled and tumbled as if it was made of nothing more than the outer coat we could see, plunging and turning with a worrying lightness on the waves. I waded further, the ice cold digging into my stomach now. A plank of jagged wood smacked into my side. I bounced up and down as the waves came in, trying to jump over each rising, cold flood of water. It was up to my chest now and I held my arms high above the waves. I reached out and grabbed for the sleeve.

It grabbed back.

There was a hand on my arm, grasping, travelling fast to my head and pushing me down. There was spume and spray in my eyes and desperate hands grabbing my face.

Aunt Charlotte dove at the hands and held hard. The head reared up. It was Bottlenose, his face livid with fear, his eyes wild against the ocean. His beard ran with chains of seawater, his hair silvered and slick against his face in the failing light. He was ashen, as if he might be made from the sea's grey surf, as though he had already died out there. But his struggling arms said otherwise. There was a strength to him that I could not have imagined.

'Get him in,' Aunt Charlotte shouted. 'I'll hold his arms.'

He kicked and flailed as if he'd been caught in a net. He was shouting and swearing all the way back to shore. We dropped him back on the sand and he looked up to heaven as if he truly believed in something he could see there. 'I was dead. I was surely dead.'

'Christ,' Mother breathed. She and Mirabelle had run from Angel. Both of them could not have been less impressed by Bottlenose's salvation.

'The Good Lord has had his fill of souls today,' the old captain gasped.

'Let's hope so, Mr Bottlenose.' Aunt Charlotte panted as she heaved him further up the dark, wet sand, dragging his legs out of the surf. 'Now, breathe deeply. Come on, man.'

71

'I need sustenance, woman. I need some of that burning liquor.' His eyes were round with fear. They jittered at the edges as if the nerves behind them were burning. 'You know what I mean, sad-eyed girly!' He flicked his gaze to me. I looked away.

'Missy . . .'

I shook my head. 'I don't have—'

He laughed. 'Believe in thy God and he will provide for thee.' He reached into his vast, heavy coat and from the inside pocket pulled out my Bible. My dad's Bible.

'Really?' Mirabelle sighed.

He held the sodden leather book out and I instinctively grabbed for it. He pulled it back fast and flicked it open, smiling. The hip flask lay naked inside the cut-out pages and this filthy man with his dirty, crusted fingers, half-moons of black beneath each nail, circled the neck of the flask before lifting it out and up to his mouth. I could have thrown him straight back into those angry waves. His cracked lips pulled back over the nicotine teeth, his laugh crude and teasing. I closed my eyes. This had been my talisman in many a dark hour, now it was no more than liquor in an old man's hands.

'Aye, the Lord provides well for his children, don't He, missy?'

I saw Mother turn away, presumably the same way that she had every time my dad had opened those old pages. Aunt Charlotte looked down with ashamed eyes.

'Secrets, eh?' Bottlenose winked. 'Always useful to someone.'

I opened my eyes and settled them sharply on him. 'Keep it. I just want the book.'

His eyes pared down into two small curves, assessing me, weighing up the worth of what he held.

'Give her the Bible,' Mother snapped.

He looked between us, his face greedy with amusement. 'What it is to have something you bastards want, eh?' He laughed and sucked on the flask.

Aunt Charlotte's hand shot out and grabbed the neck of his coat, gathering him in close to her face. 'Give her the Bible or I'll drown you. No one will know it wasn't natural. No one will know you just didn't drown when the ship went down.' She stared into the two black grains at the centre of his eyes. His eyelids were lacy with red veins, flickering constantly.

'Have it.' He threw the empty Bible into a puddle in the sand but held on to the hip flask. I scrabbled for the book, smoothing away the splatter of dirt across the worn, wet leather.

Aunt Charlotte dropped Bottlenose's collar like he was an empty bag and he fell back into the thin trickle of water heading back out to the sea.

'Someone! Anyone, please.' The voice was fractured — panicked and weak. The small outline of a woman was bent double at the shoreline further down the beach. She pulled at a body rolling on the water's edge.

Bottlenose made no attempt to move, the brandy still pouring into his mouth.

'Hey, Nemo—'

'Who?' Aunt Charlotte looked bewildered.

'Not now, Charlotte!' Mother turned her attention back to Bottlenose. 'Aren't you going to help us, man? You're our captain.'

He watched us with weary eyes, the rim of the flask resting on his bottom lip. 'Bad luck to rescue a drowning man.' He took another swig and breathed out the brandy fumes. 'Death'll come for another if you save that one.'

'Oh, really?' I started to move away. 'Perhaps we should have remembered that when *you* were drowning.'

'I wasn't drowning, foolish girl. You should learn to use those sad eyes. I was floating my way into shore. You people will never understand the—' His voice fell into the wind behind us as we ran towards the two figures.

The long stream of wet hair pulled back, some embers of colour still streaked through the damp strands. It was the woman from the boat. Jess, I remembered. But I couldn't dredge up the name of the man who lay below her now.

'He's . . . he's not breathing.' She looked at us with such wild, vulnerable eyes. 'He's not breathing,' she repeated, her voice hurried and quiet, as though she was trying not to wake him up.

I bent down and placed my Bible on the floor next to him. She looked at me for a moment, bewildered.

A thin plank of wood trailed in on a wave and clipped his ankles. He didn't move. It struck him again, but he didn't flinch. The plank seemed to pause, like a child who'd tried to wake someone, watching, waiting, before floating away aimlessly, turning back to sea.

The woman, Jess, carefully touched the man's damp, cold neck and her head fell again.

'God, no!' She seemed to crease at the middle as if her body was hinged, her hair falling in a dark amber wave across his unmoving chest.

The man looked so different without his glasses, like he'd been hurriedly woken in the night by some emergency and had had no time to grab them. But he wasn't awake. Like watching a stranger sleeping, this felt wrong, a kind of violation of his privacy. He wasn't sleeping either. His eyes were open and unfocused on some high point past me in the sky. They didn't squint against the sharp, wet wind.

'There's no pulse.' The woman's voice seemed drained of life. 'Why does he have no pulse?' She looked up at us with a childish innocence in her face and laid herself across his body as if she was protecting him. She cried as though she didn't care if she stopped breathing. Her lungs filled themselves up with pain then let it out again. She fell back onto his chest as if she was holding part of him down, part that might try to float away.

I tried not to look at her eyes. It would be real for her then. My sad resigned look would make it real. When Dad died, it wasn't real until one more person confirmed it, until they'd looked at me with those defeated eyes of acknowledgement.

74

They were Mother's eyes. When it had just been me and no one else knew, it was nothing more than a thought in my head. It wasn't real until Mother made it real.

'Ursula?' Aunt Charlotte's hand was on my shoulder.

The plank of wood swam in on another wave, insistent and jostling at the man's legs again. I still couldn't remember his name.

I watched the woman and saw the fear flooding her face, the grief being born. The loneliness was taking her, spreading through her with the cold water, washing away any warmth or comfort. A dark light was growing up through her that would never leave. I wanted to run, to not look at her, to not be the person who made it real.

The woman curled up like a leaf about to fall, as if she wanted to gather in on herself so tight that she would fold and fold until she disappeared. After Dad died, I remembered all too well trying to make myself disappear, just imagining myself as an empty outline where I lay in the bed.

'I'm so sorry,' I whispered. But no one can truly apologize for death. Death remains unapologetic, defiant in the face of all misery and grief. It is ambivalent to all our suffering. It inspires so much outpouring in others, but remains, itself, utterly emotionless. Unmoved. No matter how much you beg, it won't ever relent or change its mind. But that doesn't stop us pleading with it for mercy.

The woman let out a thin howl, rain falling into her open mouth. She barely knew me, but she would never forget my face. I looked away as if I could hide myself. Chalk clouds drew out across the wet-slate sky. Above us on the lip of the dune, I could just define the shape of a stone building, a thin dark outline sculpted against the black scrub of the land. The cross on top of the spire pierced the sky. I watched the clouds travel over it, casting it further into shadow. 'We should take him there,' I said. Her red-veined eyes followed mine towards the chapel. She nodded with an empty face.

We carried the young man's body in silence, the woman beside us. I could smell the salt on him, the seawater mingled with the last of his sweat running through his damp clothes. The rain misted our faces and the wind swallowed the sound of our sombre footsteps as they slapped on the puddled sand. The desolate chapel watched us through its solemn windows. They were such dark, neglected eyes, reflecting those eel-black waters.

An ancient damp ran through the chapel, a smell of aged, wet stone thick with lichen. It was stale, heavy. There'd been no breath in here for many years, its still, dank air undisturbed by life. We set the young body to rest at the side of one wall without any words. We said no prayers. I still could not remember his name.

CHAPTER 10: A LOST NIGHT

The first night on the island was not the worst. There were far greater fears and horrors to unfold in this place. But as the darkness took hold that first time, we watched the mist fall as if the hills themselves were breathing down on us. The fields and valleys were soon caught in a smoke-like fog. Thick, wet vapour clung to our skin and settled a dampness into our clothes that weighed heavily on us all. Our fear gathered and the hours bled into one another as if the night would never end.

I couldn't stop turning over the image of those green eyes out there. The sea is different at night. Angrier, more frightening. Depthless.

I looked out across the water, as black as the sky now. What had I seen? A woman, her desperate green eyes. Did someone push her under? Were there hands? I felt the water — how it had filled my throat, how it was in my eyes, blinding me with salt. The overwhelming memory was of being unable to breathe. Everything else was a mess of thoughts. It had to be the woman, Nell. There was no one else it could be. There'd been no sign of her or her husband yet. We'd scoured the shoreline until there was no more light. We'd called out into the wind. What more could we have done?

When we'd finally collapsed here, it still felt like we should have done more. But no one had had the strength, perhaps the will, to carry on.

The green eyes wouldn't leave me. There were no other women, other than those huddled around me, were there? Jess's eyes were green. Was it her I had seen in the waves, grappling with someone? Struggling with a man? Her dead fiancé?

I looked over at her now, shocked by grief. Surely she hadn't been fighting with him in the water before he died, had she? Had he tried to push her under and then she'd got the better of him? Jess glanced across as if she'd heard my thoughts. I looked away.

We had taken refuge by the chapel wall, the stones slippery against our backs, the ground damp and thick with the coppery smell of peat.

'Should we try some sort of signal?' I mumbled. 'A beacon?'

'No one out there but the ghosts to see it.' Bottlenose's words were heavy with drink.

'What about the other islands? A boat?'

'Too far and no one out there in this foul night.'

'Well, we're freezing.'

We lit a small fire, our hands shaking with cold and fear. What little survival training we'd had was instantly thrown out in favour of Bottlenose's water-spluttering lighter and whatever stray branches we could find near us. When it was finally lit, no one dared venture beyond that weak pool of light. I looked around at the eyes wide with shock and disbelief.

'We should be sitting inside. *We* should be in there,' Bottlenose nodded towards the tiny chapel where we'd laid the man to rest. 'The living should be inside. It's for the dead out here.'

I felt the coarse wind on my neck as if someone had breathed out near me. The cold bloomed across my skin.

'No,' Mother stated. 'We're not moving tonight.' She didn't look for agreement.

Bottlenose stood up but reeled and stumbled. He fell back against the chapel's stone wall. Mother looked away in disgust.

'I say we should be in there, watching the body all day and night. The soul's still in there,' he slurred.

'How very convenient,' Mother said. 'The answer's still no.'

I looked at Jess, but either she hadn't heard or she was far beyond any words. Angel was by her side, speaking in a low voice that she didn't acknowledge. He was making an effort to be respectful, showing her his charms and pendants in gravely slow detail.

'And *this* one, of course, is my best seller — *azogue*. It's very, *very spiritual*, you know. In my *botánica*.' He paused and looked at her unmoving face. 'Oh, did I not mention I have a shop? A *botánica* shop.'

Aunt Charlotte leaned into me. 'A few times, I believe. Nonsense — spiritual hocus-pocus. Didn't protect him out there, did it?'

Angel frowned at her but continued to speak to Jess. She didn't respond to a word.

'I sell many, many *azogue* charms. They have *ancient* powers. Here, let me give you one.' He leaned over and put the pendant around her neck. The silvery charm hung lifeless on her jacket. It had an old, familiar quality to it, like bracelets and necklaces in an old aunt's jewellery box, seen again through adult eyes. I looked at Aunt Charlotte. She'd let me play with her charm bracelet so many times as a child. I'd single out each charm for inspection — the iron, a key, a cross, oblivious to the raised voices far away in some other room of the house.

Jess seemed equally oblivious to the world. She stared ahead, unaware of anything, the firelight flickering in her green eyes. Had she fought with him? Was there something more to her broken look? She had sprawled across his chest when we found them. I'd taken that to be love. Was it the remains of something else?

'This *azogue* will keep the evil spirits away, the Evil Eye at bay.' Angel leaned closer and placed a hand on her knee. 'My belief in *Espiritismo* comes from my Hispanic mother. She was a *deeply* spiritual person and she taught me all the magic of her religion. I take the powers of that great ancestry, the powers and charms and this—' he tapped the little silver phial he'd hung around her neck — 'this can be a *very* potent love potion. I wear mine every day.' He winked at the grieving woman.

Bottlenose swayed into them, staggering over Angel's outstretched legs.

'Hey, watch—'

'Like to see it keep the evil spirits at bay here, boy.'

'Where exactly are you from, Angel?' Aunt Charlotte called over.

Angel looked up, somehow startled to be asked the question. He looked evasive. 'East Croydon.' He offered up no more information.

* * *

We burned the damp wreckage and wood from the boat that had found its way ashore. The fire pothered in bitter clouds across the darkness. It smelled of wet earth. A sharp scent of smouldering wood filled the air and caught in our dry throats.

There was a silence cut only by the rhythmic breathing of the sea. The waters had fallen into a heavy sleep. The storm had calmed, but a fine drizzle still left the air wet and cold. We stayed quiet and kept our movements small and cautious as if trying not to wake somebody, or something. Beyond the circle of light from our fire, there was a smothering darkness, one that dragged everything under. We were drowning again.

I looked around the faces. In the dark amber light of the flames, they were haggard, their eyes sunken and staring into the fire. I glanced occasionally at Jess, who sat slightly separate from us clutching her knees as if she would fall into pieces if she let go. Her face had already settled to that haunted look of grief. Angel had given up tempting her with various trinkets and edged away along the wall. He was nodding in and out of sleep, his hand clutched to his chest as if guarding the collection of chains.

A band of light slipped through the thick sky. I watched a glimpse of the moon appear through the clouds, grey and smooth as an oyster. Then it was gone, covered again by a blue-black veil of low cloud. There was a sense that we were waiting for . . . something. We didn't know what — something in the darkness.

The salt wind rubbed against our faces and dragged through our hair. Each time my eyes began to fail with exhaustion, I felt the cold infecting me, damp fingers slipping down my back. I jolted awake more than once and my eyes were quick to travel across the black fields. Shadows flitted in and out of my view. The grim tiredness was playing tricks on my eyes now, inventing small violet motes of light that skittered across then disappeared. This was like no darkness I'd ever known before. It seemed almost alive as if it was moving, or something in it was.

'You see 'em.' Bottlenose spoke too close to my shoulder and swigged again on *my* flask. 'Don't you? You see 'em.'

I cleared my throat dismissively.

'Witch lights,' he whispered softly into my ear. His words had a wet quality to them. 'That's what the locals call 'em. They rise from the marshland out yonder.'

More eyes were open and on him now, his face lit by the small fire. 'They sense a soul departing.'

I glanced quickly at Jess, but she was still locked in her own world, oblivious to everything.

'Shhh,' Mother hissed, 'it's most likely peat fires.'

'Who?' Aunt Charlotte had given every indication that she was asleep, but she does often look unconscious, so it's hard to tell.

Bottlenose spat out a laugh. 'Aye and you'd know. You'd know all about our islands from down in that London.'

'That's not what I said.'

'Oh no no no, missy, you *know* there are no witches, no faeries or kelpies. You *know* there's nothing out there in the darkness and no shadows to be afeared of.' He leaned closer towards Mother and moved his mouth around as if he was chewing the words first. He wiped a greasy hand across his lips. 'And yet you're still afraid, aren't you, missy?' he whispered.

She flinched.

'Maybe we shouldn't be sitting here on this north side of the church — the Devil's side.'

'Nonsense,' Mirabelle snapped, 'you wouldn't know one end of a compass from the other.'

'Is that right, lassie?' He looked around. 'Well, this'll be Orlon by my reckoning. No one lives here now but it did house a great and terrible witch not long ago.'

'Wait.' Bridget cradled her sleeping dog. 'You *do* know where we are?'

'Every sailor would know where he was out here.'

'Oh,' Mirabelle said with fake bemusement, 'so you are still calling yourself a competent sailor after this fiasco, are you?' She lifted her eyebrows in expectation. 'Because I would have thought every sailor would have turned back when we were heading into a storm. He might even have turned up sober.'

'You mock me, but I can taste that fear pouring out of you.' He slowly licked his bottom lip.

In the vague firelight, he seemed to take on a new malice, his eyes sharper, his features more hollowed-out. He leaned over the fumes from the fire and sniffed deeply. 'She was a beauty this island's witch — a demanding, angry beauty, but she was undeniable. Every night when her husband did sleep, she would give him her brew, cast her spell upon him and turn him into the most fabulous stallion.'

'Oh, for God's sake, really, man?' Mother's head sank.

'And she would ride him out every night far into the darkness and run with the witches across these hills. Each

82

day, her husband would wake exhausted as if a great illness had befallen him. He could barely lift his frame to work. He could not understand what ailed him. His wife, of course, would offer no answer. And yet, when that sun sank into darkness, her wickedness did rise up and she would suffer him to be her beast again. She would not stop until he nearly did expire and was spent. And again, in that grimy light of morning she would wake him, and he would be numb with tiredness. And she would say, "*Aye there my husband, you did sleep like a babe all night. You have no cause to be so tired.*"

'But she knew all right, and she did not stop. There was no taming that witch. But when he was near to his death, he did speak to a local doctor a boat's ride away. That doctor was canny, but he did not say what was in his mind. Instead, he came to watch that night from afar. And he saw the wickedness that the witch-wife brought upon her own husband, how she did turn him into that horse and permit the beast not a minute's rest. Next day, the doctor tells the man what he saw and after the husband had recovered from his shock, they did hatch a plan to exact their punishment on her.' Bottlenose paused to swig again from my flask. I watched the liquor burn its way down across the silver edge and into his mouth. The cold damp ached in my hands, legs and chest now, and I longed for just one sip of that brandy.

I looked up at the black, tragic sky, stippled with stars. Still the feeling that we were being observed lingered in the darkness. There was a growing sensation that we were not alone. This island somehow did not feel uninhabited. Something existed here, hidden. Perhaps it was animals, perhaps not. Perhaps it was Bottlenose's faeries and witches.

'Well, come on, man.' Aunt Charlotte shook her head. 'What happened to the witch and the horse-man?'

Bottlenose gave a self-satisfied smile and nodded. 'The next night, the man did not drink his witch-wife's warm brew, but poured it away secretly. When she did think he was asleep and began about her vile ritual, the man and the doctor leaped upon her and grappled her to the bed.'

'Oh, here we go.' Mirabelle tutted.

'They did tie her down—'

'Of course they did.'

'Is this some sort of filth?' Aunt Charlotte demanded. 'I've said it before and I'll say it again, I am not interested in pornography.'

We all took a moment to look at Aunt Charlotte.

'A thinly veiled attack on women, while still casting them as the predatory sexual animal,' Bridget announced. 'That's what your witches are, isn't it, Mr Bottlenose, wise women feared by men for their cunning and intelligence?'

Bottlenose looked at her in confusion. 'That *witch*—' He jabbed his finger at her — 'she had permitted him no rest and that night, for her sins, she did get shod for her crimes.'

'Shod?' Aunt Charlotte said doubtfully.

'Aye, just as the horse she had made her husband be, they did make her. They brought forth the blacksmith and that night they did nail to her feet and hands horseshoes. She was shod as a horse right here on this island.'

We looked on in horror and disbelief. Bottlenose took another long drink before leaning close into our circle. 'They say that witch's screams could be heard all the way on the mainland.' He erupted into extravagant laughing that dissolved into a thick, choking cough.

'So, some poor woman had nails hammered into her?' I said. 'Here, on this island?'

'What kind of place is this?' Mother stared at him. 'What kind of captain are you?'

'Old-school, missy.'

'I can't imagine you ever went to school.'

His eyes sharpened. 'But you're *still* scared though aren't you, missy?' He smiled at her, a crude grin of enjoyment. 'They say that witch's ghost still stalks these hills and on the deadest of nights you can hear her hooves on the ground, feel their rhythm rise up through the soil.'

We paused, each of us listening intently.

'*They*, whoever *they* are, do seem to have an awful lot to say, don't *they*?' Bridget was stroking the sleeping dog in her lap. She seemed to be the only one of us who wasn't afraid of Bottlenose's campfire ghost tale.

Quietly, I placed the flat of my hand on the cold, damp soil, feeling for some inner beat that might grow up from within the earth. Somewhere inside me, I swear I could feel that witch and see her riding towards us out of this island's dead night.

'Absolute nonsense,' Aunt Charlotte said.

'Oh, is it?' He stared past her shoulder. 'So, what are those eyes out there in the mist then?'

We all spun round. Bottlenose burst into quick and sharp laughter. 'You're all the same, you city types. All the same.' He fell back and took another dose of the brandy.

But out in the distant darkness, as the clouds moved aside for some remnants of moonlight to fall through, I *could* see something move. Its long frame was merely an outline cut from the fields. The wraith-like figure moved in slow, staggered movements as if grappling to stand. The others had all looked away and resorted to staring into the fire, casting random insults at one another to keep warm. They hadn't seen the strange figure forming from the mist, its ragged outline pulling closer.

A strip of moonlight rippled out at sea and moved across the waves. As it touched the shore, it caught the figure for a moment. Two eyes, icicle-bright, in the darkness.

I gasped and felt Mother's sharp fingers grip my arm. The dog was awake now, crouched low and emitting a deep rumbling sound. Bridget tried to calm it with a hand, but the animal remained focused on the strange figure and continued to growl and bare its teeth.

'Who's out there?' Mother called.

'Hello? Show yourself,' Aunt Charlotte demanded.

In the dark silence we stood, looking out into nothing. But there was something, something that moved in strange staccato movements, stumbling through the long grass.

Out of the ribbon of light limped a battered frame, one arm lazy at its side, the head misaligned as if in some way dislodged.

'Christ,' Mother breathed.

'No, I don't think so—'

'Be quiet, Charlotte!'

'Stay where you are, *whatever* you are,' Aunt Charlotte commanded. She turned to Mother defiantly.

'What are you saying?' Mother frowned. 'And what do you mean "*whatever you are*"? It's clearly a man. What else could it be, you bloody fool?' She marched towards the figure. 'Bottlenose, you useless mess, there's a man down. *Man down.*' Suddenly, Mother was surprisingly military.

'Stay where you are. We're coming to the rescue,' Aunt Charlotte called.

As the figure fell to one knee, he looked towards our approaching silhouettes and collapsed. His face was caught by the moonlight. It was Spear.

CHAPTER 11: FEAR

There's a point at which fear is overcome by exhaustion and we reached that pretty quickly. We dragged our delirious leader, Spear, near to the fire and unceremoniously dumped him. It seemed disrespectful, perhaps even callous, but we were beyond pleasantries now.

I bent down next to him as Mirabelle dropped his head back onto the ground. I gave her a sharp look.

'He's breathing, isn't he?' Mirabelle shot. 'What more do you want? This isn't the Ritz.' Mirabelle had never stayed at the Ritz, but she referenced it enough to make people think that she had. Mirabelle had adopted a whole cascade of fanciful airs and graces over the years because she thought Mother would be impressed. She is. My Mother is as shallow as a kids' paddling pool on the last day of summer. This is a rough estimation since Mother always thought paddling pools were not for PLU (People Like Us). Mother has a very different idea of 'Us' than the rest of the world.

I sat down next to Spear. He was still unconscious, which became increasingly unnerving. I felt sure we weren't supposed to just leave him like this but slapping him around the face seemed a bit extreme given what he'd just gone through. He'd been limping before he collapsed. Was he injured? We didn't even know that much.

The subject of what we should *do* with him slowly began to arise, which somehow seemed to have a slight *Lord of the Flies* edge to it.

'He could be injured?' I said, trying not to disturb him.

'Well, what are we going to do if he is?' Aunt Charlotte shrugged.

'We should at least examine him, shouldn't we? What if he's losing blood?'

Aunt Charlotte gave me her knowing look. 'I don't think he needs *examining* right now, do you, Ursula?'

I sighed. Aunt Charlotte could make the back of a cereal packet sound salacious.

The general consensus seemed to be that we should just leave him next to the fire and see what happened when he woke up. It was also the easiest plan of action. I'm not sure that's the recommended medical advice in such circumstances but we convinced ourselves that this was the best tactic. Bottlenose, who looked as though he knew a lot about being unconscious, didn't seem to disagree so we followed his lead of being absolutely no help whatsoever.

I sat by Spear to check that he was still breathing, and Aunt Charlotte continued to cast me knowing looks and occasionally raised her eyebrows. But I was too tired to care anymore about Aunt Charlotte's fanciful thoughts or anybody else's, for that matter.

I quickly fell into a difficult sleep and floated there for a while, aware of a few snippets of muted conversation going on around me and the distant voice of the sea. I could hear Spear's troubled breathing and I drifted further away, feeling my own breath slow and mirror the voice of the tide.

Dad's broken breath soon surfaced from the lulling rhythm. The water was rising up and into my mouth. The cold was gnawing into my bones. My clothes momentarily ballooned with air, but the seawater slipped into that warm pocket between my skin and the material and the ice flooded in.

'*Where is she?*' I could hear a broken voice close to me.

'Shhh. Someone will hear you,' Mother hissed from somewhere in the background of my thoughts. Her words were cold.

A stranger's hand reached out across the waters. I stretched out towards it, but the hand suddenly grappled for my skull. Its fingers grabbed and began to grind down, turning my head slowly like the lid of a jar. My eyes filled with brine and as I resurfaced, the saltwater ran out of me as if I was weeping. My stomach tilted and I was almost sick with the sea burning through my nose and mouth. I went down again, and the sharp water poured in over my lips. I tried to shout but my mouth flooded with water.

'Stop!' Mother whispered. 'Stop now, Ursula.' Mother gripped my hand and, as my eyes opened, she was all I could see, leaning out of the night. 'Wake up, girl. They'll think you're insane!'

'Mother, where am I? They're trying to drown me.'

'Be quiet. Do you want them all to think you really are mad?' Her eyes flicked to the various bodies lying around us.

'As mad as a hatter, that one,' Angel murmured with his eyes shut. 'Mad as a hatter. That's what they all say.' He looked like he was still asleep.

'She's not here.' It was a different man's voice who spoke now in the silence. 'Where is she?' This voice was quick with desperation.

Mother leaned forward and the dying fire lit her face with an unnerving steely glow. Her face was alive with anger and fear.

'She's not *here*.' It was Spear. He was awake and had moved. He was standing on the edge of the group staring out into a desolate field. He turned towards us, his face disturbed. 'Where is she? Where is my wife?'

We sat in silence. Aunt Charlotte was awake now and bent closer. 'This only occurs to him now?'

I could feel my heart fluttering in my chest like a frightened bird. The image of the hands pushing my head under the wild sea was still clear in my thoughts. A bead of cold sweat lingered on my temple and prickled down my skin. I quickly wiped it away with the sleeve of my cardigan, but Mother was watching me.

I looked over at Spear, separated out from us. 'Where is she?' He was so confused. Angry. There was a rawness to his voice. I watched his hands squeeze tight. Were they the hands that had pushed those green eyes into the water? Was it his wife? Surely this desperation was real. Perhaps it was more than that. Regret?

Mother stood and brushed down her trousers in a business-like manner. 'Your wife has not appeared yet.' She said it like a bank manager refusing a loan, undeniable and emotionless.

Spear turned to look at her, his eyes wild. Then he was moving towards us. His mouth was clenched tight. I saw his hands — outstretched, strong, thick hands. The green eyes surfaced from the waves of my imagination again and looked out at me from those slippery waters. It was her, his wife — Nell — staring back at me. I was the last thing she saw before she saw nothing.

'Stop! Stop right now!' Mother commanded. 'We don't know where your wife is. Why would we hide that?'

He paused and slowly fell to his knees. He didn't look at any of us. A thin, clear trail of spit fell from his mouth to the grass. 'She's all I've got.'

'Hey, man, chill. No one's got anyone in this world,' Angel spoke with smooth words that sounded so out of place. 'We're all free spirits.'

Spear lifted his head and looked at Angel with deliberate eyes. His words were purposeful. 'What did you say?' His eyes remained fixed on Angel.

Angel gave a self-satisfied smile. 'No one's *got* anyone, man. We all love freestyle, yeah?'

'What's that supposed to mean?'

'I *mean*, your *wife* . . . Well, when we met on the Isle . . .'

Aunt Charlotte looked up with sudden interest. 'Ibiza? Zanzibar?'

'No, the Isle of Wight.' Angel let a crude smile slip across his face. 'It was a festival, man. Listen . . . Let's just say she liked my *love* charms.' He held up a grubby, long phial of silver liquid on a chain around his neck. I'd seen a similar one round the neck of Spear's wife and it looked the same as the one Angel had just given to the grieving Jess.

Spear was on him in seconds, bundling him down onto the sand. Everyone held out their hands, but no one dared moved any closer.

'No!'

'Stop.'

'No, no . . .'

A flurry of words littered the air. Angel and Spear were too tightly locked together to be aware of anything beyond themselves. Spear drew back his arm and hit Angel's face with a clenched fist. It seemed to exhaust both of them. Spear lay across Angel, his fist buried into the grass below.

Angel looked at him with piercing, crazed eyes before he burst into uncontrollable anger. He kicked out repeatedly as if Spear was a stray dog. Spear was thrown back and lay sprawled by the remains of the fire. The moonlight cast both men's faces in a strange metallic light as if they were in some way unreal. Spear, in a pool of shadowy light, seemed like an animal, broken and spent. He was curled around, his hands gripping his knees, in a feeble attempt to protect himself. He spat a dark mess of blood from his mouth. It trailed in a black, sticky stream to the ground. I stepped carefully towards him, my hands still out in an attempt to calm him.

'You are crazy, man. Crazy!' Angel was on his feet. He laughed and swayed as if he was suddenly drunk. His hands twitched frantically.

'What the hell do you think you're playing at?' Mirabelle pushed Angel in the chest, and he toppled sideways to the ground as though he was now no more than a fragile shell. He lay silent on the ground.

Aunt Charlotte turned to me. 'What's wrong with him?'

I shrugged and watched as Angel moved slowly and began clutching his head, howling manically.

'Oh, I hardly touched you,' Mirabelle sighed.

'I can't see!' Angel squeezed his fingers into his temples. Every part of him was shaking now, fidgeting as if some charge was being passed through his body.

Aunt Charlotte bent towards him. 'His eyes are very bloodsho—'

Angel coughed violently before spitting into her face. He fell back, his eyes turned up and he collapsed.

Aunt Charlotte was still half-crouched, unable to move. Slowly she stood up. She didn't look at any of us as she walked, with some attempt at dignity, towards the darkness and the rhythmic sound of the waves. 'Why is it always me?'

'What just happened there?' Mother looked at me as if I was in some way to blame: her default position. She bent over Angel and started feeling his wrist for a pulse among all the bangles and chains. I assumed from the flippant way she dropped his arm that he must still be alive, but you never can tell with Mother.

'Is he OK?' Spear groaned. He was sitting, holding his knees tight. He wiped the back of his hand across his mouth.

'He'll live, no thanks to you.' Mother gave him a sour look.

'Hey, *that* little . . . incident he just had was nothing to do with me!'

'Perhaps if *you* didn't attack the guests,' Bridget said, 'we might all get along a little better and perhaps have some chance of surviving this.' She folded her arms indignantly. 'That is, after all, the idea isn't it — that we survive?'

Spear sighed and fell back, still clutching his knees. 'Yes, but this wasn't quite the plan.' He drew his thumb along his bottom lip. It didn't seem to overly bother him that he was bleeding. He didn't even look at the blood. He held his face against his knees.

'You OK?' I asked.

He shook his head.

Bottlenose finally seemed to stir, having apparently been completely undisturbed by any of this so far. Before he was fully awake or his eyes could even focus, I quickly stretched out my foot and slid the flask from his side. Mother didn't look straight at me but I'm very familiar with her peripheral vision. It had definitely not escaped her.

Aunt Charlotte returned, damp and dejected. She looked like she'd been washing her face in the sea. She let out a long weary sigh.

'Let's just all sit and calm down.' Mother motioned us towards the ground like a frustrated schoolteacher.

* * *

Eventually, when we had all settled to our various squares of grassy scrub, we made futile attempts at sleep. Spear stayed slightly separate from the group where he had been sitting and fell into another troubled nightmare.

I listened to the island. The wind was still crying like a broken spirit. Strange, distant shrieks and solemn fluting sounds seemed to ring on the air.

''Tis the island,' Bottlenose muttered without opening his eyes.

Bridget sat up, disgruntled that she'd been woken again. She was holding the dog close to her. 'Can I just ask, out of interest—' It was never purely out of interest with Bridget, there was always an agenda — 'where exactly are you from, with all this folklore and fable?'

'I'm from everywhere. All sailors are.'

'That's not what it will say on your passport.'

'I don't have a passport. Never have.'

'Which must make it challenging to be from *everywhere* when you can't travel *anywhere*.' Bridget gave him one of her more acidic smiles.

Bottlenose reached out and stirred the fire with a stick.

'What kind of sailor doesn't have a passport?'

'I tell you something, missy, that song is the island. It sings.'

'Poppycock!' Bridget said, her mouth tight and reassured.

Aunt Charlotte was awake now and looking around vaguely, 'Whose co—?'

''Tis the island, when the wind is high, it sings, all along the mountains and down the sands. It sings out to sailors, luring them in.'

'Well, we're already here, so it can shut up.' Mother's voice was final.

* * *

There was little sleep to be had in that unearthly night. The bitter air spread through our limbs. Strange, disjointed noises rose from the shadows and slipped across the darkness. I could hear the island's siren voices arcing over the dunes and down towards the sea. I was hollowed-out by fear, the cold worming its way through my joints. We couldn't see beyond our small pool of light. All we could do was imagine what might be crawling around the edges of our mean camp, waiting just outside the ring of weak light. It was a strange spirit that teased us that night and left us sick with cold terror. I lay with my eyes wide to the sky and counted the stars for a rosary. They gleamed like metal, studding the sky as if they formed barbed wire above us. It should have been gloriously beautiful to see so many stars and so much detail in the sky but somehow it made me feel irrelevant in all of this, expendable. Fear sat heavily on all of us that night.

My mind landed like a fly on those last moments in the water. It began to crawl around until it found its way to those lingering green eyes. I watched the moonlight swim over the black water and my eyes followed its path as if it was lighting the way to the green eyes, to her waiting body.

The grey-white mist crawled down the hills and spread like mould. By the first touch of daylight we were so weary, so crippled by our own imaginations, that there seemed no feasible way we could survive another night on that bleak island with all its shadows and phantoms. We didn't know then that there were much worse nights to come.

CHAPTER 12: ABANDONED

I was awake to see the first trace of light on the hilltops. It was a solemn, grey morning but I was relieved the night was over. I stood at our morose little camp by the edge of the beach. The storm was spent. It all seemed much smaller, more ordinary in the daylight. I looked down to the liver-coloured sea, sick with churned-up sand, the water heavy and motionless, the sky leaden as if it had been exhausted by some great illness. My mouth felt dirty and sour with the dry salt, even though the rest of me was damp. I could feel the dull throb in my temple and my stomach ached with hunger. We'd need to find fresh water and food, and fast.

I heard the first stirrings of our dilapidated group as they lifted from their weak and troubled sleep. No one looked capable of walking a hundred yards let alone surviving this. Damp clothes hung from our shoulders, bowing us down, our backs curved over like hags. Mother would not thank me for that analogy but as I looked at her now, she seemed older, tired. Everything about her seemed drawn further down. We were all huddled over into ourselves, our backs permanently bent trying to preserve some core warmth.

I looked out to the distant islands. They seemed further away than before. All that remained from the fierce storm was this ash-bucket sky. Listless clouds settled like smoke above the mountains. The wind was sterile now, not peaceful, but neutered in some way. Its white rapid madness was sedated for the moment but there was no suggestion of any permanency to this calm. It was just in abeyance, waiting and gathering its fire. That same strange, dull note rang across the sands, constant and discordant.

Bottlenose stood at the corner of the small chapel, retching and choking. He made no effort to disguise his phlegm-riddled cough and spat a great line out across the grey stones. The young girl Jess hadn't moved. She was still hunched by the wall, those rust-coloured curls draping her face. She was in that limbo moment, when part of you thinks that if you don't move, if you don't acknowledge the world is still turning, then perhaps it won't be real, he won't be dead yet. I remember very well that gaping blank space in the days. It was like falling through the cracks of the day, that moment when time is broken, everything is, so that it doesn't seem like the machine will ever work again. There's no way it can function anymore and the pieces won't fit, but it doesn't really matter because nothing matters.

I stopped looking at her. I'm not good at looking at grief. Bob the Therapist says I should just avoid it as if he's talking about some sort of food intolerance. '*You need to avoid wheat, gluten and death.*' I wasn't very good at avoiding any of them.

I walked through the bleached long grass that clung to the land, down to the water, and looked across the pale sands. We seemed so fragile. Even the island hung like a limpet on the edges of the waves, desolate and abandoned. Clinging on. We were at the borders of the world, that last bit of life before it falls into endless, depthless waters. There was something mesmerizing about the vast nature of it all. It was a naked beauty, with all its scars and imperfections, those iron hills above the sea, the rippling crags falling away at its extremities. This was an ancient world that had seen a lot more than our fleeting lives. There could still be monsters here. I just didn't know how close they were.

Mother came and stood beside me. We watched the waves slowly toy with a few remains of our boat.

'Someone pushed a woman under,' I said without looking at her. I stared resolutely at the barren sea and felt her almost imperceptible flinch. 'Out there.' I nodded towards the sea. I heard Mother draw in a long breath.

'Morning.' Aunt Charlotte strode towards us. 'How are our sailors today?'

'Shipwrecked.' Mother didn't look at her. My family often speak without looking at one another. It makes it easier to be insulting.

Aunt Charlotte looked old and tired in an unsettled way. She stood against that shingle-grey sky with those strange, dark vapours hanging above the hills and she looked weak. We were so small in that vast, open wilderness and yet it still felt like we were trapped.

'Well, I'm bloody starving,' Aunt Charlotte said. 'We'll have to find food. Mouth like a rabbit hutch too.' She ran her tongue over her lips.

'We're all feeling a bit shit actually, Aunt Charlotte.' I gave her a weak smile. 'But thanks for asking.'

'Come on, darling. It's not that bad. Look at the *beauty* around you.' She swung around with her arms spread and the hills behind her, like Julie Andrews in tweed.

'I've seen another murder,' I said.

She paused, her arms falling. 'Not again, darling.'

'What do you mean "not again"? You've made it sound like I've let myself down.'

'You know what I mean. Must you do this every time we go away, darling? It does make it very difficult to travel with you.'

'You should try living with her,' Mother murmured.

'I'm not the *cause* of all these deaths, you know that, don't you? Witnessing and realizing what is going on does not make me culpable or "difficult to travel with". I would like to say, for the record, I'm very easy to travel with and eminently easier to live with than my sideshow of a family.'

'But you do seem to be present for a lot of murders though, don't you?' Bridget had, as usual, materialized beside us without any warning. She was taking her dog for its morning carry, sand apparently being '*far too difficult for his coat*'.

'Good morning, Bridget,' Mother said as if there was absolutely nothing good about it. 'I see you survived the night.'

Bridget frowned. 'I wasn't aware that was in doubt, but travelling with you people, I suppose anyone could die suddenly.'

'Who said you were *travelling* with us?' Mother turned to her.

'It's so funny, Pandora—' Bridget laughed as if it genuinely was funny — 'you've improbably survived so much, done all your clever little interviews and newspaper articles, even carved out a modicum of fame for yourself from all that horror. You've been so *clever* about it all, haven't you? And yet . . .' She paused for a moment as if she was pondering something. 'Yet it was always your husband who had all the brains, wasn't it? Now, isn't that funny?' She laughed again, as if salting the words and rubbing them in deeper. 'Funny little world, isn't it? Perhaps you really are more *smart* than anyone ever gave you credit for.'

I felt Mother move forward and, even though I know she's not a fan of anyone touching her, I put my hand on her arm. Bridget saw it and her smile cut even deeper. She turned to leave with her dog and shrugged. 'I don't know, Mr Bojingles, perhaps you don't need to be *smart* to survive.'

'Tell that to Mr Bo*jangles*,' Aunt Charlotte shot.

Bridget stiffened and began to walk prissily away.

I felt the blood surge in my temple. 'Bridget, why don't you—'

'Don't.' Mother's hand was covering mine now. 'She's looking for it.'

'Forget her, Ursula.' Aunt Charlotte raised her voice. 'She's so lonely, she's even started calling herself the Lone Ranger.'

Mother and I turned to look at Aunt Charlotte. It was too late to explain it to her now.

I felt Mother squeeze my arm one last time and then let go, as if marking the end of her moment of compassion. Bridget was shuffling her little feet through the sand, shaking her head and laughing. She and the dog looked like two small wind-up toys heading into the distance.

Aunt Charlotte sighed heavily, clearing out the bad air. She rubbed her hands together. 'Right, Ursula, come on then, let's hear about this murder.' Somehow, she'd managed to make it sound implausible all over again.

'Look,' I began, 'all I'm saying is, when that ship went down, when we were in the water, I saw someone push a woman under.'

They waited for each other to speak, which is rare, so I must have made some sort of impression.

'Oh, here we go. Sharpen your pens and prepare yourself for another briefing from President Snowflake.' I hadn't noticed Mirabelle slip in as close as a pickpocket to Mother. She'd nudged me out of the way before I'd even realized what she was doing.

I watched as she settled herself in, a vicious old cat possessive of its owner. She never could cope with the sight of Mother speaking to anyone else, least of all me.

'We were all there in the Slaughter House,' Mirabelle continued, 'so don't start—'

'Yes,' Aunt Charlotte interrupted, 'And Pandora smashed you over the back of the head, Mirabelle, remember that?' Aunt Charlotte let a thin smile travel across her lips. She winked at me. 'Oh, of course you wouldn't, Mirabelle, you were almost dead. Pandora, you'll remember it though, won't you? Hitting Mirabelle over the head, I mean?'

Mother and Mirabelle both tightened their mouths as if attempting to seal in what they really wanted to say.

'That's all history. We've talked. Mirabelle understands my reasoning,' Mother used a borrowed voice, clipped and efficient to disguise any emotion.

Aunt Charlotte laughed. 'I'm sure Mirabelle does. She's always been very understanding round you, Pandora. The dog was still there paddling about in your blood though, wasn't it, Mirabelle? I distinctly remember that.'

'Well, they do say elephants never forget,' Mother snapped.

I looked out at the vast sea and, not for the first time with my family, I thought how bizarre we might seem to a passer-by. Fortunately, passers-by were not a feature of this island. 'Can we talk about the possibility of a real murder now?' I spoke quietly, almost to myself.

Mother sighed. 'We don't know that there's been any murder yet. Take it slowly. Just tell us exactly what you saw. Perhaps you were mistaken. That does happen to you quite a lot.'

'Thank you, Mother.'

'I mean, there were the hallucinations, the nightmares, the ghosts, the—'

'Yes, *all right*, Mother. The murders in the Slaughter House were real enough though, weren't they? So, you'll forgive me if, occasionally, I do see death around me or suspect people might have murderous intentions.'

'The Slaughter House was over a year ago,' Mirabelle sighed. 'George has been dead more than a decade. Get over it. *We* have. It was his f—'

I took a step towards her. I could easily have killed her right there. 'You're right, I really should forget about my father dying in my arms when I was only thirteen.' I stepped close enough to smell her sour breath. '

'*I've* always been a good friend to your mother. I've always been there for her. Living with your father was no joyride. She—'

'Don't you speak about him! Don't you ever speak about him!'

'Why not, Ursula? Because your campaign to have him canonized might be damaged by the truth? He was no bloody saint and I'm tired—'

Mother held up her hands. 'Right, that's enough.'

Mirabelle let out a long breath and shook her head. 'I'm sorry, Pandora, but I just get so tired of her eulogizing him when we both know what he was like.'

I frowned at Mother. She purposefully avoided looking at me.

It was Aunt Charlotte who finally took it upon herself to break the tense silence. 'Well, dear.' She patted me on the arm. 'You can trust me. *I'm* not your mother's friend.' She smiled. 'Relative, you see. Entirely different thing.'

'For Christ's sake,' I blurted, 'is anybody interested in the fact that I saw that woman die?' I looked between them.

'What woman?' Spear was standing like a broken shadow by the shore. He faced us, his mouth hanging slack. I had no idea how long he'd been there. I looked at Mother and then back at Spear, who seemed utterly dumbfounded.

'She's talking about back at the Slaughter House,' Mother said. 'She gets confused. She's still recovering and this hasn't helped.'

Spear pulled his head back.

'I . . . I'm sorry,' I began. Mother gave me a hard look. 'I didn't know you were there . . .' I stepped backwards into the water and almost fell over a body.

CHAPTER 13: THE FERRYMAN

I stumbled back towards Mother. The dark figure at our feet was in the shallow water with its face turned to the side. The rolling head was listing in the ebb and flow, the brown hair spiked like a drowned animal.

No one moved as the body gently rolled around on the edge of the waves. No one took a breath. A belt lay next to the hand, perhaps in a last-ditch attempt at some pointless survival skill. The fingers spread out towards it. I watched Aunt Charlotte tremble as she bent down and felt for a pulse in the cold wrist. The tiny alabaster hand seemed bird-like in her thick fingers. She shook her head and carefully let the arm fall to the sand.

Swathed in sodden clothes, the lifeless slim frame swayed on the slow current. I glanced towards Spear, who looked at the body open-mouthed. Was he hoping it was her? Or was he hoping it wasn't?

I bent down and turned the face towards me. A brief moment of recognition passed over us all. The boy from the ship. He was pallid and purple veins ran through his skin. His sightless eyes were wide open to the sky. Seaweed webbed its way across his head and knitted among his hair. His clothes rippled around his slim bones.

Mother crouched beside me. I watched a line of water that could have been seawater travel along the edge of her nose and gather in the crease. I felt the long thread of a tear run across my lip and slip down over my chin. I made no effort to wipe it away. Aunt Charlotte put her arm around my shoulders.

'I don't remember his name.' I stared into the young face. It would always be a young face now.

'Nate.' Spear's voice cracked. He was walking towards us. We all watched him. 'His name was Nate.' Spear's eyes were fixed on the cold shape of the boy.

'That it was.' Nobody had seen Bottlenose arrive. He stood over the boy, his head bowed like a preacher. He took a deep breath and held my brandy flask up as if toasting the lad. I frowned. I'd never even felt him take it back. 'In the sure and certain hope of the resurrection.' He closed his eyes and supped on the liquor.

The water breathed in and out around the boy, lulling his young, spent body, rocking him gently to and fro. The bleak hours of exhaustion in the water were etched deep into his skin. His face was taut and cracked from the long exposure to the salt water and cold. His body smelled briny as if his flesh had soaked the sea up, sponge-like.

'Best be getting this one to the church too,' Bottlenose sighed as if the boy were no more than a parcel needing delivery. 'That'll be more dead bodies than that chapel has seen for many a year.' And he laughed right over that dead young face.

Dead faces should never be young. It's unnerving — unnatural — and spreads fear. It felt too intimate somehow to be looking at his death. Almost as if we were spying on something sacred. Death is private. Precious. We didn't know him. We didn't know anything about him. We had no right to this moment. Yet, here we were, all staring at the most important thing that would ever happen in his young life. If there'd been the luxury of a headstone, I wouldn't even have known the full name that should be carved there or the dates that surrounded his life. When I'd studied Dad's grave-stone, I'd always thought how strange it was that it was just a dash in between those numbers that made up the sum total of his life. The two dates had become the most important part. The dash was nothing.

There was a sense of pity but there was an overriding feeling that this was such a pathetic end. I looked away at the layers of cloud gathering above us. The sky was darkening as if the lights were being turned out on him.

We carried the boy soundlessly to the waiting chapel. They say the human soul weighs twenty-one grams, based on the usual madcap scientist's research with methods that no longer stand up to modern-day scrutiny. A theory that's been debunked years ago, but still the romance of it remains. Even if the science is now redundant, the beauty of such an idea survives, that our souls are real and tangible, that they carry a weight to them. We want it so much that we keep a part of it as truth.

I did. Until Dad died. But he grew heavier, not lighter in my lap, as if the burden of death was taking hold and settling in on him. It was a slow and steady growth that sank further into him and I felt every moment of it. I felt the air desperate to evacuate his dying body. I felt every particle of his breath taking flight like tiny fireflies heading up into the air, each carrying a small part of him away. One was the way he laughed, one the way he hugged me, one his smell of sour, warm tobacco, another his kind touch or shrug when I had misbehaved or lost my patience. One was for the day he took me to the fair and bought me two ice creams because I dropped the first, one for the day he comforted me when I fell off my bike, one for his beige roll-neck sweaters and his old-fashioned driving gloves, for the way he tapped his hands on the steering wheel in time to the jazz. The final one was for the lasting sense of peace and joy in a moment with him that floated away that day like the dandelion clocks he used to blow with me in our little faery glen. I never went back there after he died because it would just be a park with some trees and some covered areas to sit. There wouldn't be any faeries there at all. Not anymore.

We carried the boy in silence and he too had the strange, exaggerated weight of the dead. To look at, he had been nothing, a wisp of a boy with little to weigh him down. Now, his empty frame was heavy and bloated with seawater. We formed a strange, disjointed procession towards that meagre grey chapel. The sea still stalked the shore behind us, morose and waiting, with no grief or apology for taking this boy's life.

As we surfaced over the dune, I saw Jess crouched at the corner of the chapel, her eyes flitting senselessly from the door to the wasteland around. She had a new rabid, caged nature about her.

I looked at Spear holding the boy's head and shoulders. He too had an unpredictability to him, an anxious nature, glancing around himself constantly.

As we neared the chapel, I saw Angel poking at the remains of the dwindling fire, still wearing his incongruous leather jacket and the multitude of chains and pendants. He looked over at our strange procession and frowned.

'Who is this now?' His nonchalance had a savage tone.

'The boy,' Aunt Charlotte called back. 'The boy from the boat.'

He looked confused for a moment and shrugged. It was such a callous gesture and I suddenly felt very strongly that I disliked this man, that there was something unpleasant rooted deep inside him.

He looked directly at me as if he could see my thoughts dancing around between us and gave me a long, slow smile. I looked away.

We walked on towards the chapel. My head pounded from dehydration, my stomach griped and the exhaustion dragged its way up my legs. The thought flashed through my head that we might soon begin to fill this chapel if we didn't act.

Inside, we laid the boy down carefully. I cannot say at rest. His tortured, young body looked anything but restful. There was an anguish still etched deep into his youthful face.

It looked wrong, as if it had been transferred from a much older, world-weary man.

I looked over at the other dead man. His name still lay tangled in my thoughts. A fog had wrapped itself around my mind and basic memories and words were becoming slippery. The man's eyes were closed, his skin already sallow and waxy. He was perfect — no missing limbs, no wounds or evidence of such a violent death. Drowning is such invisible violence. His body would have writhed, his eyes bursting wide, his lungs on fire. Every part of him would have fought in desperation and yet to look at him now, there was not one single imperfection. Just breath and heart and blood had stopped. Liquid had rushed into him, filling every pocket of air like an intricate system of caves flooding. And here he lay now, one perfect dead man, with no reason not to live except water — water all the way through him, where it washed away his life.

'He'll need a coin,' Bottlenose announced. 'Sailors need a coin.'

No one answered.

I searched in the many pockets that seem necessary for survival gear, none of which had assisted in my survival so far. Everything that had been in them had sunk to the bottom of the sea. Aunt Charlotte patted her damp tweed jacket.

'Wait,' Mother said, too loudly for a church with two dead men in it, 'is no one going to ask why Birdseye here is having a collection?'

Bottlenose cleared his throat and spat in the corner of the chapel. The act was so crudely disrespectful that the sound seemed to echo round the tiny room in disapproval.

'For the ferryman—'

'Oh, come on,' Mother sighed.

Bottlenose stepped so close to us that I could smell a yeasty dampness rising from him, almost like rot.

'You still got no idea where you are, girl.' His mouth pulled into a rancid smile. 'This place is older than your world. This sits *between* your world and the next. You give the lad a coin for the ferryman. Ferryman comes in the night. That's all.

106

'When I was a wee lad, there was a man in the village, folks didn't go near him. We all knew him, though.' Bottlenose paused to look into our frightened eyes. 'Sometimes he'd be awakened in the night by a voice bidding him to take his ferryboat out. And he would. He'd get up, go down to his boat and find it already low in the water, as if it had been loaded and he'd watch while it sank lower and lower. Then he'd say, "*No more.*" He'd sail out here to Orlon and when he arrived at the shore, the boat would go up bit by bit as his invisible passengers disembarked. Each one left a coin in the boat to pay his passage. That ferryman never saw no one but he heard 'em all right, heard their voices — those getting off and those waiting for 'em on the shore.'

We stood in the small, dank chapel. The quiet cold sank through us. The smell of the tomb-damp stone filled the air. Fear was tunnelling deeper into me now. I looked at the boy's bone-white eyes and fumbled with the coin I'd found in the corner of my jacket pocket.

'Take it.' My voice gave way. I pushed the coin into the old captain's hand and turned away.

'Point the lad towards the water,' Bottlenose directed. 'He needs to be looking out to sea.'

'He can't see us,' Aunt Charlotte whispered, 'can he?'

I looked at her bemused. 'No, Aunt Charlotte. He's dead.'

She nodded gravely. 'Just checking.'

Bottlenose shifted the boy round, taking care to line him up with some invisible point. 'All graves need to be staring out to sea. Lad deserves a decent *death* at least.' His words were uncharacteristically sympathetic.

'That's enough now,' Spear said, his voice sudden and sharp.

They looked at each other knowingly, waiting for the other to speak.

'Used to bury their boots up high, we did. So they can't come walking back out the sea.'

'What, the dead?' Aunt Charlotte whispered. She looked at me.

'Waste of good boots.' Spear was leaving. 'Enough of this.'

CHAPTER 14: DEAD MEN DON'T NEED SHOES

'We need to search the island,' I said. No one spoke. 'We need to salvage anything that's come ashore, search all the boxes and bags. There could be food, supplies, something to keep us warm or fresh water. Things didn't necessarily wash up here. They could be further down the beach. Then we need to form groups and map out our terrain. We need to find a source of water.'

I looked at Spear for confirmation. He seemed to have a flicker of confused understanding. I looked at each of them in turn. We were a grim group huddled round that dwindling fire. Another death had taken more than a life from us. The experience of going back inside the chapel, with the cold husk of the dead man waiting there, had shaken us all. His skin had already taken on a fragility, his head had the hulled-out nature of a wasps' nest, so delicate that one touch would shatter the delicate shell. No one touched him. Should I even say *him*? There was no essence of the man that girl Jess sat outside crying for. What remained was just his effigy.

'Come on, guys,' I said. 'What about you?' I motioned to Spear. 'No fear and all that. You must have an emergency scenario.'

He stared into the embers without looking at anyone. 'I need to find my wife.' His words were soft and confused.

I watched his hands shaking. It was the first time I'd noticed how low the fingernails were bitten. Painfully low, to a point that must hurt all the time. He gripped his hands together as if pleading with us. I saw the green eyes flash in front of me again. 'Your best way to help her at the moment is to stay alive,' I said.

He looked at me. 'OK . . . well . . . let's . . . let's start search parties. We might not all have washed up on the same shore. There might be more provisions or fresh water elsewhere.' He drew the words out as if he was pulling them from some lost place in his head. 'Nell could be somewhere. She could be hurt.'

Mother interrupted. 'You don't sound particularly convincing. You—' She nodded at Bottlenose — 'drunk man. Which island did you say this is?'

'There be many—'

'No, I didn't ask for the *Old Man and the Sea* act. You said a name earlier. You recognize it. Where are we? Just roughly will do.'

He lifted an eyebrow. 'Well, missy, if this be having this chapel and these here witches and spirits of the night—'

'No horse shit. Which island?'

'And there be those standing stones.' He pointed to a small outcrop of standing stones that none of us had even noticed before. They'd just looked like they were boulders, but our eyes had adjusted now and formed them into a circle.

'Left by the Druids they were. Buried men alive underneath them.' He glanced at Jess. 'No disrespect, lady.'

'Enough with the *Time Team* shit!' Mother snapped. 'Just tell us where we are.'

He drew his tongue across his dry, cracked lips. 'This be Orlon, missy.'

'Oh, well thank goodness,' Bridget said with faux jubilation, 'now we can just order an Uber, can't we, Mr Bojingles?'

Aunt Charlotte looked confused. 'Your dog orders taxis?'

There was a pause.

Bottlenose coughed violently before he continued. 'We is looking out to Tír na nÓg, missy.'

'Where?'

'Some sort of *Ballykissangel* nonsense,' Mirabelle said wearily.

'Who's kissing Angel?' Aunt Charlotte was struggling to keep up. We all looked at Angel, who simply grinned as though he had a salacious secret. No one asked.

''Tis Gaelic heaven,' Bottlenose wheezed. 'There ain't nothing between us and heaven, just that rolling, angry sea waiting to take us one by one. No one lives here but the faeries and kelpies. Ain't no people, just magic.'

'Nonsense.' Mother flicked her hand dismissively.

'There weren't no nonsense in the little box they found with a tiny skeleton of a faerie in it or the tiny hammer and scales.'

'Enough! Look, if someone as stupid as you knows where we are, then there'll be a boat out to find us in no time. They'll have clocked your last mayday and then . . .' She watched the vague look unfurl on his face. 'You did put in a mayday?'

'No.'

'No?'

'No. No need.' He picked something from his teeth.

'No need? When the boat was being smashed to pieces?'

'We was all going to die. No use riskin' more souls.'

Bewilderment spread round us quickly.

'You bloody fool,' Spear held his head in his hands. 'Now I've lost her.'

'Listen, when are we gonna get this little party on the road?' We all looked over. Angel was still sitting a little separate to the group, pulling on a pair of boots. He seemed remarkably sane now, as if his whole personality had suddenly changed.

'What are those?' Mirabelle nodded towards the boots.

'I know, I know,' he sang in a high voice, 'dis–gus–ting. But needs must.' He pulled on the other boot and made a gruff sound. I recognized them immediately as the custom-made boots Jess's boyfriend had worn. She was still wearing the matching ones and was watching Angel intently.

110

'Where did you get them?' Her voice sounded so disconnected it seemed unreal.

'In there.' Angel rearranged his multitude of charms and pendants.

'In where?' She still sounded detached but her voice had taken on a new, almost threatening quality now.

'There.' He nodded behind him towards the chapel. 'The chapel.'

'Where in the chapel?'

He stood up. 'Listen, lady, I get your grief. I am down with that.' His East London accent was soft and he spoke so slowly that it sounded almost patronizing. 'But, lady, I got no shoes. And dead men don't need shoes.'

'Take them off.'

We all looked at Angel, who sighed and continued with his smooth, placating voice. It was having exactly the opposite effect on her. 'It's so cold and wet here, I could die too. You would not want that, I know that, lady. You have a kind face, if a little puffy from all the crying. But—'

'Take off my dead boyfriend's boots.' Her words were unnervingly calm.

'Now, be reasonable. Come on.'

'I'm only going to ask once more. Take off my dead boyfriend's boots.' Her hand drew slowly from her pocket and the light clipped the end of the knife.

'Woah! Lady, what you pulling a blade for?'

Everyone was instantly on their feet, hands outstretched, eyes wide.

'Listen, let's all stay calm.' My voice came out uneven.

'Put the knife down.' Spear sounded unsure as well. He took a step closer towards me.

'This isn't the way, dear,' Aunt Charlotte pleaded.

Everyone started speaking at once. There was a rising sense of chaos among all the voices. This was spiralling out of control.

All eyes flicked between Jess and Angel. He was agitated and rubbing one of the pendants he wore. It glistened like

111

quicksilver in the grim light. 'Please, lady, I will freeze. I have no shoes.'

'Take them off now or I will stab you.' Her face was emotionless, her words flat, which seemed to make it all the more convincing that she would carry out her threat.

'I can't just—'

She was up and moving fast towards him.

'OK, OK!' He held out his hands. 'I need to take them off first. I'm gonna sit down, OK, lady?'

She held the knife firmly, its long, serrated blade catching fragments of light, which reflected in the surface of her green eyes.

He darted quick looks at her as he untied the laces, his fingers shaking and fumbling with the knot. 'OK. OK, no need for aggro. Peace, lady. Peace.'

No one spoke as he held out the shoes to her. She grabbed them with a fast savagery and held them to her chest with one hand, like a frightened mother. A mother who was holding a large knife in the other hand.

'Satisfied?' Angel asked and held out his hands to his bare feet. 'It is Arctic here. I'll get frostbite. I will die.'

'He can have the lad's boots,' Bottlenose murmured. 'He ain't got no one left here to care and you can't burden the rest us with your bad feet.'

Angel looked around the group as if looking for consent.

'I . . .' Spear began to speak and everyone watched. His head dropped. 'It's only a pair of boots, I suppose. He'd want you to get the benefit, I'm sure.'

Bottlenose laughed and it dissolved quickly into a rough cough that he spat the remains of onto the floor next to Spear.

Angel walked gingerly on his bare feet to the chapel, conscious of everyone watching.

'Take these and put them back on my boyfriend's feet.' Jess held out the large boots in her hand. Angel paused and she waved the knife at him again. 'Now!'

He walked slowly and uncomfortably over to her and snatched the boots from her.

'Thank you,' she said coldly.

He shook his head and ambled painfully towards the chapel.

While he was inside, I tried not to let my mind wander and settle on the scene in that small, stone room. I moved a little closer towards Jess, watching her carefully all the time and making no sudden movements.

'Hey,' I said gently.

She didn't respond. She just leaned back against the chapel wall, the knife still firmly in her hand.

'I know how it feels to lose someone suddenly . . . if you want to talk . . . you know.'

She looked at me, her eyes bulging and rubbed red. 'We were going to get married. We were going to have babies.'

I frowned. 'Are you . . .'

'No, we just talked about it. And now it is too late and there are no plans to be made and no future.'

I thought about putting my arm around her but then remembered the knife. I held back my hair as the wind dragged it over my face.

'It may seem like that now and that pain won't go away, but it will hurt in a different way, a way you won't want to let go of.' I looked at her. 'You'll want to keep the pain because it will be yours.'

I looked over at Spear. He was watching us intently. Watching the knife.

Angel walked past, wearing the boy's boots. He glanced down at Jess. 'These are warmer anyway.' He threw his head back and walked away.

'Keep the pain safe, Jess.' I nodded to her. 'Just one thing, where did you get that knife? I can't imagine you brought that with you.'

I saw Spear move towards us. He was about to speak, but Jess looked up at him. He paused and I widened my eyes as if cautioning him to wait.

She looked into my face and I could see all the anger, the resentment already starting to brand itself deep into her and I recognized so much of it. 'It dropped from his pocket,' she said. She didn't seem capable of lying at that moment but then lies can find a way through the smallest of cracks and, when they do, they take root.

I looked at the knife and then glanced at Spear. He paused and frowned at me. He took another step towards us, but I gave him a small shake of my head. Now was not the time to try and take it off her. She was too unstable, too unpredictable. We'd have to wait.

CHAPTER 15: THE HOUSE

'We need to split up,' Spear said with a new sense of purpose. I nodded to him in agreement.

'Of course,' Mother sighed. 'That will achieve maximum danger.'

'No, it's standard—'

'Standard for fools, maybe. But we're trying to avoid death. Now, you listen to me, boy,' (I'd estimate Spear's age to be about thirty-five) 'I've survived—'

'*We*,' Aunt Charlotte interrupted. '*We* survived.'

'*We* survived,' Mother continued, 'being stranded on a book club holiday where people lost their minds and four people were murdered.'

'*Oh, wait a minute*! Wait, wait wait,' Angel's face lit up. 'I didn't put it together on the boat. I get it now! I know who you are. You're the Slaughter House Five!'

Spear looked at me in confusion. 'Is this what you meant down on the beach? The Slaughter House?'

I closed my eyes.

'Five?' Aunt Charlotte asked.

'I'm included,' Bridget said. 'But Mr Bojangles wasn't deemed important enough.'

'You told us that he's dead,' Mother said.

'But he survived the house so he should still be included in the number.'

'"Slaughter House Six" doesn't have the same ring as "Slaughter House Five",' I offered quietly. I didn't look up, but I could tell Spear hadn't looked away.

Mother cleared her throat. 'We prefer the brand the "Smart Women",' she explained. 'You may remember my interviews about the incident—'

'Smart Women?' Bottlenose woke up. 'That doesn't seem to fit you.'

'It's our surname. I'm Pandora Smart, my daughter is Ursula Smart . . .'

'Oh, you're all family?'

'No,' I said quickly. 'Mirabelle and Bridget aren't.'

Mirabelle sighed. 'This again.'

'And the dog?' Angel laughed.

'Look, can we just get moving? We need to find food and water.' Spear was turning away.

My throat seemed to tighten at the mere mention of it.

'Let's put the Smart family together—'

'Like the circus?' Bridget smiled.

'Ladies,' Spear held up his hands, 'I'll go with Angel and Jess. Bottlenose, you go with the Smarts. You and Dog Woman—' He pointed at Mirabelle and Bridget — 'You can . . . you . . .'

'Oh, I see, I'm in with the dog woman now, am I?' Mirabelle shot. 'I've been Pandora's dearest friend for many years. I'm her daughter's godmother—'

'I hate you,' I said.

'Irrelevant. I still hold the title — *godmother*. I'm your god-mother and I refuse to be lumped in with the dog woman. I'm going with Pandora. Charlotte, you go with Dog Woman.'

'I'm Pandora's sister!'

'She hates you.'

Spear looked around us all. He'd been shipwrecked and lost a wife. He didn't look ready to take this fight on. His shoulders dropped. 'OK, well, Dog Woman, you come

116

with me. Hated Fairy Godmother, go with Bottlenose. The Wicked Stepsisters stick together and you can take Cinderella here as well.' He nodded towards me. I didn't know whether to be flattered or insulted. What was quite obvious though was that we made a very frightening fairy tale.

'And who are you, Prince Charming?' Bridget picked up the dog in readiness.

Angel laughed. 'No, no, that is me, I think you'll find, you wicked witch.'

'Just go with whoever you like. Packs on Backs!' Spear shouted.

'What if you don't like anyone?' Bridget asked.

'Then you shouldn't have come.' Mother turned to leave although she had no idea which direction to go. 'And for your information, Mr Spear, we haven't got any packs to go on our backs. You threw mine in the water.'

Mirabelle moved closer to Mother to ensure she was included in her group. 'She's right — and the rest went down with the ship.'

'OK, OK, wagons roll, that's all I meant.'

'We're walking,' Angel added. 'Some of us in dead man's shoes.'

Jess stared at him and clutched the knife closer to her chest.

'Let's just go.' Spear looked utterly defeated. He set off as if no one was with him and the rest of us ambled along behind as if we weren't following anyone. It seemed to work.

* * *

The upside of being with Spear was that there was a possibility that he knew what he was doing. The downside was he probably knew exactly how to kill a person and dispose of the body. I watched his hands tense at his sides. Were they the hands I'd seen on someone's head? Was Green Eyes his wife and he'd mercilessly seen an opportunity to get rid of her? Angel had made reference to her not being perhaps the most loyal wife and Spear had reacted so violently.

117

Mother certainly hadn't wanted me to let him know what I'd seen, or what I thought I'd seen. Was she trying to protect me? Would he kill me in the night if he thought I knew something? For that matter, would he kill us all if he thought I'd told the rest of them? I watched him now, imagining him as a murderer, ruthlessly killing us all.

This wasn't helpful. It was just as possible that Mother simply didn't believe me, as usual, and didn't want us to look like fools. It was obvious she didn't trust Spear though.

The facts were stark. We were shipwrecked on a desolate island with two dead bodies, a woman wielding a knife who might very well have killed her fiancé and a man who might also have pushed his wife under those ferocious waves and now suspected I'd seen him do it.

I ambled along, stumbling on the uneven ground, imagining those fingers, with their chewed-down nails, buried into his wife's scalp, grinding her head into the water.

Spear stopped and looked back at me. He was squinting into the pale, translucent sun.

'You OK back there, Ursula?' His voice seemed tinged with suspicion but then perhaps it was just my own exhaustion finding new ways to be scared.

'Fine, yes, fine thanks,' I called with a fake cheeriness. His eyes lingered for a moment then he turned and continued walking through the long scrub.

I looked towards the distant islands. The more I watched those other lands, the more remote it felt here. Bottlenose was right, this was an island for the ghosts, not the living. There were only two ways this could end, either the island let us leave or we cease to be the living.

The ground was marshy as though the land was trying to pull us in. Every step was arduous, my calf muscles ached, and I struggled to keep my breath even. The mist was falling down over the crags and hills, as though a net was drawing closer. There was a brutal beauty here in this landscape, but we were in no place to start appreciating this cold, rough land. The sands still sang in strange discordant notes as the wind travelled over the dunes, and the sea curved round us in eel-black waves. Whichever direction we looked, there was the water. Even the air was wet. It caught in my chest and settled there. The rush of the wind and the constant tumbling of the waves on the shore brought no peace. There was no calm in this place. Or perhaps there was simply no calm in me.

I couldn't settle my thoughts and every time something began to form, my body would ache or a shot of cold would travel through me and the idea was gone. Still those green eyes floated in front of me, the killer with their back to me. Repeatedly, I imagined him turning and a new face looking at me each time. Spear, harsh and aggressive, his wife disappearing below the surf. Jess struggling with her boyfriend but finally fighting back. When did she get the knife? It surely couldn't just have fallen from Spear's pocket. There was one thing I'd learned so far, and that was that these survivalists were obsessed with belts and holsters. Spear was no exception. Had she actually taken it earlier? Did she plan it?

I watched Jess wander out with the other group — Bridget, Bottlenose and Angel. The dog circled the group in excitement as if this might be a fun new game. It wasn't. It was becoming increasingly clear that this was a game not all of us might survive.

I watched them walk away and turned my view to Mother, Aunt Charlotte and Mirabelle bickering their way across the dunes like a group of middle-aged women who'd landed on the set of *Lawrence of Arabia*. Spear was quite far ahead now, striding out as if he'd never hurt his leg at all. I thought of the man who had ambled towards us, crippled in the darkness. He had a new vigour to him now, a purpose. As we left the chapel behind with its two new young inhabitants, I could hear the distant sound of whistling — one of Bottlenose's sea shanties. How could he remain so cheerful surrounded by such bleakness and death? The tune faded and the chapel sunk into the landscape. The other group dwindled into the distance. We seemed more alone than ever.

* * *

When we first saw the house, it wasn't fear we felt but exhaustion and relief. It was workhouse-grey, desolate and long-abandoned. The windows were empty eyes seeing nothing. No one had looked out from this house in many dark years. The roof of a small building at the front had collapsed. Moss grew in the jagged stone crevices of the remains as if the island was slowly growing up through the building and taking it back. This house was dying. Weathered as a gravestone, crusted lichen grew along its surface and through the cracks. The house seemed to sit in its own shadow, a dark light around it, much darker than the rest of the sky, as if the light wouldn't come any closer.

'Oh, thank God, someone lives here!' Aunt Charlotte announced. 'I must eat!'

'Why didn't you tell us about this before?' Mirabelle looked at Spear.

'No.' He was shaking his head. 'I don't think anyone lives here anymore. The last people to live here were two sisters.'

'Well, when was that?' Aunt Charlotte asked.

'About a hundred years ago, I think. People sometimes stop here. Researchers, photographers, that sort of thing. There might be basic provisions.' He strode on but we hung back and looked at one another.

Mirabelle looked suspicious. 'He seems to know a lot about this place.'

'An abandoned house?' Mother spoke slowly.

'With no phones,' Aunt Charlotte added.

'Totally isolated and nobody knows we're here,' I confirmed, more for myself than anyone else.

We felt the wind circle us and pick through our hair. We watched Spear.

'It definitely looks like the kind of place you might take someone to kill them,' I said.

They all looked at me.

'*Joke?*' I offered.

'Well, he might have mentioned that there was somewhere to shelter last night,' Mirabelle grumbled.

'Oh, come on,' I said as reasonably as I could to Mirabelle, 'he didn't look capable of mentioning very much. He'd collapsed.'

'He was certainly capable of fighting.'

We watched Spear striding off confidently. He didn't look incapable now.

'I must say he does seem to know this place better than he let on.' Aunt Charlotte shoved her hands in her pockets. 'Even knew who used to live here.'

'Let's not get ahead of ourselves.' I looked between them in turn. 'We've all been a bit preoccupied. We had two deaths to deal with and he did nearly drown.'

Mother frowned at me. 'Ursula, why are you so quick to defend the man?' She watched me suspiciously. 'Remember what Bob said about forming attachments and fixating.'

I looked at her in astonishment. Mother has absolutely no idea of what should be kept private. Mirabelle let out a snide little laugh.

'Bottlenose would have known about this house though, wouldn't he?' Aunt Charlotte asked. 'He did at least know the name of the island.'

'I'm not sure Bottlenose knows about much,' Mother sighed. 'Presumably there's some sort of witch or phantom haunting the house that makes it uninhabitable.'

'I'm happy to inhabit anywhere with anyone so long as we get out of this filthy wet cold.' Aunt Charlotte strode on ahead.

Mother gave me another one of her meaningful looks to make sure I knew she had her eye on me then followed on with Mirabelle.

As we drew closer, the house looked as if it had been constructed from the same stones as the chapel and the graves of the ancient Druids Bottlenose had pointed out. It was so weather-worn, its edges blurred as though merging into the grey stone hills behind. There was little evidence of any life here — only one window had the remains of a curtain that flickered in the wind. Some of the panes were smashed or cracked, their eyes blinded by storms and neglect. The heavy wooden door had once been painted a muddied green that was peeled and warped, its hinges dark with rust. There was nothing on the door, no lock or letterbox, no knocker. There was no need for it here. The door was slightly open as though in anticipation and Spear had already gone inside. I looked above the door frame. There was some form of frayed ornament nailed up. As I looked closer, it was clearly a ring of plaited human hair no bigger than a small child's head. The faded red strip of ribbon dangled from the end and flickered in the wind.

'Oh Christ,' Aunt Charlotte said, looking up at the knotted ring, 'We can't go in here, surely. It's definitely haunted. Just look at the place!'

'Don't be so ridiculous.' Mother pushed her out the way.

'Of course it's ridiculous, Mother. I mean, what could possibly go wrong? A deserted house in the middle of nowhere and no way out.'

She gave me *The Look*. And walked in.

The wooden door was swollen from the peat-soaked air. It scraped across the slate floor. The first thing we saw was Spear's pack looking out of place in the abandoned hall, resting among a pile of dry leaves. It hadn't escaped any of us that he'd been careful not to throw his own rucksack overboard.

It took some moments for our eyes to adjust to the half-light. A series of closed doors led off from the entrance, each with the paint split and peeling as if age was burning it off from inside the wood. There was a strange, undisturbed smell. The air was grey with dust. Thick layers of it coated the small remembrances of life — a side table with no marks in the powdered surface, a chair leaning into the corner as if it was cowering away. The sense of abandonment and loss ran through everything as if the house and everything in it was in mourning. Sadness drifted freely as though it owned the house now.

Aunt Charlotte looked around. 'I like what they've done with the place.'

'I'm not surprised. It looks like yours.'

Aunt Charlotte turned to Mother. 'And you would know that how? You haven't been since—'

'Mum! Aunt Charlotte!' I looked at them in disbelief. 'We've just walked into *Hill House* and you're bickering already. You'll scare the bloody ghosts.'

'Oh, I see.' Aunt Charlotte folded her arms. 'You know the name of the place and exactly where we are as well, do you? And that it's haunted. You all seem to know an awful lot about this place.'

'No doubt from chatting up Spear.' Mirabelle didn't miss an opportunity.

'No, Aunt Charlotte, I meant . . . Never mind.' I walked further in and looked up at the high ceiling.

Every corner and light fitting was knitted with grey-white cobweb. It was so thick on the chandelier above us that it had formed a pale gauze all around it, as though it had been wrapped in a sheet when the house was abandoned. I took another step forward. As I slowly breathed in, I could taste the mildew. It was a sick air where it was easy to imagine all manner of spores flooding my mouth and lungs.

Picture nails sat nude on the yellowing plaster. There were marks where old pictures had hung, outlines that had once had faces in them, long dead now. I still had the over-whelming sense that those blank spaces were looking down on us now.

Spear came through the door straight ahead of us. I could just make out a kitchen behind him. As he walked, his thick boots seemed almost too heavy for the old boards. They groaned under his tread, sending up plumes of dust that sifted through the air. 'Right,' he was trying to sound efficient, 'there's no food and no electricity. There is running water though.'

'Oh thank God!' I breathed, my mouth grainy and throat raw.

We all hurried to the kitchen. I didn't wait for cups or mugs but just hung my open mouth under the tap. The water was clean and cool on my tongue, the relief shocking.

When we finally all stood clutching full mugs of water, we had a chance to look at the kitchen more closely.

'There's a little tea and coffee left over from someone. Nothing else.' Spear said.

'What the hell is this place?' Mother looked at him sharply. She used that clipped voice she has when I know she's afraid. 'And what is that little Voodoo doll there?' She pointed towards the wall to our left, opposite the stairs.

'It's not Voodoo.' He looked around distractedly, as though something was bothering him.

We all looked at where Mother was pointing to the little tattered poppet strung from a nail by the door. The doll's chequered dress was ripped and the hair braids pulled and uneven. It watched us with its solitary eye.

'Looks like one of yours.' Mirabelle smirked at me.

'Oh, you mean the one I stick pins in when I'm thinking about you, *Godmother*.' We stared at each other.

Spear shook his head. 'Can you not stop jibing at one another for one second?' He walked purposefully into the hallway, looking around as if scoping enemy territory. He was clearly agitated and this in itself was disturbing, quite apart from the fact that there was a hanged doll above us.

'We're sorry, OK, Spear.' He looked at me. 'I mean . . . what I mean is, there's human hair over the front door and this dead poppet here. I'm . . . we're just scared. OK? That's all. We just tend to do this when we're scared.'

His eyes settled on me and studied me for a moment, with a look that seemed to be trying to work out if I was actually mad or just sad. I'm well acquainted with that look.

Mother decided to break the tension. 'What sort of people lived here?'

'Lonely ones—' Spear turned away distractedly and looked up the dark stairs — 'I should imagine.'

'I'm sure they were, but—'

'It's all from a long time ago. Let's not great freaked out, OK? There's nothing here to be scared of.' He glanced over at me. 'OK? They were just two old sisters and they didn't go out much. One was a little . . . *childish* for her age.'

Mother and Aunt Charlotte eyed each other as if that was familiar.

'You seem to know a lot about it all of a sudden.' Mirabelle stood with her hands on her hips.

'I don't know that much about it. Bottlenose said it was Orlon. I've not been here before, but the locals talk about it. We pick up info about various islands when we're gathering ideas for trips. This one didn't sound too great. I'm not into all these old folk tales.' He tested the banister carefully with his hand. 'Ask Bottlenose when he arrives. He's a local. I'm not. It's just nonsense.' Spear started to walk up the bare boards of the stairs. Each step he took sent weak groans up from the wood.

Mother looked at him curiously. 'Why didn't you mention this place? Why have we spent a whole night freezing—'

Tap.

He stopped, his foot hovering over the step.

Tap.

It was above us.

'It's nothing. This is an old house,' he said unconvincingly, 'there's a lot of broken windows and the wind will howl through here.'

He carried on and walked carefully to the top of the stairs.

'I don't think you should go up there.'

He turned and looked at me. 'It's fine. You people are so jumpy.' He shook his head and started looking around him.

'Wait!' Aunt Charlotte said. 'There's something up there.'

'Don't be so ridiculous.'

Aunt Charlotte turned to Mother. 'Why must you always say things like that? All you do is criticize. I just . . .'

Mother and Aunt Charlotte's arguing faded into the background as I watched Spear disappear through a door on the left at the top of the stairs.

Tap.

We fell silent. A smooth blade of cold air travelled across the back of my neck. There was still that strange, discordant tune in the distance, beneath the sound of the wind. But the outside world seemed very far away now.

'It'll be a cupboard or a window banging in the wind,' Mother said.

'It didn't sound like a window or a cupboard to me.'

'And you can tell from down here, can you, Charlotte?'

'Oh, always got to have a little dig, haven't you?' Aunt Charlotte turned to face her. 'Is now really the time?'

Spear cried out.

A sharp thud.

Then there was silence. We waited, unable to speak or move.

It was followed by a flurry of noise from the room above. Heavy boots running and then falling, chaotic banging and scratching in some great explosion above us.

There was no time to think if it was a good time to run up the stairs. I was first, Mother a couple of steps behind. Mirabelle and Aunt Charlotte jostled with each other to make sure they weren't last. Although my chest was surging with fear, it seemed to move me faster. We raced up the stairs. The door was closed. Spear wasn't making any sound. All we could hear were the *taps* we'd heard earlier interspersed with dull thuds.

'Spear?' I tried the door. 'Spear, it's jammed.'

'Mr Spear?' Mother shouted. She likes to be formal in a crisis. 'Can you hear me?'

There was a loud rushing as if the room was suddenly flooding with water.

Thud.

Thud.

Thud.

A trickle of noise slipped under the rough door, a whimpering sound, keening like a child. A very frightened child. I thought of the doll downstairs, strung up in its rotting clothes. This was no place for a child — it was no place for

126

the living. I looked around at the dark landing. Yellowing wallpaper hung from the walls, its flowers wilted and dying onto the bare boards as they peeled away. An animal's head was strung up above one door.

'Spear, can you hear me?' I pushed the door again but it didn't move.

Mother's face was rigid and intent. 'Force the door. Come on, Charlotte get your weight behind it.'

'Why can you never be nice, Pandora?'

'Now is not the time for *nice*. Just get the bloody door open. Mirabelle, come on, you always help.'

She doesn't. Mirabelle just likes to give Mother that impression and Mother loves all forms of flattery.

'Come on!' Mother is actually quite good at rallying people. Mostly because no one dares do otherwise.

We all leaned our shoulders hard against the door, although I suspected Mirabelle wasn't pushing at all. It did nothing.

We stood back for a moment. Aunt Charlotte leaned over me and turned the handle. This time it opened. She looked at me and smiled. 'Little trick I learned.' She winked.

'Oh, Ursula, why didn't you try the handle for God's sake?' There was always time for Mother to be disappointed, even in an emergency.

The door buffered against something. The fringing of a rug was just visible through the crack. It had rucked up into folds behind the door. We shoved again. The fast pattering and the thudding paused, as if something was now aware of us and it paused to watch the door.

Another groan came from the room.

'Spear, we're nearly in,' I called. 'Hang on.'

We pushed again and made enough room for me to squeeze round. As I edged slowly through the small gap, I could see the long dark gouges in the wood, cracks and scratches of age. I ran my fingers down the seam of the long scars embedded in the grain. It was almost as if something had tried to get in, or out.

127

Spear was lying on the floor, his head next to an empty fire grate. A single berry of blood formed on his temple and slipped in a thin line across his face to the floor, where it pooled on the black hearth tiles.

I closed my eyes and felt the familiar quick beat of panic swill through my chest. I've never been good with blood. I screwed my fingernails deep into the palms of my hands: the cold, wet skin gave easily as if there was no substance to it at all, as though I could drill the nails right through the skin if I just pushed a little harder.

There was a sudden flurry and scratching that sounded as if it was coming from the corner by the open window. I opened my eyes, but in that moment there was a frantic smattering of noise and the air was alive. I held my arms over my head. I was panting for breath. The room was moving all around me. I squeezed my eyes shut and my head filled with flashing light. A strange, high-pitched whistling rang in my ears as if it was inside my head. It began to form into a tune that was fading away. I was falling.

I felt a hand gripping my arm so tight it sparked with pain. 'Ursula,' Mother's voice rose above all the other noise. 'Ursula, can you hear me?'

I was drowning. I was flailing and couldn't breathe. I felt the sweat prickle down my face, a weight push down on my chest. My legs buckled and the noise grew louder, the air whisking round me. My face was flooded with strange beating. I saw the green eyes again as my knees hit the floorboards.

'Ursula! Ursula!' Mother shouted above the noise. She bent and held my shoulders. 'It's birds. Ursula, it's birds. Just birds.'

The desperate air beating against my face and raking through my hair seemed to lessen slightly. I curled myself tight and held Mother's hand on my shoulder. I kept my eyes almost shut until only a curl of light could come through. The rotten smell of animal mess and feathers circled me and settled over my face and in my mouth. I felt the bile rise under my tongue.

'Ursula, it's birds coming down the chimney and through that window.' She was pointing to something I couldn't make out.

'There's Spear!' Aunt Charlotte shouted above the rattling sound of the birds hurtling into the walls, their claws scratching at the bare plaster.

I let a slit of light through my eyelids and saw the black cloud of birds. Aunt Charlotte ran forward and bent over Spear's motionless body. She felt his neck in a way that was disturbingly brusque.

'I think he's alive!' she called back to us.

'What do you mean, you *think* he's alive?' Mother shouted.

'I don't know how to find a pulse. I just . . .'

It hadn't even occurred to me that he might be dead until that moment.

'What? You're kidding! For God's sake, Charlotte! Just get him out.' Mother said.

Aunt Charlotte grabbed him under the arms and Mirabelle ran forward, crouching low with the birds swarming above her. It panicked them and their noise rained down on us again, their bodies pattering into the ceiling.

'I'll get Ursula out,' Mother shouted. 'You two focus on Spear.' I felt her thin, sharp fingers under my armpits and my legs were dragging through the mess and feathers along the rough wooden boards. The light drifted over my eyes and then there was nothing.

But the green eyes still lingered there in my darkness.

CHAPTER 16: SOMETHING ELSE LIVES HERE

The line between the things that live and those that don't can sometimes blur. It is not always binary. My eyes began to focus and my mind drifted back into the room. I didn't recognize anything. I glanced around the dark walls. Mother was asleep opposite me by the wall, Aunt Charlotte and Mirabelle either side of her. Spear? I remembered him being dragged, a line of blood down his head. I sat up and looked around. He was there, next to the door. I watched him for a moment. He was breathing. He was alive. His eyes were shut, and he looked as though he might be asleep. Given how much his face was twisting and frowning, he must have been dreaming. Did he see those green eyes again?

I couldn't make out much more of the room. There was a small table near me under the window and two rickety chairs. The rest was hidden in shadows. I looked up to the window. There were no curtains. Through the filaments of glass that splintered out from the window frame, I could see mist circling the moon, a blind eye above us in the sky. We were deep into the night. I must have been out for hours.

Those strange lights were still flickering out there in the desolate fields. Witch lights, Bottlenose had called them. I thought of his tale of the poor, tortured woman with her shod feet and hands: the two sisters who'd lived here. Perhaps there were once witches here. Driven out. As strong or artful as they were, this island could cripple any spirit. How could they endure this? The long, slow nights of cold and days of ragged hunger, everywhere wet with rain and sea spray, a world like that could burden even the most beguiling witch. Women out here, struggling at the edges of survival and all the tales of them bent and twisted so they became the thing to fear. Men who came and told stories about them saw them as the evil, not the sea or the cold or the rabid storms.

My eyes lingered on those moments of light in the black hills. They were groundless, fleeting in the darkness. Were they witch lights? Were they something to fear? I lay down, my head throbbing and exhausted, my stomach empty and griping. I watched the flickering points in the distance until they finally lulled me, and my world slipped back into stark dreams. Maybe Green Eyes was out there with them now. Or maybe she was here.

* * *

The day was broken before it had even begun. A new frail light stalked the horizon slowly, insistently dripping into my eyes until I opened them fully. I looked up at that window. The vague beginnings of dawn were touching the hilltops. It had been a fitful few hours of sleep. Spear had cried out for his wife more than once. Whether it was deep anguish, loss or guilt, there was no telling. But with each new cry, I had stumbled into my own dreams of those green eyes — sometimes desperate, sometimes strangely cruel, always looking at me as if they could see right through me. I had woken regularly to sounds of Mother and Aunt Charlotte breathing and snoring. It had been steadying among the nightmares.

There'd been only snatches of sleep, and I'd wished for the night to end, but now that dawn was finally surfacing, the day seemed already exhausted. My teeth and mouth were coated with a sour taste now. I thought of that original kit

131

list we'd been sent. What I wouldn't give for a toothbrush wrapped in cling film now. I watched the melancholy light, reluctant to break through the mist. The rest of them were still asleep, or pretending to be. Either way, no one was ready for one another yet.

I lay with my drained-out thoughts, staring into the ceiling. The plaster was damp and stained with a bitter shade of neglect. That's when I was first aware of him being on the island, standing still in the corner of the room, his head bowed but eyes fixed on me. He held no fear for me. When you lose someone so dear you are no longer afraid of those ghosts and phantoms of the night because you want nothing more than to see them one last time, whatever state they turn up in.

I knew the figure in the corner was only in the corner of my thoughts. Dad wasn't real, he never is anymore. But still he watched me with eyes that said, '*I could be real for a moment if you believe.*' But I don't. I can't let myself be tempted. That way, true madness lies, and I can't go back there again. I used to think I saw him all the time when I was younger but that faded and disappeared. Then after the Slaughter House, he came back clearer than ever before. Bob the Therapist reckons it's a manifestation of my extreme anxiety. Give that man the Nobel Prize. Whatever it is, I wasn't about to start analyzing it away right now. I needed any comfort I could cling to.

That was when I heard it. My dark spectre in the corner heard it too. I knew he did because his ivory eyes travelled along and looked up at the ceiling.

Clunk. Slare. Clunk.

Clunk. Slare. Clunk.

I glanced around the room. They were still in exhausted sleep, their spent minds and bodies totally surrendering to it.

Clunk. Slare. Clunk.

I looked back to Dad but he'd gone. He always does. That's the trouble with ghosts, they're never there when you need them.

Clunk. Slare. Clunk.

It was directly above me, a constant, rhythmic sound, beating out the seconds. I sat up. Mother was a few feet away sleeping as usual as if it was her who was dead. I have always thought she must have a very clear conscience to sleep so heavily, that or the build-up of medication over the years has completely stupefied her.

Mirabelle and Aunt Charlotte hadn't moved and looked like they were still asleep, although I wouldn't be surprised if one of them was watching. Like all dragons, they both sleep with one eye open.

Across the other side of the room, Spear slept fitfully, still muttering names from the dark sea of his dreams. I couldn't make any words out over the sound of Aunt Charlotte snoring like a drunk at closing-time. A sound I know very well. Aunt Charlotte's favourite watering hole, The Foot and Glove, have had my number on speed dial ever since they discovered Mother had given them a fake one. Mother's never any use at that time of night anyway.

Clunk. Slare. Clunk.

The noise, although muffled by the floorboards, was insistent and clear but the others seemed to be utterly oblivious to it. I pulled my coat tightly around me. The cold memory of the sea still clung to my clothes. The damp coat made little difference. It was as if the sea had washed through this room in an icy wave while we slept and had pooled once more in our clothes, our skin and hair. It had got a taste for us, had settled deep into our bones. The thought of our drowning remained, an invisible scar.

Clunk. Slare. Clunk.

I was on my feet. I walked thief-like through the long shadows. There was little to avoid, except for sleeping bodies. I passed the old dining table, cut deep with the marks of long-forgotten meals. The two wooden chairs sat primly under it. I thought of those two sisters again. Spear had said they were the last to live here. Did they die here or did the island finally drive them out when it was too much for their old bent backs and aching joints? Were they out there in the lights or did part of them linger on here, in these decaying rooms, watching us now, these strange invaders?

In the hall, I could see that the front door had been left slightly open and great flurries of leaves had blown in, filling corners and littering the floor. They crumbled beneath my boots, crackling with every step. Strange, I thought Mirabelle had closed the door. She'd said she had, but then she says a lot.

I made my way slowly to the bottom of the stairs.

A window at the top of the stairs gave just enough fragile light to draw out the shape of the staircase and the thick wooden settle in the hallway. I reached out for the banister and felt a quick breath on my hand. I pulled it back as if I'd been scalded.

Clunk. Slare. Clunk.

The noise grew louder. And a strange, distant tune began. Whistling. I was sure of it now. I even thought I might have recognized it, but I couldn't place it. I looked back to the sitting room and could still see the bodies of the others laying out on the floor as if they'd been pulled from the sea and dumped there. Still, no one else stirred but the slight melody carried on the air. It had a familiar, old nature — like a school hymn or playground song half-remembered. A quick little jig, the notes happily sailing up and down as it drifted and grew faint.

It paused as if it was aware of my presence. I waited. Nothing. The distant hush of the sea was the only sound. I took a step, the rush of my own pulse sharp down my neck.

Each stair was worn, ashen wood, weak and stressed beneath my feet. I glanced back through the open sitting room door. The cracks and moans didn't seem to be disturbing the sleeping bodies. But something was waking. I could hear it moving again.

Clunk. Slare. Clunk.

I stopped. Now I could hear voices whispering. Hurried voices that were alert, hissing anxiously in the darkness. Something had alarmed them, disturbed them. Me.

The click of a door and my chest flushed with blood. I was caught, unable to move up or down. I looked back for Dad's spectre. Gone as always.

A rush of noise filled my head.

Footsteps. Quick, eager feet were scuttling above me. Towards me.

'Hello?' My voice came out broken. 'Who's there?'

More panicked steps, moving busily towards the stairs. My stomach tilted. There was a figure.

'Who's there?'

'It's us! Who else would it be on a deserted island?' Bridget stood, dog in hand, looking down. 'Were you expecting someone else?'

Bottlenose appeared beside her and spat by way of announcement. 'Got that brandy, girl?'

'No.'

'Liar.'

I was suddenly very conscious of being caught in a no man's land on the stairs, standing awkwardly with one foot above the other. 'What are you doing here?' I tried to look a little more natural.

'Same as you, lady.' Angel had surfaced from the other door straight ahead at the top of the stairs. He was crudely adjusting the zip on his trousers before rearranging the bracelets on his arm. His face fell into a frown and his voice grew distracted. 'We're getting some shelter for the night. Didn't want to wake you all when we came in.' He paused and looked up at me. 'Nice little surprise for you in the morning though, hey—' He winked — 'to find me sleeping upstairs in your house.'

All eyes turned to him.

'I don't think "nice" would be the word for that, do you?' It was Spear. He was walking out of the sitting room, his hand cautiously touching the side of his head. He paused and looked at me. 'What are you doing on the stairs?'

I looked down as if I hadn't realized where I was. 'I heard a noise.'

'Maybe she was making her way up to my room, you never know, Spear.'

'Just be quiet, Angel.' Spear glanced at the dried blood on his hand. 'Someone hit me,' he said.

'Don't look at me, man. I'm a lover, not a fighter.' Angel shrugged and went back to rearranging his multitude of charms and bracelets.

'It was the birds. The birds in that room.' I pointed to the left up the stairs. 'We've closed it. You fell. Hit your head on the hearth. You remember?'

He didn't speak but walked towards the stairs. I looked up at Angel and Bridget. Bottlenose was staggering back into the room he'd come out of.

'Well, you have been busy, haven't you, Ursula.' Bridget stroked Mr Bojingles. 'Looks like you just can't go anywhere without someone having a life-threatening injury inflicted on them. Makes you wonder if you're the thing that links them all together, doesn't it?'

'She didn't hit me. She came in afterwards.'

I looked at Spear. I could have sworn he was unconscious when I got in the room.

He'd started up the stairs and I didn't know whether to stay where I was or carry on walking. I took one step forward but he spoke again, so I stopped.

'Where's the other woman?' Spear frowned.

'What *woman*?' Angel was still trying to look distracted by his bracelets.

'Boots Woman!' Spear said, clearly frustrated by his own inability to remember her name.

'Jess,' I whispered.

'Thank you.' Spear was alongside me now and I could see the brown-black blood matted into his hair. The cut was deep but had stopped bleeding.

Angel continued nonchalantly counting through his beads and charms. He held one of the chains round his neck between his teeth and pulled it to and fro. It glimmered against his lip. Then he turned with a sudden savage glare.

136

'What? How would I know where she is? Why are you even speaking to me? Why is everyone looking at me? Don't even look at me. Don't ever look at me!'

We all looked at him.

He held the palms of both hands to the sides of his head and began pushing. 'I don't know! I don't know!' His eyes sparked with a strange fury. 'It hurts.'

Bridget frowned and held Mr Bojingles closer. 'Is something wrong, Mr Angel?' The tone was more suspicion than concern. 'Are you in some way ill? You are disturbing Mr Bojingles.'

'Me?' He paused, his hands still either side of his head. 'Ill? Don't you even dare—'

'She didn't mean anything by it,' I added quickly. I walked up the final few stairs, my hands outstretched as if calming a wounded animal. Spear walked in front of me and reached across me for the banister. He held his arm there so I couldn't walk any further.

'We're all just tired and tense,' Spear said. 'Let's just take it easy.'

'You take it easy!' Angel dropped his hands. 'You and your crazy bitch there.' He snorted. 'I thought you were missing your whore of a wife. You don't even know if she's dead and you're moving on. That's real quick, man.'

Spear took a fast breath. 'I'm warning you, Angel.'

'Oh, oh you hear that, little lady?' He jutted his chin out towards me. 'Your new stud is warning me.'

'I don't know what you mean but—'

'You ask him. You ask him, little sad lady, about him and his wife. She was leaving him and he knew it.'

I looked quickly at the side of Spear's head. He purposefully didn't look back at me. There was a new threatening tone to his voice. 'Angel, stop. You know absolutely nothing about this.'

'Oh, don't I, Mr SAS? I know she'd asked for a divorce. I know she slept around, with anyone but you.'

'You fucking . . .' Spear was moving fast up the stairs.

'Save yourselves!' Bridget shouted and ran through the door to the right with Mr Bojingles under her arm.

'Don't!' I reached out and grabbed Spear's wrist.

He paused and looked down, then back at me.

'Please don't.' I kept a tight hold. 'There's been enough death.'

'I wasn't thinking of killing him.' He frowned before letting out a long sigh. 'You can let go of me now.'

Angel laughed and I felt Spear clench his fist.

'You sure?'

Spear closed his eyes. 'Yes, I'm sure.'

I slowly let my grip loosen.

'Oh, she's got you good and—'

'Just be quiet, Angel,' I said. 'If you wouldn't mind, please.' I could feel Spear's hand relax and I let it go. 'Now, if we can just start being civil to one another, we might survive.'

'I'll survive, with or without fucking Jason Bourne here,' Angel sneered.

'Who?' It was Aunt Charlotte, bleary-eyed at the bottom of the stairs. I was glad to see her face, full of sleep, fresh and pink as a boiled ham.

'Oh, Aunt Charlotte, thank goodness you're here. We were just asking Mr Angel a few questions.'

'About his outfit?'

I paused. 'No, not about his outfit, Aunt Charlotte. About the missing girl.'

'Oh, the one you saw pushed under?'

I looked quickly at Spear, who was staring at me. 'You saw someone pushed under? Under where?'

'No. I mean, yes. I don't know. I don't know what I saw.'

His mouth hung open for a moment. 'What do you mean, you don't know? How can you not know? This is what you were talking about on the beach, isn't it?'

The words stumbled out of me. 'I was drowning. We all were. I saw . . . I saw a woman. At least, I think it was a woman. She was . . . She had green eyes and she was struggling with someone.'

'Who?' Spear's face was pleading. 'Who was she struggling with?'

I shook my head and looked at the stairs. 'I don't know. I didn't see. I only saw the back of their head.'

'And you think it was me?'

I looked up. 'No, I didn't say that. I don't even know who the woman was. It could have been your . . . your wife. It could have been Jess. She has green eyes. Her fiancé turned up dead with her lying across him. I don't know. I don't know what I think.'

Angel was laughing and turning away. 'Of course she thinks it's you. Who else would take the chance to bump off your wife? I'd be surprised if you hadn't planned the whole thing, sunk the boat and then killed her.'

'Everyone stop!' I said. 'Look, has anyone seen Jess?'

'Who, dear?' Aunt Charlotte was on the stairs walking towards us.

'The woman with the red hair? Angel, we just want to know, was she with you?'

Angel looked at me for a moment as if a cloud was parting. 'You mean the crazy little bitch who made me take off my shoes?'

'I'm here.' Jess appeared from the door to the left, where we'd found Spear with the birds. She looked at me. There was no way she hadn't just heard what I'd said about her and the possibility she'd been fighting with her fiancé in the water and killed him.

She was different, changed somehow. She looked dazed. Grief was weaving its spell fast. The thin light from behind cast her as a gaunt silhouette now, with tails of lank hair down her shoulders. All the colour had leached out of her so that she could almost have been a ghost standing there, thin and bent.

I hesitated. 'Are you OK?'

She nodded.

But it was Angel who was twitching erratically beside her. 'I'm fine! I'm fine!' His voice was fractured.

139

'All right,' I said. I slowly edged around Spear, being careful not to touch him or look at him. He stared resolutely ahead.

'So that's everyone accounted for, is it?' Bridget poked her head through the door she'd scurried into. She spoke efficiently as if she hadn't just dramatically run for cover.

I nodded. I didn't bother to tell them about the extra, silent figure that had stood watching me from the corner of the sitting room. As Bob the Therapist says, if I go around telling everyone my dead dad is in the corner of the room, they'll think I'm mad. I'm not sure that's a technical term, but I take his point.

'Who's in that room, then?' I nodded towards the closed door on the left of the stairs, next to the room Jess had just come out of. It had to be where the noise had been coming from, I was sure of it. 'Is someone using that room as well?'

They all looked at me with rising concern. Angel leaned against the door frame to the room he'd slept in, winding his pendants round his finger and picking his way through the bracelets, a seething little mess of anxiety — that's what Mother calls me when I do that.

'What exactly is going on, Ursula?' Aunt Charlotte was alongside me now at the top of the stairs, her voice still bleary with sleep.

Angel paused, beaded bracelet in hand. 'We just told you, or weren't you listening, you stupid old—'

'Don't speak to her like that. In fact—' I held my face up defiantly — 'don't speak at all.' I walked past him towards the closed door.

'You better watch yourself, crazy girl.'

'She doesn't like being called crazy,' Aunt Charlotte muttered. 'Not since—'

'Leave her alone, Angel,' Spear interrupted in a low voice. He was at the top of the stairs now too. It was getting pretty tight there.

'What the hell is going on?' Mother's voice was already well-stoked with irritation. 'Why is everyone awake? And why are *you* defending my daughter?' Her eyes were clamped on Spear.

'I heard something, Mother,' I called.

'Oh, you've always *heard something.*'

'She's creeping around like she thinks she's some sort of sleuth, your daughter, that's what's happening.' Angel looked down at Mother.

Aunt Charlotte looked confused.

'*I* am the victim of a crime.' He announced it as though he was almost proud of the fact. 'Someone stole from me.' He took a moment to enjoy the attention, but I watched his frenetic fingers jitter through the chains round his neck.

'Someone stole from *you*?' Bridget said in disbelief.

'OK,' Mother sighed, walking slowly up the stairs. 'Come on then. Out with it.'

Angel placed his hands on his hips and repeated, '*I* am the victim of a theft.'

Mr Bojingles yapped. Angel glared at the dog as if he could be a suspect. 'Well, why is everyone looking at me as if I haven't got anything worth nicking. This jewellery is from all over the world!' The words quick-fired out of him with nervous energy.

'Oh, so it didn't come from Garrard's then?' Mother never misses an opportunity. 'You do surprise me.'

Angel laughed at her, his head shaking slowly. He sounded crazed. 'These are treasures.' He held up a fistful of necklaces and pendants, then plucked at the bracelets on his arms. 'Like I told *her*—' He nodded towards Jess, who was utterly unresponsive — 'I got charms and talismans here to heal all regret and loss, ward off the Evil Eye, and some that might even make a person fall in love with the likes of you.' He widened his eyes at me. 'If anyone is going to survive this nightmare, it's me. I always travel with protection.'

'Oh, they all say that,' Aunt Charlotte sighed.

We paused.

'What?' She looked around at us.

141

'Superstitious nonsense,' Mother sniffed. 'Utterly worthless.' We were all clustered in the small landing now, which was starting to get a little bit claustrophobic.

Angel pushed his face close to Mother's. 'Nonsense, is it? Well, if it's so *worthless*, you tell me why someone has stolen one of my bracelets.'

Mother didn't blink. She shook her head. Angel scanned our disbelieving faces. 'Hey! This is no joke! Someone has stolen from me. Someone here is a thief, I tell you.' He shook his fist and a great jumble of bracelets ran down to his wrist. Like trinkets from a child's jewellery box, they were all shapes and sizes, colours and charms from various religions. He had icons and crucifixes dangling from his neck, jostling for position with miniature perfume bottles, bike chains and long links of paper clips. He was the kind of man who had more friendship bracelets than friends.

'Listen,' I said, 'we've been through the worst the Sound of Harris has to offer us—'

'Them again.' Aunt Charlotte shook her head.

'We've been shipwrecked on a deserted island that has nothing but driving rain and frozen air.' I leaned so close to Angel now that I could smell the lingering remains of his Paco Rabanne mingled with sour sweat. I lowered my voice to something barely above a whisper. 'There will be losses.' I patted him on the arm and turned to the closed door. 'You just have to stay calm. We must all try to be rational and think clearly. Now, I just need to go in this room for a moment and see if it's haunted.'

No one said a word as I walked towards the closed door. Although, I thought I might have heard Angel murmur, 'Mad as a hatter,' again. But I could have been mistaken.

The paint had blistered and peeled on this door as well, as if something had tried to burn its way out of the room. I reached for the handle and turned it. I pushed and the door slowly scraped along the planks of the coffin-wood floorboards, groaning as if it was unused to this action.

I looked into the one room none of us had been in yet.

CHAPTER 17: SKULDUGGERY

Inside was dead. This whole house was dying but here seemed to be where all the rot stemmed from — this place. I could smell it, the ripe decay growing through everything, rotten tendrils infesting every crack and pipe. The house occasionally let out a resigned groan as another part of it perished. On the far wall, an old spinning wheel stood silent as if abandoned at the end of a dark fairy tale, banished to this broken room until some foolish traveller might lose their way and find themselves opening this door.

Two old banister ends leaned in a corner. A cold fireplace was framed by a blackened mantelpiece. Its iron fireguard was bent and bulging out as though something had pushed hard against it from inside the fireplace. As I looked closer, I saw tiny porcelain-white bones clustered in the hearth in small piles. They were chalky with age, falling to dust at the edges. A small smattering of dry, crumbling droppings and ragged feathers betrayed that there had once been birds in this room too, lost and frantic with life, exhausted from battering at this cage. Finally, they'd succumbed to this strange new world. Nothing lived here anymore.

I looked back towards the landing, where all the voices had gone silent. Spear watched me from the door. He didn't speak.

There was a sadness in here, a confusion, as if this room, this house, could not understand why it had been left behind. What had happened? One day there was life — beds that were warm with sleep, fires burning pockets of light into the dark cold. But the flames had flickered and grown weak, dwindling into loss. And then they were gone. No one was left and there was no explanation. Something took those last two sisters away — death or a life elsewhere. Spear knew something about it. Could I trust he'd tell me the truth? This house, though, would never know what had happened or why it now echoed to the sound of so much desolate emptiness.

The rain tapped incessantly at the window. It had been left half-open as though the old women had just deserted the place and fled for the hills with no care for securing the place from the weather. A cruel little draught scuttled through the room making it seem even more bleak.

Outside on the landing, Angel was murmuring about how he'd been the victim of a theft and nobody cared. Bridget and the others were talking as if they'd forgotten I was there. Their muted voices seemed to drift further away.

Only tokens of life remained in this room, in the superstitions nailed up in more dolls and tangles of hair above the door frame. Over the mantelpiece was an old etching of some joyful Victorian scene, a man playing with three children, one child pulling at his coat insistently. I could hear the room ring with their broken laughter.

It stopped, as if they'd seen me watching, as if they'd been painted into that moment and all they could do was turn their eyes to look at me. They watched me now from the picture, their eyes following the smallest movement.

Suddenly, the figures were distracted. I thought I saw their eyes glance towards the large bay window as if something else had moved, as if someone else was here. I followed their gaze. There was no one. I looked back to the picture but still they watched the area just beyond me by the bay window. There was something like fear in their eyes now.

The windows let only the faintest sense of dawn's light through the dust. Beneath the dull glass was a lame, old rocking horse. A breeze whispered through the horse's mane, tugging at it like a child's eager hands. I took a step towards it. Did the horse move or was it just my crude disturbance of this untouched space? Did it see out, see me through those sorrowful eyes?

It must have taken many long years for this weak light to strip this horse of so much colour. A ghost of its glories remained in a single, frayed rosette and the occasional memory of scarlet paint on its saddle and down its rich brown mane. Someone's favourite, a forgotten Derby winner left in its stable with no riders. Any children who remembered hours here and glory days, had long since grown up and been blown far away by the years.

I reached out and cautiously pushed it.

Clunk. Slare. Clunk.

'Ursula?' I'd forgotten Spear was at the door. 'Ursula, what is it?'

'I'm fine,' my eyes remained fixed on the rocking horse. 'There's nothing here.'

But as I looked to the floor, the bare footprints that led across the carpet of dust said otherwise. I didn't mention them to Spear.

Mother was by his shoulder at the open door. 'What are you doing?' Her cold eyes looked around the room before settling on me. 'Why are you in here?' Her words were sharp with suspicion. 'What are you up to?'

'Looking for things to steal? Like my bracelets?' Angel called from behind them.

Mother turned and gave him *The Look*. He immediately turned his attention back to his jewellery.

Mr Bojingles gave out a quick, sudden bark and jumped down. He ran panting across the room, disrupting all the dust on the floor.

'Control your bloody dog!' Mirabelle snapped. 'What the devil's going on here? What's *she* doing in there?'

'There's been a theft.' Angel folded his arms across his chest. 'And Little Miss Crazy thought someone or *something* was in this room.'

'Oh, here we go again.' Mirabelle gave a dramatic sigh and shook her head.

'Perhaps it was another one of those sealed-up door mysteries you like, dear,' Aunt Charlotte said, as if I was the one who was struggling to keep up. 'It did look quite difficult to open. In fact, all the doors—'

'Thank you, Aunt Charlotte, but we have been through this before, haven't we?' I said. 'It's "locked-room". They're called "locked-room mysteries" and they're not in any way relevant here as there is no mystery and no one is dead.'

'They are,' Jess's voice was solemn and definite. We all turned to look at her. She seemed even more sallow than before, as if the grief was infecting every part of her.

'I think she meant inside that room,' Bridget offered with a smile. 'Now, come on, Mr Bojingles, let's get you some rest. You need a little more sleep.'

'I think we all do.' Mother looked at me pointedly. 'It's only just dawn. If we're going to stand any chance today we need a few more hours' rest. *All of us.*' She held my gaze before moving closer and lowering her voice. 'You know what Bob said about a full night's rest, don't you? Remember Bob's Bedtime Rules?'

'You mean the ones involving sleeping with my mother?'

She looked round quickly at everyone. 'I'm sure I don't know what you mean! I've never been so—'

'Yes, you have, so let's not bother rehearsing this again.'

'Wait, is no one going to *do* anything—' Angel's voice was beginning to sound disjointed — 'about the theft?'

'No,' Mother said with finality.

She walked towards the stairs. Jess drifted to her room beside this one, the bird room. Angel had chosen a dilapidated bed in a small room on his own directly opposite the top of the stairs and between this one and the room Bridget and Bottlenose had slept in. There was a large dead cow's

146

head above the door but rather than inspiring a gentleman's-club aesthetic, it brought more of an abandoned-abattoir feel to the house. Its black glass eyes looked out at us forlornly, reflecting every movement.

'You'll all regret this,' Angel shot before slamming the door. A singed cowhide fell from its hanging on the wall. We all stopped.

'Oh,' Bottlenose slurred. I'd forgotten he was there. 'That be there to ward off faeries, daemons, witches and the like. He'll be unprotected now!'

'Perhaps you could offer to replace the animal,' Mirabelle sniped.

'All these poppets and paraphernalia around the house is just grim.' Mother turned to me. 'It's worse than your bedroom, Ursula.'

'Nice.'

'At least you haven't resorted to nailing up plaited hair.'

'Maybe I have, Mother. Snip, snip.' I mimed cutting her hair and she looked suitably horrified.

Bottlenose spat something into the corner, which rolled around collecting dust. 'When the head o' the family dies, custom is to nail a large piece of their hair to the door frame to keep away faeries.' He staggered a little before laughing and stumbling back into the room next to Angel's.

'Shame you didn't remember all this about the house last night,' Mother called, 'or perhaps even the fact that there was a house, before we slept outside and nearly died of exposure.'

'Who's been exposing—'

'Be quiet, Charlotte.'

Mirabelle nodded along with Mother as usual. 'Yes, exactly, what Pandora said. How could you have left us out in the wind and rain when you knew which island this was? You must have known there was a house here.'

Bottlenose coughed again and threatened to clear whatever there was blocking it into the hallway. 'Aye, I knew. But no one would sleep here who was in their right mind. This

147

place is haunted. *Evil* walks here.' He grinned as if he might very well be the malevolence he spoke of.

Bridget and the dog trotted into the bedroom after him. 'I don't care what evil there is. I'm happy to sleep anywhere so long as Mr Bojingles has a comfortable bed.' There was a large nest of threadbare blankets in one corner that she and the dog settled into. Bottlenose sprawled himself out under the window. Bridget and the dog watched him closely as he proceeded to slowly cover himself with the faery-repelling cowhide that had fallen down earlier.

The floorboards creaked behind me. Jess had wandered into the rocking horse room and was crouching down next to the toy looking up at it hopefully. She seemed calmer now but walked with the hunched-over shoulders of someone who didn't want to see the world anymore.

I couldn't bring myself to disturb her and what more could I say to her? He would always be dead? It wouldn't get easier, just different? She didn't look at me but drifted back out of the room as if it was her who had died and become the ghost. There was nothing I could do. Nothing I could say. No one can navigate grief for you.

As I walked away, I saw a small cabinet standing just beside the door to the room. There was a single photograph of two middle-aged women, neither smiling, just caught in a moment of their lives. They weren't young and, from the photograph, it was hard to imagine they ever had been. Yet, there was the rocking horse in the corner of the picture, its mouth wide, with its lips pulled back over the teeth, its eyes staring straight back at the viewer. Perhaps it had been a childhood memento they'd kept. Perhaps.

They'd all gone and I was alone. Mother, Mirabelle and Aunt Charlotte had gone downstairs, Angel and Jess to their own rooms and Bridget with Bottlenose and Mr Bojingles, of course.

Like the eyes in the painting, the women's eyes in the photograph seemed to follow me then flick away when I looked back. I peered closer. Behind them I could just see through the window, down towards the dark outline of the chapel. Had their deaths been mourned there?

A rusted handle caught my eye. There was a small door just behind the cabinet that I hadn't noticed before. There were still so many things we hadn't discovered here. This house had so many layers, but I wasn't sure how many I should peel back. But then a large handle on a cupboard door wasn't something anyone would have left unturned. Even if they should have.

It wasn't as big as the other doors and the handle was much lower down, as if it was more of a large cupboard than the door to another room. I reached out and again that quick draught passed over my skin. I'd left the window open in the rocking horse room and the door was still open. There was always a rational explanation. I just had to keep reminding myself of that.

The opening to the cupboard was stiff and I could see where it had been painted shut previously. But someone had forced it open, cracking through the paint and leaving a sharp, jagged edge around the door frame.

As I eased it open, I quickly looked behind me to see if anyone had heard. I waited. No one came out. I can't really explain my need for secrecy, only that it increasingly felt like a currency here, as if there was a value in the things we knew that others did not.

The stale air escaped as if it had been crouched waiting behind that small door ready to be released. Inside, there was complete darkness. As my eyes slowly grew accustomed, it seemed like some sort of linen cupboard with shelving down both sides. It was bigger than it had first appeared and there was enough room to walk in.

It was cooler in the cupboard than out on the landing as if there was some sort of vent or small window to the outside. The weak light from the hallway fell across the strange pale shapes stacked in perfect rows. It wasn't linen at all but something like large ivory pots. They had a dull sheen to them that the light glanced off.

The cupboard, although small, stretched far enough for the back of it to be entirely in shadow. The shelves were floor-to-ceiling and there must have been almost a hundred of these strange, domed bowls. I stepped closer to one shelf and the floor creaked noisily. I looked back at the landing behind me again, keen to keep my secret for the moment at least. The dust stuck in my throat and made my skin itch. I reached out to touch one of the strange matching pots but as I stepped closer, two dark hollows looked back at me.

I fell against the opposite wall and into another shelf. The pots clicked together and one fell to the floor by my feet. I carefully bent to pick it up and felt with my fingers around the rough stone of the bowl.

I'd broken it. A sharp section lay next to me and I picked it up to look. I stared open-mouthed.

There in the palm of my hand was a long, thin tooth.

I looked down at my feet. The dull-white pot was staring up at me with empty eyes. It was a skull, a human skull.

My eyes travelled frantically down the long shelves. I could still barely see but as I stepped closer and peered down the line, I could see the uneven curve of each head. Row upon row, placed in perfect lines, many were turned with their faces away from me. My pulse raced through my head, my breath stuttered in my chest. Slowly, I reached out.

It felt like smooth chalk beneath my fingers and as I turned it, I could feel it grate slightly against the shelf. It clicked against the neighbouring skull. There it was, staring out at me from the dark holes where its eyes should be.

I stood utterly motionless, staring back at it and felt my legs begin to slowly buckle at the knees. I could feel myself gasping for air. I looked down the long rows of domes that had morphed so easily into menacing faces.

'Oh . . . I . . .' I staggered back towards the door and a hand reached out from the darkness and grabbed my shoulder.

'What are you doing in here?'

I was about to scream.

'Ursula, it's me.' A face pulled towards me.

'Spear?' I stared at him. 'Is this your cupboard?'

'What?'

'Are these your skulls?'

'What the hell are you talking about? Skulls?'

I pointed and he looked past me. 'Christ! What is this place?' He looked back at me. 'You seriously thought I had my own little catacomb going on here?'

'No, no, no.' I laughed a little. 'Of course not.' It didn't sound convincing.

He raised his eyebrows before turning back to look further into the cupboard. 'What is this place?' He reached out for the skull I'd knocked to the floor and picked it up. 'It's got a label on it.' He squinted closer. 'It's just a number.'

'What the bloody hell is going on now?' Mother stood framed by the small door. 'And why is he holding *that* and being all *Alas, poor Yorick*?'

'Poor who?' Aunt Charlotte was just behind Mother. My family like to travel as a pack.

'I knew I shouldn't have left you up here alone.' She looked knowingly at Spear. 'Only you're not alone, are you?'

'Mother, surely the noticeable thing here is that there are rows of skulls, not the fact that I'm in a cupboard with some man.'

'Some man?' Spear stared at me, still holding the skull.

'Yes, she means you, SAS Boy!' Mother folded her arms and began scanning along the shelves. 'And what the hell is this? This is worse than your bedroom when you decided to go goth for a year.'

'It was the man.' Bottlenose had arrived.

'Oh, here he is, Captain Jack Sparrow,' Mother sighed.

'Yes, I thought Bottlenose must be a nickname.' Aunt Charlotte nodded confidently.

'Still floundering around, are we?' Bridget stood by the door with Mr Bojingles by her feet.

'We need to listen,' I said. 'Bottlenose, please explain what you mean by that.' I turned to Spear. 'You can put the skull down now.'

He looked at me and paused before carefully placing the skull back on the shelf. 'Can we get out of the cupboard now, as well?' he asked.

I nodded. 'Let's just close the door on this for a second, shall we?' I pushed the door to and looked around at the silent faces.

'The man,' Bottlenose repeated. 'He collected skulls. Not here anymore. Just upped and left. Didn't take his skulls, neither. All a long time ago now.' He grinned and wiped the spit from the sides of his mouth.

'Let's go downstairs.' I looked around the confused faces.

They nodded slowly. 'This changes everything. We need to talk about this,' Mother said sternly as if it was in some way my fault that there was a large cupboard lined with skulls.

They walked down the stairs and I hung back a little, staring at the cupboard door. I looked up to where the light touched the outlines of various antlers and dead animal heads. Dark spindles of shadow were thrown out, their broken fingers lifting as if appealing to something. This was a desperate place, a place where people reached up for salvation, pleading for nothing more than to be allowed to leave. My mind lingered on one idea — how long before we were dead heads, nothing more than skulls in a cupboard?

I could tell Spear was hanging back too.

'Sorry,' he looked away. 'I just wanted to ask . . . well . . . what exactly did you see? Out there in the water.'

I closed my eyes. 'I don't know. I've told you everything I saw.' When I opened my eyes again and looked at him, there was anguish in his face but something else as well. It wasn't quite anger but it was close. 'Spear, I . . .'

'Look.' He stepped closer and for some reason, I stepped back. His face tensed. 'You don't have to move away. I wouldn't hurt you or anyone else, no matter what they'd done.'

'Spear, wait—'

He turned and brushed past me, leaving me standing alone at the top of the stairs.

CHAPTER 18: A DEATH

We discovered Angel's body later that morning at around eight o'clock. No one could be exactly sure of the time as most of us had replaced watches with mobile phones and the sea had either taken them or flooded them beyond repair. Spear had some sort of diver's watch, which only functioned eighteen metres below sea level and might have been useful if we had drowned but was of no use whatsoever on land. Bottlenose said he was a human sundial which, in the absence of any sunlight, was completely useless. Time was becoming very difficult and it felt like there were too many gaps in the day.

We'd all tried to get some more sleep but that had proved to be almost impossible in a house with a cupboard full of human skulls. Bottlenose, having collapsed into a drunken stupor, could provide no further details as to who the mystery man was that liked to collect human remains. So we'd lain there in the darkness with nothing more than our imaginations to fill the spaces.

I'd stayed awake and watched more of the witch lights prickle the dawn sky. Everyone else had settled back to their floor spaces. I could tell Spear was still awake. He'd occasionally glanced over and I'd wished he'd just fall asleep. I had prayed that he wouldn't come and start asking more about his wife. I'd told him everything. What more could I do? It wasn't as if I was hiding anything from him. I'd definitely not seen who pushed her under or even if it was actually his wife. I was beginning to doubt that I'd really seen anything at all. But whatever I said about my recollections didn't seem good enough, at least not for Spear.

Dad's shadow had lingered unseen by everyone else in the corner in those early hours. I wanted to sit and talk it through with him. But finally, exhaustion had dragged me under again. I'd drifted fitfully in dream-soaked sleep for at least a couple of hours after the skull discovery, when we'd finally all managed to resettle. I'd dreamed of cupboards full of skulls pouring out over me and the rocking horse trampling across it all. The strange clunking noise had stopped but my mind still drifted to that room.

So I had no real idea of what time it was or even where I was when Bridget first started shouting and calling out for Mr Bojingles to 'stop licking the dead man'. We all stumbled up the stairs to find Angel's body still in his bed, rigid and contorted with death, his eyes turned up into his head as if he had to take one last look at his thoughts. Perhaps he knew his killer. Perhaps he tried to look away. Whatever reason it was, his face had already started to take on the gaunt, empty look of the skulls in the cupboard next door, his mouth stretched taut into a rictus death-grin. People are very quick to lose the look of life when they die. They don't just look like they're sleeping. They don't look the same. They look dead.

His skin was already anaemic, smooth and eggshell-dull. The life had stopped in his veins. Exhausted, the blood had finally given up trying to move anymore. It couldn't have happened that long ago, we'd all been up here at dawn. We'd been right next to his room when we were looking at all the skulls. Was he dying then or was it later while we slept? Had he been alone?

Something sudden and desperate had torn a frantic path through his limbs until he couldn't cling to life any longer.

Finally, he'd just let the life evaporate from him as if it was no more than that one last breath of air.

But before that, he'd struggled, that was for sure. Battled. He'd grappled to hold on to those last seconds, rising and falling. A hand hung limp over the side of the bed and I could see the faint white crescent moons in the palm where he'd gripped his hands so tight that he'd left the imprint of his fingernails. All this suffering when we could have been standing right outside his door.

'Poison,' Bridget pronounced, as if she was a judge deciding on the form his execution should take.

'Aye, Sibyl,' Bottlenose said gravely.

'Her name is Bridget. The dog's the one with the ridiculous name.'

'No, Aunt Charlotte, I believe what he was referring to was that Sibyl is a witch, a wise woman—'

'Well, that's definitely not Bridget then, is it?' Mirabelle sniffed.

We had all clustered at the small doorway to the bedroom, our faces wedged round. If Angel could have looked back at us out of that room now, we would have looked just like a painting in a frame, a cluster of shocked and disbelieving faces.

Aunt Charlotte was the first to step forward, but Mother blocked her with her arm. 'What do you think you're doing?' Mother frowned. 'He could have died of anything.'

'I need to take his pulse.'

'But you said you didn't know how to?'

'Well, I won't learn unless I try.'

Mother paused. 'Can I suggest learning on *living* people first, not the dead, who don't have a pulse?'

Aunt Charlotte looked bemused for a moment, then pulled her mouth down and nodded as if the idea was somehow novel.

Bottlenose was taking none of this. He pushed away Mother's arm and walked towards Angel. He stood over the body as if he was studying it, then laid his hand flat on Angel's face.

155

'He's not stiff yet,' Bottlenose said.

We frowned but no one spoke.

'If he don't stiffen up, there'll be another death in the family before the end of the year.' He nodded to himself, his fingers still splayed out on Angel's face.

'I'm afraid we don't know his family. Perhaps Mr Spear might be able to help with that,' Mother said with aggressive expectation.

'What's happening here?' Spear's dreary, broken voice was behind us. He still seemed drugged with sleep, his weary eyes barely able to open. A dried brown smear of blood was still visible on the side of his face, the cut even more livid and bruised.

'We were just commenting on who his family was—'

'Was? Whose family?' Spear was suddenly awake, his eyes darting between us.

'The dead man.'

'The dead man?' He eased his way to the front and peered into the room. 'He's dead!'

'That's why we're calling him "the dead man",' Aunt Charlotte said.

He frowned at her. 'He's dead,' he said in disbelief. He almost seemed too shocked.

'It's Angel, the man you were fighting with, remember?' Jess had appeared from the bedroom to the left of us — the bird room. She spoke in an empty voice. 'He's dead now. Someone killed him.'

'What?' Spear stared in confusion at the broken body on the bed. 'I . . . I barely touched him. He can't . . .' He held out his hands as if to show they were clean, and I watched as his face twisted with a bitter look. He turned to Jess and there was a new ripple of anger in his voice. 'Hang on, *you* were the one who pulled a knife on him though, weren't you? Over a pair of boots, wasn't it?' He leaned his head to the side in mock curiosity.

'Oh, I see. I see you.' She had a sharp, vicious smile now as if something in her was waking up. 'Let's fling some blame around so it doesn't land on you. I saw how you looked at

156

him. We all saw your arguments, heard what he said about your wife. We all know what had been going on there. You know what, he showed me his love potions, his little charm. It was remarkably similar to the one your *wife* was wearing, wasn't it? Didn't he say he'd given it to her?'

'And where exactly is yours?'

She paused. 'I threw it away.'

No one said anything for a moment.

'You threw it away?' Spear repeated. 'Where?'

'I don't know. I can't remember.'

Spear drew his head back and looked up at the ceiling as if he was trying to gather his patience. 'We've got a dead man. We need to act.'

Bridget and the dog shuffled in front of Spear and both of them looked up into his face. 'Don't worry, Mr Spear, although you look ridiculously guilty, this man did not die from your violent fists or indeed your arguments about your philandering wife.

'Wait a minute.'

Bridget placed a hand on Spear's shoulder which was a surprisingly awkward moment for all of us. 'This was some form of poison, Mr Spear. The dead man—' She pointed towards him as if we were in any doubt as to who she was talking about — 'This dead Angel, he ingested something.'

'Oh now, hang on, we don't know that. It could be natural causes,' Mirabelle said. 'This could very easily be a heart attack or some other—'

'No, it couldn't,' Bridget continued. 'Look at his mouth. Look at the discolouration and the contours of the body. He was gripped by something so potent that nothing could have saved him even if we'd heard his wretched, pathetic attempts to get help.'

We waited in stunned silence.

'What?' Mother stared at her. 'You heard him?'

'They just never listen, do they, Mr Bojingles? I said "*if* we'd heard". I'm just trying to set the scene, dear. Bring a little drama to it.'

'Bring a little drama to it?' Spear stared at her. 'The man's dead, what more drama do you want?'

'Well, in fairness, I think if he had been screaming for help it might have been more dramatic.' Aunt Charlotte looked round for agreement. 'I'm just saying, he's just a . . . a dead body, really.'

'Charlotte, we've spoken about this before.' Mother sighed. 'Thoughts and speech. Two entirely different things.'

The self-satisfied smile spread across Bridget's lips. 'You never change, do you. Coming on this trip with you this time—'

'Woah, woah—' Mother held up her hands — 'Who said you'd come *with* us? You're just here.'

Bridget's tight smile didn't shift. 'After our last little *expedition* to the Slaughter House, I became very interested in poisons and their effects. It's a wonderful world! Do you know he may well have died within minutes? How fabulous is that?'

We listened in appalled silence.

She shook her head knowingly. 'Did you know that if major governments could harness the real power of the planet's most poisonous substances rather than messing around with perfume bottles and umbrellas to dispense it, we'd have no need for all these silly nuclear weapons? These substances could wipe out millions if they were properly used.' She turned and began to trot off with her little dog just as if she was on her way to church. 'Now, Mr Bojingles, do we think cyanide? No, not again. Something new, I think. Very odd that Ursula didn't hear anything when she was creeping around in that cupboard, don't you think?'

'She's talking to the dog, isn't she?' Aunt Charlotte said quietly. 'Imagine if they harnessed the poison of those two.'

We watched in fascination as they disappeared into the bedroom.

'We need to get everyone away from this room,' Spear said firmly. 'We actually don't know what killed him yet and it could still be active in there or on him.'

'That's right, move us away from the murder scene.' I had no idea why Jess had taken so badly against Spear, but she wasn't letting it go. There was so much animosity between these two now. Spear didn't respond.

'Right, everyone downstairs.' Mirabelle put her arm round Mother's shoulder. 'Come on, Pandora, you don't need this at your stage in recovery.'

Mother has been in "recovery" ever since I can remember. She'd have to be the dead one to need this much recovery. She and Mirabelle started to move away slowly, heads bowed, as if we were already leaving his funeral.

'Come on, Ursula, dear.' Aunt Charlotte guided me away from the room. 'I know how much you like looking at dead bodies, but let's call it a day here, OK?'

I frowned. 'I *don't* like looking at dead bodies. I just happen to have been around a lot of them.'

'You all have,' Jess murmured. She kept her eyes locked on me. Her expression was no longer simply that of the grieving widow. There was a new suspicion in her eyes. I looked at her neck. She'd said she'd thrown the silver phial away that he'd given her. Angel had been wearing one just the same as Spear's wife when we met her on the boat. *Azogue*, he'd called it, part of his *Espiritismo*, to ward off the Evil Eye or bring love. It brought him neither and it certainly couldn't have saved him from this. By the look of his tortured body, nothing on Earth could have done that.

'Come on, Ursula.' Pandora was edging down the stairs with the others.

'I'll be there in a minute, Mother.'

She watched me closely.

'Mother, I'm fine. I'm a big girl now. I don't need a chaperone.'

'Your mother's just worried, like I am, that you're looking at the body too long, dear.' Aunt Charlotte looked at me and raised her eyebrows.

'No, Aunt Charlotte,' I sighed. 'That's not what Mother's worried about.'

Mother tutted then turned away.

They wandered down the stairs and Jess shut herself back in the bedroom where the birds had been.

Spear was leaning back into the corner beside the chest of drawers with the photograph of the two women on it, near to the skull cupboard. He'd come from nowhere when I'd been in there. The landing had been empty before I went in, I was sure of it. He was half in shadow now and I couldn't really make out the look on his face. His eyes shone beetle-black in the half-light and I could tell he was watching me. I suddenly didn't feel very comfortable, standing in that hallway with a man who'd just been accused of murder and the body lying a few feet away.

'Can I trust you?' I said.

He took a deep breath. 'Why?'

I shrugged. 'Oh, I don't know, maybe because I'm stranded on an island with three dead men and a possible murderer among the rest of us.'

'Why do you always make a joke of death?'

'You've known me less than forty-eight hours. You don't know anything about me and death or what I *always* do.'

He took a step closer and again, without thinking, I took a step back.

He stopped. 'OK—' He held up his hands as if he was showing me that he wasn't armed, or perhaps he thought *I* was the dangerous one — 'look, we've got to try and work together if we're going to get out of here. That's all I'm saying.'

I looked over at what was left of Angel, an empty bundle of clothes, just bones and skin. His face was marbled grey and wrought with so much pain that it had twisted into shapes it had never known in life. The charms and symbols hung worthlessly round his neck. Love potions, a good luck talisman, a crucifix, an Egyptian ankh — all reduced to nothing more than pointless trinkets now that they hung from a dead man's neck. The silver phial dangled across his partially bare chest.

He'd said he had a *botánica*, selling all his snake oil and an armoury of life-affirming, enhancing and preserving tonics and charms. But it had all ended here, with this grotesque death. As I stepped forward, my foot crunched on some of the broken beads and chains that had scattered out from his frantic hands. All those plans and dreams, beliefs and convictions had become meaningless in that last moment, all gone in that one final breath.

'Do you think she was right? Do you think he was poisoned?'

'Maybe.'

I looked into Angel's drained face, blanched with horror, his eyes cold stones, his jaw rigid with pain. The right arm dangled down, a waterfall of bracelets and beads that ended in a broken pool below. The left hand clutched his chest and chains. I looked closer at the liquid silver *azogue* charm he'd explained and doled out copies of to various women. It wasn't silver anymore. It was empty. The lid had been dislodged, perhaps by him as he grasped, and the liquid silver had gone.

'Look at that.'

Spear frowned.

'The liquid silver charm. The same as the one he gave . . .' I glanced at Spear.

'It's OK. I know he did.'

I looked back at Angel and the poisonous shapes his body had been bent into. *Liquid silver.*

My hands were shaking. I started to see the familiar pattern of speckled blue lights behind my eyes. My legs dipped in the middle and a slow droplet of sweat traced down my spine.

'Ursula?' Spear put a hand under my elbow. 'Are you OK?'

I steadied my breathing just how Bob the Therapist had recommended. As with most of his advice, it was utterly useless and achieved nothing. 'I'm fine. I'm fine.' I pushed myself away from the room, the nausea building in a sour pool beneath my tongue. 'I just get a little dizzy sometimes. I . . .' I stumbled and felt the floor drifting away. Spear held my arm and guided me towards the banister. The doors to Jess's room and the room with Bridget and Bottlenose were both closed. There was a stillness around us. I suddenly felt very alone on that landing with Spear. Mother was right, I should have gone downstairs.

'OK. Take it easy.'

'I'm fine.' I tried to pull my arm away. 'Where were you?'

'What?'

'When I was first in the skull cupboard.'

'I don't know, out here, I suppose. What's the matter with you?'

I tried to steady myself again. 'I just faint a bit, that's all. I get . . . a bit stressed, you know. Bob says it's anxiety.'

'Bob?'

'It's not important. I just pass out sometimes.'

He gave me an overly sincere smile. 'Well, Ursula, that is a bit inconvenient for you when you find yourself on your own with the killer, isn't it?'

I stopped — instantly petrified at the top of the stairs. I felt my breath quicken.

He leaned close towards me and whispered in my ear. 'I'm joking, you idiot.' He pulled back and smiled. 'Now, lean on me and just take a minute.'

I could feel the panic rising. I looked at him. I couldn't tell if he was joking or a murderer. It's strange how many times that's happened to me and I still don't know.

'Liquid silver,' I whispered. My foot slipped from under me and I felt his grip tighten round my waist.

'Shhh.' His voice made a sharp sound. 'Don't want to disturb anyone. We just need to get you downstairs. Don't worry, I'm here.' It didn't make me feel very safe.

'Liquid silver.' My voice split.

'You said. Now leave it! Come on.'

I felt his grip tighten on me again. We were at the top of the stairs.

'I can't feel my legs,' I breathed.

'That doesn't matter. You're not going to need them now.' His hand moved to my back. 'You can lean on me.'

I could see Mother at the bottom of the stairs frowning up at me. Mirabelle was beside her and Aunt Charlotte was coming out of the sitting room door.

'Mother,' I breathed. I tried to pull away from Spear but he dragged me back in with his other arm.

'Don't move,' he said quietly at my ear.

'Ursula?' Mother was looking exasperated. 'What on earth are you doing? You, Action Man, what are you doing with my daughter?'

'She's ill,' he called.

'She's always bloody ill.' I heard Mirabelle but I couldn't focus on anyone now.

'It's liquid silver. His chain. The one Jess had and Nell. The *azogue*. It's mercury.'

'Stop, Ursula! Just be quiet.' Spear's face rippled with anger.

'You . . . It's . . .' I looked down the stairs at Mother. 'Angel has been poisoned with mercury. His charms were mercury. It's open. The liquid's gone.'

I looked defiantly at Spear and took one step down. I felt the stairs slip from beneath my foot.

I could feel Spear's hand on my back. I was falling.

Everything disappeared.

CHAPTER 19: THE MADNESS OF VATICINATION

In the distance, I could hear the words repeating over and over. 'She's mad as a hatter.' I could hear Angel laughing hysterically somewhere in the back of my dream. 'Look at her! Mad as a hatter, the crazy b—'

I remembered Aunt Charlotte whispering on the stairs, 'She doesn't like being called crazy. Not after the . . .'

'Mad as a hatter,' I murmured. 'Mad as a hatter.' My eyes snapped open and there they all were, leaning over me with distorted faces.

'What are you saying, dear?' Aunt Charlotte looked confused.

'It's nothing.' Mother was there, somewhere.

I could feel the bare boards beneath me. The weak sunlight was falling through the sitting room window onto the chair at the table as if it was trying to throw light on whoever sat there. The chair was empty.

I pushed myself up onto my elbows and looked around the room. Spear was sitting by the wall, fiddling with some sort of small knife. I closed my eyes. The top of the stairs. His hand on my back. I remembered.

'He tried to push me down the stairs.' I gripped Mother's arm.

Her mouth turned down and I could see Mirabelle shaking her head.

'He told me to be quiet. He had his hand on my back . . .'

'He also caught you and carried you all the way down the stairs.' Aunt Charlotte leaned closer. 'It was all very . . .'

'Stop, Charlotte!' Mother flashed *The Look* at Spear.

He just continued to fiddle with the penknife.

Mother stood up and put her hands on her hips. 'Right.' It sounded like there was going to be more, but she just waited.

'I need to get some air.' Spear folded up the penknife and walked towards the door.

'Now, wait a minute,' Aunt Charlotte said, 'you can't just walk out like that. There's a body here!'

'And I'm going to help with that, am I?' He stared at us. 'So far, you've accused me of killing my wife, killing one of my passengers and trying to push one of them down the stairs. Men don't rank very highly in your world, do they, ladies? I think you might just be able to cope without me for two minutes.' He strode out the room without looking back, nearly knocking Bridget over as she came through.

'Not Mr Bojingles! Spare him,' she shouted at him and held the dog close.

He paused, astonished. 'Christ! You are all utterly insane!' I could hear his boots stomp out into the hall and the front door slam heavily.

'How rude.' Bridget motored into the room with the dog at her feet. 'Now, what have I missed?' She passed her smile over us all.

I sat back against the wall and let out a sigh.

'I thought he tried to push me but perhaps . . .'

'Never mind, dear. We all make mistakes.' Aunt Charlotte patted my shoulder.

'Some more frequently than others.' Mirabelle turned and looked out the window at Spear, who was in the process of kicking a large rock.

'He is a very odd man, isn't he?' Bridget said to the dog. 'Best you don't look.' She covered the dog's eyes with her hand and said quietly to us, 'That's Mr Bojingles's favourite rock.'

We looked back out the window and Spear was frowning at his foot. He seemed to swear then proceed to wipe his foot vigorously on the grass.

'Mad as a hatter, that's what he said.'

'Ursula.' Mother leaned closer and gritted her teeth. 'Will you stop saying that or they might just think you're the mad one.'

'She is, isn't she?' As usual, Mirabelle was quick to stick the knife in.

'No, Mother—' I looked into her face — '*He's* as mad as a hatter, not me.'

'Who's as mad as a hatter?' Bridget continued to stroke Mr Bojingles slowly and rhythmically, as though she was performing some sort of interrogation technique. It wouldn't really be too much of a surprise if we discovered Bridget had been a spy or a sleeper all of these years, deep undercover in Mother's book group. To be fair, we'd all been sleepers there.

'We need to honour the dead.' Bottlenose stumbled into the door. It was hard to imagine how he'd maintained such a consistent level of drunkenness given that there'd been no available alcohol except for my brandy in a Bible. Perhaps he was just topping up the general toxicity level of his blood.

'I'm not honouring that bastard.' Jess wasn't far behind him. 'He stole my fiancé's boots and didn't even bother to put them back on.'

Bridget tilted her head to one side and folded her arms. 'You mean the boots you threatened to kill him for wearing? You did hold a knife to the man, my dear.'

'Oh, I see.' Jess's anger seemed to rise very quickly. 'Blame the vulnerable woman. The man wasn't stabbed, was he?'

'Oh, I think you're very far from *vulnerable*, my dear,' Bridget smiled. 'I take it you still have the knife, do you?'

She looked away.

'Mr Spear's knife I believe,' Bridget added.

Jess looked at her strangely with those sharp green eyes, as if she might be contemplating using that knife right now.

'Well, it was Spear who was the one brawling with Angel because he'd slept with his wife,' Jess retorted. I was starting to understand what Bridget meant. Jess certainly wasn't as vulnerable as we'd all first imagined. 'And let's just take a minute to remember that we're talking about the wife who happens to still be missing.'

'Right, that's enough!' Mother said firmly. 'We—'

'We need to get that body to the church,' Bottlenose interrupted. He looked at our less-than-enthusiastic faces.

Aunt Charlotte sighed. 'I suppose you're going to tell us it's bad luck or some such nonsense.'

'And you don't think we're in the middle of a lot of that already?' Mirabelle said.

'I think it might be wise to have a little less vaticination.' Bridget let the word linger before looking round with the smug face of a *Countdown* contestant who knows an obscure word. 'Oh, I'm sorry. Should I explain?'

'No.'

She ignored Mother and launched into a definition. 'Vaticination is the art of prophecy or prediction. Thus, our smelly friend here, Captain Bottlenose, is in fact a vaticinator.'

'You'll take that back or I'll make you.' Bottlenose staggered to his feet.

'No, no, Captain Bottlenose, I'm simply saying . . .'

He took a step closer.

'Very well, Captain. Very well. You are not a vaticinator. You are simply a very odd man indeed.'

'I'll take that.' He nodded in satisfaction.

'But that does not alter the fact,' Mother interrupted, 'that something did that to Angel and we don't know what. We need to get Angel's body out of here. It's full of toxins.' She made it sound like he'd just rocked up for one of her colonic sessions. To be honest, I'm not sure they'd notice if someone was dead anyway.

'Like the old woman says—' Bottlenose nodded towards Mother who looked suitably horrified — 'we need to get that body out or he'll stink the place up.'

Everyone waited for someone to speak.

'I suppose he does have a point. We don't know what he died from,' Mirabelle said. 'He could still be toxic.' She looked at Bottlenose. 'You and Spear can carry him.'

'Not a chance.' Bottlenose didn't seem to be in an accommodating mood.

'*We* are the paying guests,' Mother said as if we were at a hotel reception desk. I know this because she's used this phrase at a hundred hotel reception desks.

'I'm not being paid to carry contaminated corpses around.'

It was a fair point that Bottlenose was making.

Bridget grimaced, or smiled — it's hard to tell sometimes. 'But you were paid to sail a boat, weren't you? And in light of the fact that there is no longer a boat and you were incapable of sailing the one we had, I think undertaker will do for now as your occupation on this island.'

He staggered in a way that didn't instil confidence in his ability to transport dead bodies.

'I think you're going to need some help.' I looked out of the window to where Spear was now poking at his shoe with a stick and still swearing heavily.

Mother followed my gaze. 'Leave him.'

'I'll just go and ask him.' I stood up shakily.

'You're in no state to go anywhere. Sit down, Ursula.' Mother was being remarkably firm, even for her.

'I'll be fine.'

'I said, sit down!' She seemed somehow concerned.

'Mother, this tired old drunk isn't going to be able to carry that body to that chapel on his own. So unless you want to start dragging Angel across the wilderness, I'm going to speak to him.' I paused. 'I owe him an apology, at least.'

'You owe him nothing at all!' Mother blustered.

'And we're quite capable of carrying a dead body,' Mirabelle leaped in again. 'We don't need a *man*.'

'Oh, let her go, Pandora,' Aunt Charlotte said. 'Just let her talk to the guy.'

Mother shifted her guns. 'And what would you know about it, Charlotte? Your experience of men extends to a series of fictional encounters on public transport!'

Mirabelle let out a laugh.

'How dare you! Both of you.' Aunt Charlotte turned away.

There was an awkward silence behind which we could hear the distant rush of the sea. Bridget was enjoying the moment, rocking her dog in her arms and smiling.

'This is ridiculous,' I sighed and began to walk out of the room.

'Ursula!'

I didn't answer Mother. She could wait.

* * *

The frozen air rushed into my lungs the minute I stepped out into the wind. The thick, grey sea fret pulled in over the distant islands so there was no distinguishing the land from the sky anymore. The small chapel was now only a vague outline against the wall of clouds. But its shape was still a very real and constant reminder of the dead men inside it and the one waiting in the house.

Spear was standing with his back to me, looking down towards the shore. I could tell he knew I was there as his shoulders flinched with the sound of the door slamming behind me. He didn't look round.

I took another breath and walked towards him. The sands stretched out in front of him in the same faded colours as the sky. The constant sound of the sea was like the wind rushing through a thick forest. But there was no place for trees here. This land was beaten low by persistent gales. The air hadn't been still since we got here.

I stood alongside him and cleared my throat. 'OK?'

He frowned and gave a single nod.

I turned to him. 'Look, I'm really sorry about the whole throwing-me-down-the-stairs thing. I wasn't thinking straight. I . . . have a few issues . . . just with my balance, that is.'

'It's fine.' His words were clipped.

'Oh, come on, don't do this. I—'

Now he did turn to face me, and I wished he hadn't. His face was a tight cluster of anger. 'Don't do what, exactly? I'm stuck on this island with you and your carnival of fools! My wife is out there somewhere, most likely dead, a fact you decided to hide from me. I still don't even know what you saw or even if you're telling the truth.'

'That's not fair! I was drowning. We'd been capsized in a massive storm at sea. You'll forgive me if I was fighting to survive waves the size of a bloody house. You took us out there. You were in charge.'

'Look, whatever you saw out there, it wasn't me. OK? Yes, we were separated, we were getting a divorce. But like so many married couples, we'd taken the route of paperwork rather than elaborate murder schemes involving scuppering my own ship so that I could drown her and maroon myself in this godforsaken hole without any food or any way of getting off.' He stepped closer towards me. 'I'm not trying to hurt you or any of your bizarre selection of relatives. I'm just trying to survive, find my wife and get us all to safety.'

'There's no need to be so—'

'So what? Dramatic? Because that, lady, is your bloody calling card.'

'It's not, actually. It says *The Smart Women*, Mother got a job lot made when she did an article about the Slaughter House. They thought it might be a nice brand. Better than *Slaughter House Five*.'

He stood there looking at me. 'I just can't believe you people. You're like some sort of lunatic Girl Guides' camp! Your mother is an utter control—'

'Hey, I didn't ask you to get personal.'

'This is personal, Ursula. We are shipwrecked together on a deserted island with a killer on the loose. How much more personal do you want this to get?'

We waited, with the wind circling us.

'I'm . . . we're all just scared.' I was determined not to cry.

'Well, so am I!' He looked away, towards the sea. 'My wife's out there. It's my fault.'

'I thought you said it wasn't.'

He shook his head. 'For Christ's sake, I meant that she was on this trip because of me. I said, "*one last trip*". I asked her to come. For old times' sake. She didn't want to come back to Lewis, to Leverburgh. She hated the place. She'd not been back for years but I had to ask her, didn't I? Had to say we could do it, have one last trip before we sailed our separate ways. And now look. It's such a bloody mess.'

'It'll be OK,' I didn't sound very convinced. 'It always is.'

He frowned at me. 'It always is? You've got to be kidding me. Listen, let me get this straight right now, I don't want to know what you did last summer, it's way too scary for normal people. My life doesn't feature murders at regular intervals.'

'That's not fair. That's not fair at all.' I moved away and he grabbed my sleeve. 'Don't.' I pushed his hand away. 'Yes, you're right, I spent a weekend in the Slaughter House fighting for my life — so I suppose in some way, I must deserve all this.' I started to walk off.

'I'm sorry. I'm sorry, Ursula.'

I turned to face him and the wind dragged my hair back. 'You're sorry, everyone's sorry. Mother's sorry, they're all sorry. You know what they're in there discussing now? How Jess got hold of your knife.'

'What?'

'That's right. You're the one who runs around with dangerous weapons on a campsite, not me.'

'Wait a minute, I didn't pull the knife, she did.'

'But it was your knife.'

'Well, no one's been bloody stabbed, have they? So what does that matter?'

'You didn't want me to tell them what I saw, did you? The mercury gone from his charm. You knew about those charms all too well, didn't you? Given that your own wife wore one.'

He moved towards me. 'I don't know what you're talking about. I didn't stop you saying anything. In fact, I think you've said enough.'

I walked away, back to the house before he could see any tears.

As I opened the door, I saw Mother standing in the hallway like a one-woman firing squad. She saw me wipe my eyes on my sleeve.

'What the hell are you doing?'

'Nothing. Just leave it, Mother.' I looked down.

'You didn't need to go bounding after the man like some sort of idiotic puppy. We don't need him or any of the weaponry he chose to bring on this little jaunt. Never trust a man who packs a knife to go on holiday.' Mother has a cute little phrase for everything.

'He's the best chance we've got of getting off this island.'

'Oh, spare me. Ursula, if I've taught you nothing else, it's that you don't need some man to *save* you.'

'Mother, I don't need saving at all . . . Well, except for now with the whole marooned thing. I mean generally. I'm not in need of saving.'

We locked eyes. 'He's trouble, Ursula.'

'Aren't they all, according to you? What do you suggest, Mother, that I live with you for ever? Not all of us can be lucky enough to find someone like Dad.'

'Lucky? You call that lucky?' She looked at me as if she wanted to say a lot more.

The door to the sitting room opened and Aunt Charlotte came out.

'Oh, for God's sake.' Mother turned and marched up the stairs as if there wasn't a dead body waiting in one of the rooms at the top of them.

I sat down on the settle in the hallway, dust clouding up around me. I let a stray tear fall unchecked.

'Oh, my girly, come on now. It can't be that bad.' Aunt Charlotte sat down next to me and the wood groaned. She put her heavy arm around me. 'You've got to cut her some slack, Ursula. Especially where *men* are concerned.' She said it like they were a disease.

'She had Dad.'

'Exactly, my dear.'

I looked up into her face. A few of my tears fell onto her tweed jacket and rested there for a moment like perfect silver droplets. 'I don't understand.'

'Well, dear . . .' She shifted uncomfortably. 'I suppose I'd say he was like most of us — not all saint, not all sinner.'

I stared at her and she squeezed her lips together as if she was scared of what else might slip out. 'Aunt Charlotte? What exactly is that supposed to mean?'

She shook her head. 'I shouldn't . . .'

I gripped her arm. 'What do you mean, "you shouldn't"? Shouldn't what?'

She glanced up the stairs. I don't know if she was checking whether Mother had gone or hoping she was still there. 'I can't say any more, Ursula.'

I squeezed her arm tighter. 'You have to! You can't say that and just leave it.'

'Say what?' Mirabelle was at the sitting room door. I don't know how long she'd been there but she was looking at us suspiciously.

'Nothing, Mirabelle.' Aunt Charlotte stood up with a look of guilt.

'It's never *nothing* with you, Charlotte.'

'Oh, I'm sorry, what I meant was, it's nothing to do with *you*. Family matter.' She pushed past Mirabelle into the sitting room.

Mirabelle looked over at me, her eyelids narrow. 'I'm warning you, if this has anything to do with Pandora . . .'

'Ladies.' Leaves flurried across the floor as if they were running away from whatever was coming through the door. Spear strode across the hallway with a new purpose. 'Let's get moving this body.'

'Now you're talking!' Bottlenose leaned into the door frame to the sitting room and winked. He smiled at me before falling into another round of his hacking cough.

CHAPTER 20: THE THREE BAREFOOTED DEAD MEN

Bottlenose and Spear struggled to carry the limp corpse. Aunt Charlotte kept trying to intervene and help but continued to trip on Spear's feet.

As we walked in yet another solemn procession towards the waiting chapel, I tried to picture where everyone had been last night, but my mind was a tight mess. I looked along the line of faces. Now that everyone was a suspect, no one looked innocent anymore. I was even worried that I might be starting to look guilty. I tried to walk respectfully, yet innocently. I had no idea what that should look like.

I remembered Dad's funeral, a sour memory now. There's none of him in it anymore. That day was for everyone else, for all those eyes to watch me and see how a young mind deals with death. They watched me like a specimen. A room of awkward strangers all dressed up, low voices sharing memories of him around like bits of stale cake. One woman even took a photograph. Mother was furious, which the woman seemed to enjoy. I remember it because it was the only emotion Mother had shown all day. 'Get her out! Get her out now!' I'd never seen the woman before. She didn't seem angry or embarrassed, just satisfied. I didn't see her again after she was asked to leave by Mirabelle and some more of Mother's henchwomen. It seemed cruel, but then Mother never was very good at sharing grief.

As soon as Spear opened the door to the small, mean chapel, the rough wind greeted us with renewed vigour, eagerly tracing round our strange, sombre group like a keen animal. It was certainly a funereal sky with no more than a blank, insipid light to guide us in.

Spear and Bottlenose made less-than-perfect pallbearers, Bottlenose staggering and dropping Angel's legs, Spear increasingly frustrated with his captain's inadequacies.

Spear resolutely did not look back. The cut to the side of his head had bloomed with a yellowing bruise now. I thought of him there again, lying in that room full of frantic birds. He was on the hearth. There was blood. I'd assumed he'd fallen, disorientated by the birds around him, his head striking the fireplace somehow. But how? I hadn't asked that until now. No one had. I'd assumed he'd stumbled with all the birds circling his head.

He'd been on his side, facing the door. There was blood on his face. It had been trickling down his temple from the cut. So the cut was on the upper side of his head, not the side that hit the hearth. The wound couldn't have happened when he fell because when we saw him he was still lying where he'd fallen. Something else had caused that injury. Something else had struck him. It definitely wasn't the fight with Angel. That had happened before we'd even got to the house and there was no injury then. That injury happened inside the house, inside that room.

I watched Spear carrying the dead man now. He'd been so angry with Angel, about his wife, his missing wife with her sea-green eyes. And it wasn't the first time Spear had been angry. On the ship, hurling the backpacks into the water, he'd been livid. What had happened to make him do such a ridiculous thing? I pictured him on the boat. He was standing, the boat lurched. His wife stumbled and fell . . .

Nothing would focus. The deaths were taking a heavy toll now. And the fear.

Had Spear been in the room with us all last night? I'd thought he was downstairs but perhaps exhaustion had anaesthetized us all enough for any one of us to have sneaked out of the room.

I pictured the sitting room in my mind. Spear was there, definitely, when I drifted into unconsciousness, and certainly when I'd woken at dawn to the noise of the rocking horse.

Mother and Mirabelle had been opposite me and close to each other, Aunt Charlotte the other side of Mother. The growl of her snoring had been constant. She would have had to cross the whole of that rickety floor without waking anyone up.

I watched her stumbling around on the uneven ground, her feet catching in the tails of long grass. No, she could not have crossed that creaking floor without us hearing.

Mother and Mirabelle would have woken each other up and then Spear on the way out. So either they'd gone together or not at all. Most importantly, neither of them had any reason to kill Angel. There were plenty of people Mother would cheerfully kill, but Angel was not on that list.

It was far easier for the people upstairs to have gone into his room.

Jess sprang to mind first. She'd stayed in the bird room by herself. She could easily have sneaked into Angel's room, poured the mercury into his mouth and run back to her room. She was familiar with those necklaces. She had one of the phials too and yet she said she'd just thrown it away. She couldn't remember where. Maybe she'd used the contents of hers as well to make sure of the job.

She definitely had the instinct for it. As Spear pointed out, she had pulled a knife on Angel. But then, it was Spear's knife. What kind of trip had he planned that required such a weapon? It seemed entirely over the top. But why had Jess been so angry over some boots? I know only too well how grief can cripple someone. Even the slightest thing the dead person has touched is somehow imbued with sacred status, a relic of their life. Still, that was a long way from justifying pulling a knife on someone over a pair of boots.

Jess had refused to come with us to lay Angel to rest in the chapel. It was entirely possible that she just didn't want to see the dead body of her fiancé. That was completely understandable. But she'd definitely had more opportunity than any of the rest of us to kill Angel. Apart from Angel, she was the only other one who had slept alone. Bridget and Bottlenose had been in the room with Mr Bojingles, who certainly wouldn't have let anyone leave that room without the *yap* alarm going off.

I watched Bottlenose and Spear carrying the lifeless body. Angel was still in the uncompromising black leather jacket and jeans, just a thin hammock now sagging between the two men. There was no dignity in this. It was all so wrong. He looked like he was no more than a binbag being slung out in the rubbish.

'This is horrible.' Aunt Charlotte shook her head. There was genuine anguish in her soft, old face. 'He was young. He had all his life ahead and such plans. His bot . . . his botan . . . you know, his odd little shop.'

'And that's making you sad?' Mother's voice hardened. 'Not the fact that we're stuck on the Isle of Death?'

'Oh my God, Pandora! Why? Why would you say that?'

'She's working on her next TV interview,' Bridget said in a long, sly voice as if she was concentrating hard on sharpening her blade. 'I can see it now: *Slaughter House Survivor Tells of Horror Mark II on the Isle of Death*.' She laughed in a way people don't usually do around dead people.

'What exactly is wrong with you, Bridget?'

'I got involved with you, Ursula, and your family.'

'You are not in any way *involved* with us.'

'Please,' Spear said, pausing for a second to readjust his hold on Angel, 'can we just stop with the sniping while I carry this dead body?'

We all looked a little ashamed, except for Mother of course. Mother doesn't do shame. 'No one made you the priest.' She looked at him with a cold, challenging stare.

Spear waited for a moment at the chapel door. 'I didn't say I was. Now, we're going to go in and place Angel under the altar.'

''Tis bad luck to—'

'I don't care, Bottlenose! Three dead bodies is pretty bad luck, wouldn't you say? There's no other space. He'll have to go there.' Spear didn't wait for any other suggestions or criticism. He gripped Angel tight under the arms. Bottlenose had dropped the legs again and now the bare feet were being dragged pitifully across the cold stone floor.

A butcher's smell of cold, wet meat had already begun to build. It ran with the sharp taint of seawater that leached from the damp clothes and pooled on the flagstones below. The bodies were barefoot as if they had taken their shoes off in some great pious act before coming to lay down here and die. Angel had brought the boots back as ordered by Jess but had petulantly thrown them by the side of Ryan's feet, not bothering to put them back on the body. Ironically, although I'm sure Angel would not describe it as that, he'd died in the night with no boots on either. They had walked out of this world with their feet as bare as the day they came into it.

It was crowded in that little chapel, no bigger than the size of the smallest bedroom back home — mine. We were trying hard not to knock into the bodies but it was almost impossible to avoid, especially for Aunt Charlotte.

'Careful,' I whispered and bent down to pick up the coin that she'd knocked to the floor. I looked at the young lad, his eyelids so thin with death that I could make out the shape of the eye below.

I was caught by panic. I didn't know what to do. I held the coin out for inspection as if I'd found some marvellous treasure, but I had no idea what should come next. There was no way I could make my hand reach out and place it back on that dead eye.

Bottlenose had seen me stall. He shook his head and took the coin. I could feel his hands, rough and impolite.

'You people out there in your real world, you're all allergic to death these days.' He placed it back on the boy's eye. He gave a rasping laugh that ended in him spitting a great ball of phlegm into the corner. It was no less shocking than if he'd spat on someone's grave.

'Bottlenose, please!' Spear hissed. He dragged Angel's body round and laid it carefully across the top width of the chapel under the simple altar. 'Altar' was perhaps too grand a word. It was more of a small, wooden bench. We stood in the cramped silence for a moment, listening to the rabid wind desperately trying to find a way in.

I looked around the chapel. So many years that were due to be lived, taken in such meaningless gestures. And now Angel, his life cut far too short. Had he really been murdered? Was he poisoned, perhaps by his own mercury? Perhaps it was some natural cause, a heart condition? He could have already been ill. We knew nothing about him, not even his surname or if he left any family to grieve. He'd spoken about his Puerto Rican mother, but we didn't know if she was alive or if she'd even been real. Maybe she was just part of this strange fictional character he'd created with all his charms and the rag-and-bone collection of beliefs. What I did know was that he'd left the world surrounded by strangers in a strange land.

As we walked back into the mournful light, I turned and watched Spear close over the door to the makeshift tomb. There was one thought close to the top of all our thoughts right then — would we be opening that door again?

The answer was a resounding yes.

CHAPTER 21: MORE BODIES

We were silent. There were no more words now. Words could wait. We walked along the strip of beach in front of the house but if we'd thought the long grass was exhausting, this was even more draining. The sand was being driven hard on the wind, scouring our faces. Fleshy seaweed dragged around our feet with pieces of driftwood ensnared among it. I walked slightly behind the others, my feet shuffling through the damp white sand. Aunt Charlotte was wandering by my side.

'Let's just say he *was* murdered—'

'He was murdered,' Aunt Charlotte parroted.

'No, no, I mean "say" as in "say for instance" or "just imagine".'

She looked confused. 'Oh, I see.' From the look on her face, she clearly didn't.

I continued regardless. 'If we assume that the murderer is not one of us—'

'And why would we do that, dear? It wasn't a very good idea the last time we were trapped in an isolated house with a killer.'

'True, but just say they're not—'

'They're not.'

I gave Aunt Charlotte my best approximation of *The Look*. 'That leaves only one other possibility. Someone else is on this island with us.'

The others had begun to slow down and were listening now.

'You mean someone else survived the shipwreck?' As Aunt Charlotte spoke, I watched them look back and their faces fall.

'We know no one lives on the island,' I continued, 'and they haven't for some time. We arrived in a storm so it's unlikely anyone was out there sailing as well.'

'Only a fool would have been doing that.' Mother glared at Bottlenose.

'Then there's only one other person on board unaccounted for,' I said.

Spear turned. 'If you're suggesting my *wife* had anything to do with this, I swear—'

'We don't need you to swear to anything yet, Mr Spear.' Bridget walked assuredly up the steps to the house. 'Shall we go inside, have a nice cup of tea and talk it over?'

'Charlotte ate all the tea,' Mirabelle said and pushed past everyone. Even Bridget looked lost for words.

'Ate it?' I looked at Aunt Charlotte.

'I'm starving, darling.'

'We all are!' My stomach seemed to respond with a sour turn. Aunt Charlotte shrugged.

Back inside the house, my eyes struggled to adjust to the heavy light. The shape of Jess moved quickly across the top of the stairs. She looked almost ghost-like with her ethereal skin and floating hair. She flickered across my vision in one brief, silvery moment. Then she was gone.

She'd been alone in the house. What would I have done if I'd been alone here? It's a long time since I was alone in a house. Mother is always just *there* — like the furniture but slightly more judgemental.

'Hello?' I called.

No one answered.

'We don't have time for this.' Spear strode into the sitting room. 'We need to get out there and find some food and my wife.'

'In that order?'

He stared at Bridget but she didn't flinch.

'You really should have brought some food with you.'

'We were supposed to forage. Nell . . . Nell was very good . . .' His voice trailed to nothing.

'You clearly know nothing about middle-aged women,' Aunt Charlotte sniffed.

He lifted his head and I felt sure his eyes had a filmy glaze. He sniffed. 'There weren't supposed to be any middle-aged women booked on my course. You got on the wrong boat, remember? And even if there were, they'd be treated no different from anyone else.'

'I'm glad to hear it!' Bridget said.

'Well, I'm not!' Aunt Charlotte blustered.

'I'm not middle-aged,' I was about to say, but Mother got there first.

'Mother is fifty-seven.' I find it's important to make sure everyone knows that. Mother doesn't agree.

'Ursula! No one needs to know my *personal* details.'

'I'm sure everyone could guess your age anyway, Mother.'

Spear made a strange growling sound that sounded like frustration or possibly indigestion. 'However old you are, you still need to eat.'

'No, she doesn't,' I said as an aside, but nothing is an aside with Mother.

She gave me *The Look*.

'I've checked the kitchen again and there's just tea and coffee.' He looked at Aunt Charlotte. 'Well, there was until someone ate the tea, of course.'

'I thought it was something like quinoa or . . . or bulgur whatever. You know, hipster stuff.'

We took a moment.

'We need to get foraging.' Spear stood, hands on hips. He seemed strangely enthused. He was, after all, a survivalist

183

facing a real-life survival situation. There had to be some part of him that was at least a little bit excited. A bit like a doctor faced with his first genuinely ill patient. There was the unfortunate, underlying concern that there might be a death though.

'We need to get out there and scope the island. There might be . . . there might be a survivor.' He said it like he didn't think there was. We watched him closely. 'There might be food sources. Look for anything that might have washed ashore and could be useful. Remember, this is not a training exercise.' Spear was starting to look like he might even be enjoying this. 'We need to stop sitting back waiting to die. We need to grab this place by the cojones.' Mr Bojingles had walked over to him and was sitting at his feet looking up at him expectantly. Spear glanced down at the dog and then back at our expectant faces.

'Do we just grab any cojones to hand?' Aunt Charlotte mimed gripping. Mother slapped her hands down.

Bottlenose leaned into Mother's side and smiled with a very wet-lipped mouth. Mother pulled away in disgust.

We divided into teams in a nightmarish recreation of a school netball team selection. Spear was leading our little party that included me, Mother, Aunt Charlotte and Mirabelle — the Smarts, or 'not-so-Smarts', as Bridget kindly renamed us. Bottlenose was to remain at the house with Jess, Bridget and Mr Bojingles.

I looked back at them as we walked away. They stood there in front of the house looking faintly reminiscent of the cast of *Scooby-Doo*, if they'd been arrested and put in a line-up.

The rest of us set off with a quiet sense of purpose and Aunt Charlotte's complaints about her bunions. The sky was laid out in grey layers like perfect fish-scales. The shadow of every heavy cloud left its dark reflection across the sea. We were under a watery light that barely left any space for daytime in the hours between dawn and dusk. But as we walked out from the house and I looked across the sands, there was a stillness, almost a pureness to the island's muted colour.

There was a simplicity to all this that brought a new sense of calm.

The cold air rushed over me and was fresh in my pounding head. There was an energy in this astringent air, a vibrancy in the white foam on the end of each wave. But there was also something quite terrifying to this isolation, the remoteness of it all. A real danger. I just wasn't sure where that danger was.

There were no paths, so we made a decision to hug the shoreline on our journey round the island. We skirted the beach, through long scrub grass and over dunes. Every step away from the house felt like we were casting ourselves adrift into a wild, unforgiving no man's land.

As we journeyed on, our sense of purpose started to flag quite quickly. We'd fallen into an uneasy silence, each of us looking around the undeniable beauty of it all but also its ferocity. The sea battled at the edges of the landscape. There was no part of it that was sheltered. The hills of far islands stood defiant. With every step, I began to feel even more that we were such insignificant moments in this island's history. Mists flowed down like grey water running from the hills. The sands lay in such sea-dark shadows that there was no telling where the land ended and the water began.

Those strange, moving lights I'd seen before perforated the sky, droplets of light appearing then vanishing in a moment.

'The witch lights are back again,' I said.

No one responded. As my mind wandered, the idea began to rise up that perhaps not everyone could see them. Was it just me? I quickly banished the thought.

I listened to the wind playing again with that strange tune. It rippled through the grass, over the dunes and across the surface of the beach, raking up a fine dusting of sand. A flock of birds took flight as if something had scared them.

A dark outline lay across the beach.

It moved.

As we drew closer, it formed into the shape of a seal that lazed and pulled its head up before looking in our direction.

'Wildlife now as well.' Mother sounded appalled. 'What next?'

'Some people think this is heaven,' Spear said.

'Dead people, presumably.'

We continued to shuffle through the bone-white sand. In fact, as I looked closely around my feet, there *were* white bones in the sand. I stopped and bent down. What looked like a long femur bone was poking out. I turned it over with my foot and more bones began to move to the surface. And then a skull. A human skull. There were bodies all around us, sections of them poking through the sand.

My hand went to my mouth but it didn't stifle the scream.

'What now?' Mirabelle blew out in frustration.

The rest of them had stopped and were standing there, watching me.

'Have you thought for a minute that if it wasn't one of us who murdered Angel,' I spoke slowly, carefully choosing each word, 'then it has to be someone else, someone here on the island?'

'Oh my God.' Mirabelle turned to Mother. 'I thought you'd explained to her that this sort of behaviour isn't acceptable outside the house?'

'There could be a killer, on this island who—'

'Wait.' Aunt Charlotte looked down. 'What the hell is that?'

I stood back to reveal the skull. 'Look at the sand,' I said. 'It's full of them! Bones! Human bones!'

Aunt Charlotte stared at me wild-eyed. 'Oh God, we're all going to die!'

'Be quiet, Charlotte.'

'No, you *be quiet* for once, Pandora. Look at this place, it's . . . it's . . . the Hebridean Chainsaw Massacre!'

Spear was shaking his head. 'No, no, you don't understand—'

'Oh, I think I do! I see it now. This is your lair. You've brought us here to kill us. It's you! You're disposing of the bodies here. You're the Leatherjacket.' Aunt Charlotte stood pointing at Spear.

He sighed and shook his head. 'You need to calm down.'

'What, so you can kill us without a fuss?'

'Oh you'd make plenty of fuss.' Mirabelle started to look more closely at the sand.

Spear closed his eyes as if trying hard to keep his patience. 'Firstly, it's "Leatherface", not "Leatherjacket" and secondly, no, I'm not bringing people here for some sort of killing sport. This is an old burial ground.' He pointed to a battered sign nailed to a wooden board. 'It's where the skulls come from. The skulls in the house. Bottlenose explained it to me.'

'When? Not to us, he didn't.'

'Oh my God, what is it with people building on old burial grounds? Have they not watched *Poltergeist*? Have they learned nothing?'

'Aunt Charlotte, no one's built on it.'

She took a moment to digest this, turned her mouth down and shrugged. 'Not yet, dear.' She had that look as if she'd said something profound. She calls this her 'Aramis face' — she means 'Amis'.

'The sign explains it.' Spear turned to look out at the sea.

I looked around. There was, of course, a very large and obvious sign by the edge of the sand. We read it in silence.

This is the ancient burial ground of the island, year by year more exposed by erosion. The area has been registered by the authorities in Edinburgh as an Ancient Monument of considerable importance and therefore may not be excavated without permission.

Every year human remains become exposed and, since 1966, are regularly rescued and cared for by Professor Miles of the Royal College of Surgeons in London. The building at the centre came to light in 1971 and is a chapel, thought to be of the fourteenth century, which became buried by sand blows in the sixteenth century.

Please do not move any bones or pottery that may be exposed and please walk over the site with care.

'Oh.' Aunt Charlotte looked down at the bones. 'I suppose that does seem to explain it quite fully.'

I tried to carefully reposition the bone I'd moved with my foot.

'Sorry,' Aunt Charlotte called over to Spear sheepishly. 'I thought—'

'I know what you thought.' He looked round at her, then at all of us. 'First, you thought my wife was hiding out somewhere and killing people. Then you thought I was a serial killer using an uninhabited island as my *lair*.'

It was fairly undeniable that these allegations had all been laid against him.

Aunt Charlotte leaned closer towards me. 'He does seem to be taking it all a bit to heart, doesn't he?'

'Grief can make people see things in a very odd light.' Mother was scanning the horizon trying to look distracted. This was a strange comment from Mother. Mother doesn't do empathy, not usually. I watched her and Aunt Charlotte share a look. It was only for a moment, but it's rare that Mother would do this too. It was all becoming very disorientating.

The lights still flickered out in the distant mist. But they seemed more than just random. There was a purpose to their movements as if they were being guided by something or someone. My exhausted mind was too quick to settle on the idea of some sort of hand moving those lights. I watched them flare and float with a new vigour.

The wind had picked up again. It was growing increasingly frantic and cold against our skin. Rain dappled our faces. Every step was a trial for our weak legs now. We dragged our fatigued bodies through the sand and grass. The ground was becoming more loamy beneath our feet as we moved further away from the shore, a thick mixture of sandy soil, wet and clinging to our feet. The land rose steeply into the cold steel sky and as we stumbled over the top edge of the hill, we saw it — another building. Another light. Another life. Someone else *was* here with us on the island.

CHAPTER 22: AN UNEXPECTED GUEST

Visitors can be disturbing at the best of times and there was nothing best about these times. Mother, of course, has her own unique way of dealing with guests, or 'intruders', as she calls them. She has many mottos that she uses in place of offering any real guidance in life, one of which is, '*Always be visitor-ready.*' This basically means keeping your home spartan so it looks like nobody lives in it. Some guests admittedly might find it disorientating that there are no personal items or photographs whatsoever. It can also be confusing that Mother doesn't know where any cups are because she always gets a takeaway coffee, but then they discover that there's no tea or coffee in the house anyway, or milk, or a kettle.

Our house is always kept clean and ready for the estate agent pictures to be taken. But Mother never gets around to calling them. She's not even started looking for a new place to live and Dad's been dead a long time now.

The main thing Mother was quick to strip out of our house was Dad's existence. After he died, she scrubbed every inch of it as if he'd left a residue of himself there or something she didn't want reminding of. I'd always assumed that we'd just move. She'd said we would often enough. But something seemed to keep her there.

At least she could say we were always *visitor-ready*. It didn't matter that the only visitors we ever had were Aunt Charlotte and Mirabelle.

This new visitor to our island, however, was even more disturbing than them. Ever since our arrival, Bottlenose had talked endlessly about witches, faeries and evil spirits and here stood the very embodiment of a fairy-tale witch's house.

It was a small and gnarled, weathered stone building no bigger than a shed, with a single room. There was no glass in the dark hole that served as a window and the door was cut from crude wood, not finished or painted. No one could possibly live here in such conditions. Both Spear and Bottlenose had told us this was an uninhabited island. Yet, a thin trail of smoke curled out of the chimney and there, moving inside that black window, was one of the lights I'd been seeing: the witch light.

'I thought you said no one lived here.' Mother angled herself aggressively towards Spear.

'They don't. That's a bothy, a kind of place for travellers to shelter in for a night maybe. No one lives in them. I didn't even know there was a bothy on this island. I doubt many people do.'

'Well, there's certainly not a lot of passing trade,' Mirabelle sniffed.

Slowly, we walked towards the small building. My thoughts quickly tumbled with all the impossible images of witches and supernatural horrors. I knew it was nonsense, but here, now, with the waves rolling round us and the world so far away, anything seemed possible. Perhaps there really was a woman with horseshoes nailed to her or a small man in the Devil's coffin riding out there on the waves.

All these strange, bewildering images were quickly dismissed when a face appeared at the window. Neatly framed by the damp grey stone, was the stodgy, grinning face of . . .

'Kempmobil!' I said in disbelief.

'Who?'

'It's the man, Aunt Charlotte, the guide . . . the man with the whip belt.'

'Brendan?' Spear's face rippled with confusion.

'Oh, hi!' Kemp called and waved as if it was the most natural thing in the world that he would be in a tiny stone hut on this uninhabited island we'd been shipwrecked on.

All those strange, impossible thoughts I'd had of us being watched, of there being someone else here, an outside presence that had stalked us from our very first moment on the island and maybe even killed one of us, were all starting to look a little less far-fetched.

Suspicion spread through each of our faces in turn. In the background of the hut, just behind Kemp, I could see small candles flickering, their wax dripping on the floor below.

'You're the witch,' I whispered.

'I'm sorry?'

'The witch lights I kept seeing, it's you.'

'Witch lights?' He stepped forward out of the door and we all instinctively took a step back.

I looked at Spear, then Mother. 'Ever since we got here, I've been seeing the lights in the hills. I thought it was just the witch lights Bottlenose told us about.'

Kemp paused, looking dishevelled in khaki — his signature look. 'But I've only just arrived.'

'Really?' Mirabelle looked at him in disbelief. 'We've all seen how long it takes you to light a fire.'

'It was already lit.'

The weak smoke rose from the chimney and I could see past Kemp that there was a smouldering fire that looked like it was burning down.

'What are you doing here?' Spear asked, unconvinced.

'I was . . . looking for you guys. I can't believe I've found you!' Kemp's enthusiasm seemed a little contrived. He frowned. 'I might ask, though, what you're doing here, ladies? I wouldn't have had you down for jumping ship onto the hardcore trip — or were you shanghaied?' He laughed and looked over at Spear.

'We've been here all along, over the other side of that hill. How much looking did you do?' Mother folded her arms. 'The island's the size of a playground with one big house on it. We were hardly difficult to find.'

'Like I say, I only just got here. I was about to start up my reconnaissance mission.' Kemp started to walk towards us again and we all took another step back.

'Hey!' He held up his hands. 'I thought you guys would be pleased to see me. I'm the rescue party.'

We couldn't have looked less thrilled. We stood there in a dissolute line, exhausted, hungry and desperate with fear. Even Kemp could see that his announcement hadn't quite created the excitement he'd been hoping for.

He tried to placate us. 'Look, by the time I got to the harbour, I realized you guys had gone. We checked your rooms and you weren't there either. I tried your phones — no luck. I figured from the way you'd been the day before that you'd gone home and couldn't hack it.'

'Couldn't hack it? You must be joking!' Mother rolled her eyes.

'I had to get my tour off. So I took them to the first island but we had to come straight back because of the weather. When they told me there'd still been no sign of Spear's boat and they'd lost communication, I said I'd come out and take a look for them.' He looked round at our dubious faces. 'I know Spear, he likes to go off-grid a bit. So I told them I'd scout around and get back to them. The boys back at Leverburgh were happy with that. I've done it before. They weren't worried. There'd been no distress call lodged from *The Terror*. I figured you must have been forced to land on one of the islands in the sound for a bit, so I started searching.'

'Alone?' Spear's voice was quiet. 'You didn't think to bring help?'

'I'm a survivalist! I didn't need help. Anyway, how come you stole my clients?'

'I didn't realize they were your clients. As far as I knew, they were standing there waiting for the boat.'

'What? You're kidding me right, mate?' Kemp snorted. 'Look at them!'

192

Aunt Charlotte looked confused. 'Whatever do you mean, young man?'

Spear looked ruffled. 'I don't keep the list of clients, Nell did all that sort of thing and handed it to the captain. He'd have the list, not me. It's how we always work. Worked.' He looked at the ground.

I watched him closely. Was his wife really past tense to him now?

'Look, I'm sorry, mate, but this is what I'm always saying about you guys who aren't locals doing these trips. You sail here once in a blue moon, you've no idea about the local conditions or our systems or our ways and look what happens. Chaos, that's what.'

'You're kidding me now, right?' Spear pushed his face towards Kemp. 'We should just step aside for jokers like you with your Boy Scout courses? I bet you're still skinning your pet rabbits on day one.'

We all raised our eyebrows, but no one wanted to interrupt this.

Kemp held his chin up as if he was daring Spear to punch it. 'We're very cutting-edge. We've got mindfulness, yoga, life skills. It's blue sky thinking.'

'It's been nothing but grey,' Aunt Charlotte sighed.

Spear stepped closer towards him. 'Mate, we are the real deal. We're a *survival course*. People don't want your old-fashioned *Carry On Camping* crap anymore.'

'What's wrong with *Carry On Camping*?' Aunt Charlotte looked genuinely insulted.

'Weren't you in it?'

'No, Mirabelle, I wasn't in it.'

'Anyway, we've got that useless beer sack Bottlenose to add a bit of local colour.' An aggressive smile spread across Spear's mouth. 'People like you, your days are numbered, *mate*.'

These were not the words anyone wanted to hear on this rock in the middle of nowhere with a murderer on the loose.

'Oh,' Kemp said, 'is that right? Look at the state you're in! You come along and wreak havoc on small communities and you've got no idea of the mess you leave behind. It's us who are left holding the baby . . . trying to clean up what you lot leave behind.'

Spear watched him. There was definitely more than an undercurrent here. Something else was going on. It seemed like a very inappropriate moment to speak, so Mother did. 'When you two have finished playing at Rambo, can you just explain to us why you didn't make any effort at all to tell us you were here? Perhaps you could have dropped in to say hi, have a cup of tea like a good new neighbour.'

'We haven't got any tea.' Everyone took a moment to look at Aunt Charlotte again.

'I've explained this! I was *starving*.'

'Look, Brendan, mate, there's no need for us to fall out,' Spear sighed, 'but this makes no sense. You're telling us you've come to the rescue, but you've not even searched the island for us and we're pretty easy to find. I don't mean to sound—'

'I think you should know, there've been deaths,' Mirabelle announced in a flat voice.

'I . . . what . . . deaths?' Kemp looked between us in turn as if trying to get confirmation.

'Yes.' Mother's eyes narrowed. 'Deaths as in deceased, no longer breathing.'

'Oh.'

She gave him *The Look*. 'And? That's your only reaction?'

'I don't understand.' Something about the way he was responding made me feel the need to analyse his reactions very closely.

'What's not to understand?' Mother snapped. 'We're on the Isle of the Dead—'

'Please stop saying that, Pandora!' Aunt Charlotte was looking increasingly disturbed.

'She'll trademark it soon.'

'Ursula, how dare you?' Mother put her hands on her hips and turned to face me.

'Please, come on, ladies.' Spear was shaking his head. 'Look, Brown, how did you get here?'

Aunt Charlotte drew in a quick breath. 'He must have a boat.'

'Brilliant! Thanks for another fiendish deduction,' Mirabelle said dismissively.

'Of course I have a boat,' Kemp said proudly. 'Not even I can swim those waters. But, come on, what deaths are you talking about?'

'And a radio?' Spear asked.

'Sure! What do you take me for?'

'You don't need me to answer that.'

Spear and Kemp stared at each other again.

'Any food?' Aunt Charlotte asked.

'No.'

'Unbelievable. What kind of survivalists are you?'

I couldn't shake the feeling that everything about meeting Kemp here was frankly very odd. This man had been on the island with us long enough to have walked to this place and maybe even set a fire. He'd made no visible effort to look for us, even though it would only have taken two hours to walk all the way round the island at a leisurely stroll. None of it made any sense. And I knew those lights had been flickering up here ever since we'd arrived. I could see how far the candles had burned down.

'Well, what are you waiting for, Brown?' Spear said. 'Let's get moving.'

There was a pause, both of them waiting to see who was going to move first.

We left the hut and began walking slowly, Kemp and Spear up ahead as we drifted along after them.

As we walked on over the small hill towards the sea, snippets of their conversation fell behind.

'This is a definite situation you got here then, Spear. There've been deaths? What are we talking about here? Passengers or . . .'

'Listen, mate.' Spear was suddenly very distracted. He paused a moment before adding in a less combative voice, 'She's missing. Nell.'

195

Kemp slowed and stared at Spear. 'What? I don't . . . What happened?' His voice was quiet, almost sad. 'Is she . . .'

'She just didn't appear . . . she—' Spear gripped his forehead — 'I don't know. The boat went down and I haven't found her. I don't know. I've got three dead. One of them might have been murdered. We think maybe poisoning.'

Kemp stopped. He looked at Spear in disbelief. 'Christ,' he whispered. 'Poisoning? Are you sure?'

Spear let out a long sigh then lowered his voice. 'He looks like he might have been . . . given something. I don't know.'

'Given something? Like what?'

'I have no idea. Maybe mercury. He was a bloody mess though. Look, mate, I'm sorry about back there. I'm just not myself. The whole thing is such a disaster and I can't find Nell.'

'She's tough. She'll turn up. I know she will.'

I couldn't hear much more as Mother and Aunt Charlotte were bickering about whether eating tea was acceptable. But as Spear and Kemp rounded the next small turn of the hill, I heard the very distinct cry of 'What the bloody hell!'

We ran after them.

'My boat!' was the next thing we heard.

And then we saw it, smashed on one side and tilting dangerously into the lapping waves. Water had already pooled on the small deck and it was clearly unusable. The damage was very obviously deliberate.

A distant white flash lit the dark air above the hills.

'Lightning,' murmured Spear.

Two large birds spread across the clouds and wheeled above us, their long calls drifting over the sea. It felt like the carrion were already circling. Spear and Kemp sprinted towards the boat.

'Scuppered.' Kemp stood open-mouthed.

'The radio?' Spear asked.

'Smashed.'

'Shit.'

'This is sabotage!' Aunt Charlotte announced.

Spear turned and looked at Aunt Charlotte, Mother and Mirabelle arrayed on the brow of the small hill. 'Well, thank God Charlie's Angels turned up to clarify that.'

Mother interrupted sharply, 'We need to think rationally and try to salvage something—'

'Salvage?' Spear left his mouth hanging open. 'What the hell is there to salvage? We're not going to get out of here. None of us.'

Aunt Charlotte gave a sympathetic smile. 'Now, Mr Spear, we need a positive mental attitude. I want you to try and remember, you're a survivalist.'

'Shut up. Just shut up all of you.' He was shaking. 'Just stop your bloody arguing and ceaseless prattle for one fucking second. My wife is out there! My *wife*! And it's brutal and crushing and now we can't get out there and find her. Every minute I waste here with you ridiculous clowns is another minute further away from finding her, from saving her. We have a boat and then we don't have a boat or a radio anymore . . . I can't . . . I just can't . . .' He fell slowly to his knees and bent his head as if he was in silent prayer. He let out a deep, low cry like an animal in anguish. 'This was our chance. I can't . . .'

'What exactly is going on?' Mirabelle murmured to Mother. 'What does he think he's playing at?'

Mother squeezed her lips so tight they turned white. Her sharp eyes didn't leave him for a minute.

Kemp watched but didn't speak, then looked away in embarrassment.

'Well, isn't anyone going to help him?' I asked them all. I started to walk towards him.

'Ursula! Leave him.' Mother's voice was so harsh, so strict that I flinched. I took a deep breath and kept walking. 'Ursula, that man is trouble. You need to stay back here with us.'

I could feel everyone looking at us.

I paused and looked at Mother. 'Because you're not trouble? Your dreadful friends, they're not trouble?'

'Wait a minute,' Mirabelle began.

'Leave it, Mirabelle.'

'No, Pandora, I will not stand by anymore and watch her eating away at you and eulogizing that bastard husband of yours.'

'Mirabelle, stop.'

Everything seemed to slow down. 'Why are you calling my father a bastard? Don't you speak about him.'

Mother didn't move her gaze from me, but it was Mirabelle she was speaking to. 'We've discussed this, Mirabelle. That's enough.'

'I'm fed up of having to listen to the lies—'

'I said *no*, Mirabelle!'

'Lies, Mother?'

'We don't have time for this.' Spear wiped the back of his sleeve across his eyes and nose. 'We need to do something, anything. Standing around here with a storm rising, listening to another of your petty arguments is not happening. I'm not going to let this happen. I'm going to find her!' He lifted his head and tears fell from his swollen eyes. 'I need her to be OK. No matter what she did, I just need her to be safe.'

We stood in an awkward silence, the rain beating down again.

It was Mother who broke first. Mother doesn't do embarrassment. 'Mr Spear, you need to leave here, go back to the house and try to calm down.'

'Come on, mate, let's have you.' Kemp put his arm around Spear's shoulder.

He immediately shook himself free. 'Get your bloody hands off me.' Spear staggered forward and wiped more tears from his face. 'I can sort myself out. Don't *you* come any- where near me. The last person in the world I need right now is you, Brown.'

It wasn't clear why the tide of animosity between these two had risen again so quickly, almost unnaturally quickly, one might say.

I tried to keep my voice even. 'Why don't you all just calm down and—'

Spear turned to me. 'You mean be calm like you — running around screaming and fainting?'

I stared at him.

'Don't speak to my daughter like that!'

Spear laughed. 'Why not? You do.' He turned and strode away. No one tried to call him back.

When he was far enough away that he couldn't hear, Mirabelle spoke quickly and efficiently. 'Just exactly how long have you had that boat here?'

'I told you,' Kemp sighed, lifting up pieces of broken equipment from the boat, 'I only just arrived.'

'And the fire, smouldering away down there in the bothy?'

'I *told* you, it was already burning.' It could easily have been a lie but then nothing here seemed true anymore.

I'm sure there are low points in everyone's survival journey. All the handbooks I'd read (one) had been at pains to point that out. But I don't know if they'd envisaged a shipwreck on a deserted island with a defunct book club and a random killer on the loose. What was certain, however, was that no one could have foreseen what would happen next.

CHAPTER 23: ANOTHER DEATH

We stumbled down the hill, our bodies bending into the rising wind. The smell of rain and the coming storm drifted on the air, a sulphurous scent driven over the sea. The darkness was gathering in thick folds over the mountains and distant islands. The salt-white sand was already stippled with rain. It was as if everything was bracing itself for something.

The house sat waiting by the edge of the beach. A dark silence seemed to shroud it. Its thickset stone stood firm as if readying itself. All the clear, sharp beauty of the landscape we'd seen fleetingly earlier had withered beneath this rising storm. There was a sense of expectation, of fear in this dark pause.

Spear was far ahead of us now and I could only just make him out as he disappeared into the house.

Pins of rain fell fast across our faces. We didn't bother to wipe them away. Our walk back was slow and dejected — a penitent's walk. My head throbbed incessantly from lack of sleep and hunger now. As we drew closer, the rain dappled the house's windows and rolled down through the grime as the sky broke with another slash of lightning. The house had almost started to look like shelter, maybe even safety. How wrong we were again.

A broken scream and the door was pulled back. It was Bridget, her face stark with horror.

'Bottlenose is dead.' Her voice was flat. She didn't move. Her hands remained crossed in front of her as if in prayer. The dog bounded out towards us and, as though in confirmation of his master's voice, held his face up to show us his bloodstained muzzle. A loose smear of blood ran through the fur, which he proceeded to wipe against Mirabelle's leg.

She kicked out. 'Get your bloodhound off me!'

'How could you let the bloody thing kill Bottlenose?' Aunt Charlotte said in disbelief.

'What?' Bridget walked towards us. 'Mr Bojingles did not kill Captain Bottlenose.'

We took a moment to comprehend this.

'Where is he?' I was trying to calm myself, breathing steadily through each word.

'Just what is going on, Bridget?' Mother sounded more weary than concerned.

Bridget caught sight of Kemp and frowned. 'Where did he come from?'

'Who knows. We don't have time for this!' I began to walk faster towards the house before breaking into a jog.

'It seems he fell on Mr Spear's knife with his back,' Bridget called.

* * *

Darkness was being ushered into the hallway. Someone had lit candles along the length of the settle, but they brought nothing more than a grim light and long shadows. Jess sat in one corner, her face as pale as the moon, deep hollows carved in her cheeks. Her green eyes were bleak as though she was looking out from somewhere a long way away. She made no effort to acknowledge us. It was as if she couldn't see me at all.

I stood on the dark stone, damp puddles forming around my soaking wet feet. My shadow reached out towards the stairs as if pointing out the way I should go.

'He's up in the bedroom.' Bridget was behind me, her voice solemn.

'What the hell happened, Bridget?' Mother arrived, out of breath and already angry as if she was trying to apportion blame.

Bridget stood with the unswayable conviction of a jury foreperson. To be fair, it's a role she's very familiar with. She's done jury service three times so far and been foreperson every time.

She began her recount. 'Mr Spear entered the house in a state of great excitement. He stormed up the stairs uttering words I've never heard someone use in public before.' (She's heard plenty, I've seen people shouting them at her in the street.) 'There was then a period of stomping around before everything went silent for approximately four minutes. Mr Spear then shouted, "*Christ, get up here!*" I assumed he meant us, so I proceeded to run up the stairs with Mr Bojingles in pursuit and saw Jess standing on the landing looking as vacant as you see her now. Mr Spear emerged from the room I had slept in the previous night. He had a rather blank expression and blood on his hands. I looked beyond him, into the room and saw the distinctive outline of Captain Bottlenose lying face down on the floor with the large knife that belonged to Mr Spear sticking out of his back. This was the same knife that the young lady Jess had previously threatened Mr Angel with, you will recall.

'I examined Captain Bottlenose and he was clearly dead. Mr Spear confirmed this by stating—' She paused to take out a small pocketbook and began reading — '"*He's dead, you stupid bag.*" I assumed Mr Spear must be in shock. Unfortunately, while I was questioning him and examining the dead body, no one was taking proper care of Mr Bojingles and he had been allowed to enter the room. He began lapping at the blood of the deceased. However, I do not think the footprints were in any way disturbed.'

'Wait,' I said and held up my hand. 'Footprints?'

'Yes, that's what I said, young lady. Prints made by a foot.'

I approached the stairs and saw Spear sitting just outside the bedroom door at the top. He looked at me with pitiful eyes, as if he just wanted me to say this hadn't happened.

'You OK?' I walked slowly up the stairs, my eyes fixed on him as though I was scared of what he might do.

He shook his head. 'Not so much.'

'No, I can see that.'

'Before you ask, he is dead and no, I didn't kill him.' Spear didn't sound as if he cared whether I believed him or not.

As I reached the top step, there was a new, ferrous taste to the air. My breathing seemed to grow shallow in response. I could feel the surge of my pulse in the side of my head.

I looked around the edge of the door. I saw him. Bottlenose, sprawled face down as if he'd done no more than fallen over, but the great, thick blade sticking through the back of his coat made it so much more than that. The material of his coat had bunched around the blade and been pushed down into him with some force. A thick, black wreath of blood bloomed out across the navy jacket. Without the knife, it could have been anything, just a simple mark. The blue material disguised any tell-tale red. It was just a dark brown stain. It was only the blade that made it very obviously blood. The way he lay face down on the floor, it had allowed very little to leak across the boards. It had stayed inside him, pooling and thickening, slowing. His arm was stretched out where he'd fallen, my hip flask just out of reach.

I stepped a little closer.

'Careful.' It was Mother. 'Don't disturb anything. Look.' She pointed to the bare floorboards. Next to his out-stretched hand and faintly etched into the grey dust was a word. 'It's a name.'

By the side of his hand, he had tried to draw out the broken letters in his last moment. They were shaky but still distinct.

'It makes no sense.' Mother looked up at me, frowning. 'Mardiv?'

'What's . . . ? What's . . . ?' Aunt Charlotte stood at the door, 'Oh God!' She held her hand over her mouth. No matter how many times you see a murdered body, it's still shocking. As they all looked towards her, I took the opportunity to draw my hip flask back towards me with my foot and slip it in my pocket.

'He's written a name in the dust,' I said in a whisper. A church-like quiet had descended on the room.

'Macdiv?' Aunt Charlotte read.

'How are you getting "Macdiv"?' Mother tilted her head to the side.

'They're Scottish, aren't they?'

Mother sighed.

'We should photograph the body.' Bridget entered in a flurry of efficiency.

'Keep your bloodthirsty dog out,' Mother snapped.

'If you want to be helpful, look at this. He's written a name in the dust.' Aunt Charlotte pointed towards the lettering.

Bridget picked up the dog, 'Do you hear that, Mr Bojingles, the victim wrote the killer's name with his dying act! It's just too marvellous.' She looked genuinely excited standing over the impaled body of the old man.

'Have a little respect, Bridget.' Mirabelle stood frowning at the door. Her eyes flitted to the corners as if the killer could still be there. That hadn't occurred to me before and I started scanning the small bedroom. There was a heap of old blankets near the door where I'd seen Bridget and Mr Bojingles sleeping the night before and the dirty animal fur that had fallen from the wall was in a heap under the window where Bottlenose had slept. There was nothing else in the room. There was nowhere to hide.

'He's dead.' Bridget stared intently at the corpse. 'He can't hear me now. You showed him no respect when he was alive and could hear you. So, I fear that you are the greater sinner.' She smiled piously. 'Now, does anyone have a phone that isn't waterlogged?'

'Mine's good. No signal though.' It was Kemp at the door, his face nervous, his fingers picking at one another. His hand visibly shaking, he unlocked the phone and held it out.

Bridget looked at him suspiciously. 'I don't understand why you are even here?'

He frowned as if the answer was perfectly obvious. 'I was looking for you.'

She looked surprised.

'Not just you,' he added. 'All of you.'

'You came by boat?'

'It's broken.'

'Well, that's not very helpful then, is it?'

'I . . .'

'I have no idea how you fit into all this but since you are here, you might as well be useful.' She took the phone and began photographing.

'Wait!' Kemp moved towards her. 'What the hell do you think you're doing? I don't want pictures of a dead body on my phone!'

'Why not?'

He didn't seem to have an immediate answer to this question but just looked at her as though it should be obvious.

She took a deep breath and let it out as slowly as an impatient schoolmarm. When she spoke, she picked out each word carefully. 'We need a record of it as it stands now.'

Kemp looked at her dubiously.

'Look, you do it.' Bridget turned to me and held out the phone.

'Why me?'

'You're young, you know how to do these things.'

'What? Everyone knows how to take a photo.'

'It needs to be a selfie, that way we have context. They'd usually use a newspaper in such shots but my watch shows the date and time and it's still going.'

'That would have been nice to know earlier,' Mother said.

She shrugged.

205

I stared at Bridget in disbelief. 'You're kidding, right?'

'Oh, I can assure you I know what I'm talking about. It creates a full record — a person discovering the body in this exact state and at this date and time. It is also conclusive proof of the person who took the photo. There can be no arguments at a later date then. It's all there in one shot — scene, evidence, date, time and photographer who produces the exhibit. They can't use the photo in court if they can't prove who took it with certainty. If there's any doubt, it's out!'

Aunt Charlotte nodded. 'It does sound sensible to me.'

'Oh, that makes me feel so much more reassured. I'm not sure we should even stay here, let alone mess about being all Kardashian.'

'Who?' Aunt Charlotte looked at me. 'Is that someone who photographs dead people?'

I frowned. 'All I'm trying to say is this is a real dead man, meaning there's a real killer somewhere and possibly very close by. We shouldn't be hanging around taking selfies.'

Mother closed her eyes. 'Just do it, Ursula, and then we can get out of this room.'

'Really, Mother?'

'What's the harm?'

'I'll do it.' Mirabelle stepped forward as if she was so much more capable than me. She reached for the phone and I instinctively pulled it away.

'Don't worry, it's fine! I can do it.' I held the phone as far away from her as possible.

'Here, take the watch.' Bridget held it out to me. 'Make sure it's visible and crouch down nice and low. You want yourself, the watch, the name in the dust and the dead body in the shot.'

'Oh, is that all?'

'Come on, girl. This is a crime scene. We need evidence, evidence, evidence.' It sounded like the title of a new police drama with Kirstie and Phil. 'We've got to start making a record of this. If we believe we're going to get off this island alive, we're going to have to explain all this. This is you recording exactly what we've found and when. Do you see?'

I stepped forward gingerly, looking around at them all, their expectant faces anxious and tight. 'This is such . . .' I murmured.

I squatted down, holding the phone out from me and trying hard to only look at the body through the screen. My hand was shaking and my greasy finger marks smeared across the glass. My pulse hammered in my ears.

'Get the watch in, remember,' Bridget prompted.

They all looked on keenly like students in an old-fashioned operating theatre.

I paused. Something had occurred to me. I looked at them tentatively. 'You're sure I'm not going to look like a killer taking a trophy picture?'

'Don't be so ridiculous,' Bridget snapped. 'Just take the picture.'

'I can't believe I'm doing this.'

I carried on looking at the shaking screen. The body with the long knife sticking out of it was in the bottom corner of the screen, the word in the dust just above. My hand was holding up the watch above his head, dangling in the top left. My finger hovered over the button but as I took the photograph, something seemed odd.

I quickly turned the phone to me and looked at it. All the elements were there, all just as I could see them in front of me now.

'OK?' Mother leaned over to look at the picture.

I nodded but still looked at the screen and then back again to the body.

'Ursula?'

'I'm fine. I'm fine,' I said quickly and stood up. 'Just not one for the album. I hope you're satisfied.' I gave Bridget a sharp look.

Aunt Charlotte leaned towards me. 'Well done anyway, darling. Now, let's get you downstairs.' She put a warm, soft arm round my shoulders. It was reassuring but still I felt wary. Something was out of place. Something was wrong.

I tentatively handed the phone to Kemp on my way out.

'Thanks.' He looked at the photograph. 'One for the kids.'

'You've got kids?'

His face fell a little and he walked away.

CHAPTER 24: THERE ARE NO SILVER LININGS

We walked out the room in a solemn line. Aunt Charlotte murmured about checking the house for food again and the possibility of dying of starvation. To be fair, my stomach was cut through with hunger now. I was feeling sick and weak.

'I'd keep my head down if I was you, Charlotte,' Bridget smiled.

'What?'

'Well, today we've had Angel — A, then Bottlenose — B. You might be C.' She laughed.

Aunt Charlotte looked nonplussed. 'Why would she say that? Why?'

I took one last look at Bottlenose's death scene before I closed the door.

Spear was still there, lingering in the thin pool of light by the grimy window. He stood at the entrance to the small bedroom where Angel had slept and died. The door to that room was open. The empty deathbed was all that remained.

'We should think about what to do with Bottlenose's body, I suppose.' Spear was rubbing his forehead intently as if it might in some way help him to think.

'Yes,' I whispered.

'He'd want us to do all the things he held dear.' Spear looked down at his feet. 'It's all such a mess, isn't it?'

'A bit, I suppose.'

He looked at me. 'I want to ask you something.'

I waited for him to speak.

'Do you have someone you . . . Sorry, I mean, well, what I wanted to say was, why do you hang out with all those dreadful women all the time?'

'You mean my mother, my aunt and my godmother?'

'Yes. Right. Yes, I'm sorry. I hadn't really . . . I didn't mean to be rude. I'm stressed — ignore me. You just seem to argue . . .'

I smiled. 'You're right. They can be dreadful, and I suppose it is a bit strange, but . . . they're all I've got left. And anyway, Mother needs me around.'

'Really? She doesn't act like it.'

'Wait a minute, no one's analyzing your relationships.'

He took a step back. 'Oh, I think they are. My marriage has certainly needed a lot of explanation.'

'Underneath it all, Mother is very . . . loyal.'

'So are stalkers.' He looked at me. 'Sorry, that was . . . Look, I know you think I killed my wife. I know I'm a suspect. But I didn't. She was all I'd got. We were done, but it doesn't mean I was going to kill her.'

I shook my head. 'I don't think that at all.' I'd made it sound very similar to a lie.

'Let's be honest, we all suspect one another. It's that or there's someone else here. Truth be told, I even suspect you and your ladies. I don't understand anything about any of you and you definitely weren't supposed to be on my boat.'

'Fair.' Something occurred to me. 'The list. The list of people on your trip. You said Bottlenose had it.'

He shook his head. 'It's gone. I checked his pockets.'

'Do the others know that?'

'No. I wasn't sure who to trust.'

I tried to imagine him, running into the house and up the stairs. Had there been time for him to check through

Bottlenose's pockets before everyone else came in? Bridget had been pretty precise putting Spear in the room for four minutes. Every time I came close to trusting him, he started looking suspicious again. Perhaps Mother was right to be wary of him.

We stared into the derelict bedroom that had been Angel's last view of the world. The mattress hung with great shreds of faded pink silk that fell down in a mass of fine cobwebs. There was a delicacy to all this decay, a grandeur that had been left to age and die. I looked towards the window and could see the distant grim face of the small chapel, so full of lives that would no longer age. They were all young.

'Someone hit me, I think.' Spear's hand went to his head.

'I know.'

His eyes flashed towards me. 'You?'

'No.'

'I walked in . . . I'd heard something. A noise. There were birds and I was surrounded, all over my head. I couldn't see much. I could hear whistling. But a figure came from nowhere.' He paused. 'Then there was nothing. The next thing I knew, you guys were dragging me out. Someone was there before you came in — a shape. I'm sure of it.' He drew a breath and then looked at me. 'Ursula, I could have sworn it was a ghost.'

I watched him closely and there was no trace of a lie on his face. He was bewildered, lost in that moment.

'I know that sounds crazy but I just had to tell someone. I saw someone, something in the corner of the room.' This time he did look sincere and I think part of me was starting to believe him. This house, this island could make a person believe all manner of unnatural spirits stalked an unlit world, living in some sort of half-life around us.

My eyes travelled over the dim room. The remains of Angel's jewellery speckled the floor with cheap beads and baubles, like the remnants of an abandoned Christmas. There were glimpses of silver and tinsel colours glimmering in the shadows. One caught my eye, the red beads still clinging to their threads. A bracelet perhaps. I thought of Angel lying there all adorned and bejewelled, a magpie dead in this dirty little nest. I remembered it there, on his wrist. I stepped forward to look but Spear's hand went across the door and blocked me.

'You don't know what killed him.' He looked earnestly into my face. 'No more deaths, hey?'

I watched him closely. He didn't move his arm.

'Spear? We all moved him. No one got ill . . .'

He looked away quickly, back to the room.

'I think I do know what killed him,' I said. 'The mercury. The necklace he wore with the silver phial. I'm sure of it. It makes complete sense.'

'That's very interesting.' I swung round. It was Bridget. I don't know how long she'd been there, but she'd definitely made sure she'd not made a sound coming up those stairs. I could have sworn she'd gone downstairs with the others. Maybe I was wrong. Maybe she'd been hiding out in one of the other rooms. Listening in to our every word. 'Let's hear what you've got to say then, Dr Scarpetta—'

'Who?' Aunt Charlotte popped her head out of the rocking horse room next to us. She'd been up here too. Were they all just lying in wait, listening at doors? Secrecy is very important to my family. They just don't believe in it for others.

Bridget cleared her throat. 'She's a pathologist.'

'Are you, Ursula? I did wonder what you did all day.'

I sighed. 'No, Aunt Charlotte, she meant . . .'

'So you've put together a little theory, have you?' Bridget smiled. 'You think that Angel's *love charm* was anything but that. Is that correct?'

She nodded at me to continue.

'Oh, for God's sake, get on with it, Ursula.' It was Mother this time, peering out of the bird room, already wearing *The Look*.

'Mother! You're up here too? What are you all doing?'

'Gathering clues.'

This was like a bad game of hide-and-seek. I've always hated playing that. Whenever I used to play it with Mother, she'd slip out to the shop.

'Come on then, let's have it.' Bridget was becoming impatient.

They all waited in expectation.

I began slowly. 'Well, the thing round his neck — the *azogue*, I think he called it — I think it was mercury. It looked like quicksilver. I think he even said that himself and . . . well, his behaviour. He was all crazed and angry one minute, then joking around the next. He had the headaches and . . . and . . .'

'Yes?' Mother said.

'Just hear me out. This is going to sound a little odd—'

'You surprise me.'

'Mother, please! It was what he said about mad as a hatter.'

'Yes!' Aunt Charlotte gasped. 'I know exactly what you're talking about.'

'I doubt it,' Mother muttered.

Aunt Charlotte continued. 'Hat makers used mercury and it sent them doolally. That's why people say "mad as a hatter". Happened to Millicent Armitage, don't you remember, Pandora?'

'Millicent Armitage was already mad. Her ridiculous hats had nothing to do with it!'

'She always used to say, "*Charlotte dear, I've literally no idea who I am today!*" Oh, we did used to laugh. Family was in toilets. Armitage Shanks. Went to work at *Horse and Hound* magazine, I think, as their resident millinery expert. Or it could have been bathrooms.'

Everyone paused.

'The phial was empty round Angel's neck,' I continued. 'He was acting very strangely. Jess's phial is also missing. She says she threw it away but what if she used it on Angel along with his own? Or someone else could have found it?'

Bridget laughed at me and I'm fairly sure the dog did too.

'Someone here knew what was in that charm and realized its possibilities. Angel had one, Jess had one she claims she chucked somewhere. Spear, your wife had one.'

'Oh, here we go again.' He looked away.

Bridget held up her hand. 'I think it's time we explained, isn't it, Mr Bojingles?'

'It was you and the dog! I knew it.' Aunt Charlotte nodded firmly.

Bridget laughed. 'Oh dear, aren't they silly? Yes, mercury is a poison, Ursula. And it was undoubtedly the substance Angel wore around his neck and doled out like noxious little sweeties to all who took his fancy. Quicksilver, or *azogue*, he used the Spanish word, is well known as a spiritual talisman or charm.'

'Is it?' Aunt Charlotte looked bemused.

'He did tell you that was what he was selling. You should really listen more and then you wouldn't end up being so stupid.' She turned to me. 'Sadly, it won't work in the manner you are suggesting, Ursula. Mercury takes a person piece by piece, very, very slowly.' She smiled and ran her tongue over the roll of her bottom lip.

'And how the hell do you know?'

'Mr Spear, I went on a course.'

'In how to poison people?' He looked at her suspiciously.

'It was actually a course *about* poisons not how to poison people. Although I'm sure people go on it for a variety of reasons.' She laughed a little and it looked terrifying. She dabbed the corners of her mouth with a lacy handkerchief. 'It was in Chelsea, actually, at some beautiful apothecary gardens there.'

Aunt Charlotte suddenly stood up very straight. 'I know it very well! The Chelsea Psychic Gardens.'

Bridget frowned. 'Physic.'

'What?'

'*Physic* Gardens. The Chelsea Physic Gardens. Not the Psychic Gardens. How could a garden be psychic?'

Aunt Charlotte looked confused.

Mother was holding her head again. 'Just bloody well get on with it.'

'As I was saying—' Bridget looked pointedly at Aunt Charlotte — 'it is long-term exposure that is the problem with mercury. The simple act of opening that phial around the victim's neck would not come anywhere near killing him immediately, nor would swallowing it usually. And if I'm not mistaken, which I never am, Angel's erratic behaviour began well before last night and definitely before that phial was opened.' She smiled as if she was enjoying something illicit. 'No, no, something else killed him. Something much worse.'

The atmosphere had grown distinctly tense.

Bridget peeled off another vicious smile. 'The mercury was your first red herring.'

'Or silver herring.' Aunt Charlotte laughed then stopped suddenly when she realized we were all silently staring at her.

'What do you mean "first"?' I said.

'Oh, I'm sure there'll be plenty more.'

There was a creak on the stairs and footsteps in the hall. We all looked over the banister to see Jess disappearing into the sitting room. How much had she heard? Had she heard me accuse her of perhaps poisoning Angel? Why hadn't she let us know she was there?

Everyone looked around the group at one another. We'd reached that moment when everyone was afraid to speak. It was staring us in the face now. We were on an uninhabited island. Angel and Bottlenose had definitely both been murdered. The murderer was one of us.

CHAPTER 25: ALL THAT GLITTERS

'So if the mercury didn't kill him, what did? You know, don't you?'

Bridget watched me, enjoying the moment. She nodded once.

'Wait, you know what killed Angel?' Mother was looking fierce. 'And you didn't say?'

'I needed to be sure.'

'Unbelievable! Utterly unbelievable. We're dying and you decide to—'

'Mother, perhaps we should let her speak.'

Mother shot *The Look*.

'The answer is right in front of you.' Bridget was enjoying this far too much.

'Where? Is it close?'

'For God's sake!' Mother was becoming increasingly infuriated.

'The ghostly killer! It's here. I knew it! Does anyone know how to perform an exorcism? I'd be happy to give it a go.'

We all looked at Aunt Charlotte, stunned but not surprised. Even Bridget and Mr Bojingles were momentarily silenced.

'Look into the room. Look very carefully.'

We did as Bridget said. Nothing was leaping out. Thank goodness.

'Shall we help them out, Mr B—'

'Did you know, Bridget, that out here it's still technically legal to kill someone if it's part of a traditional religious ceremony?' I said, stony-faced.

'Really?'

'No, not really. But I'm sorely tempted.'

Bridget blew out a long, disgruntled breath and shook her head. 'You think you're so smart, you Smart Women, don't you? Yet, you've got no clue, have you? You're just scrabbling about, trying desperately to understand how you always end up in a mess.'

Mother started walking towards the top of the stairs. 'I don't need to hear this.'

'Well, if you don't want to know what killed him . . .'

Spear stepped towards Bridget. 'Speak.'

She and the dog looked up. The smile had gone from both their faces. 'It was the beads, wasn't it, Mr Spear?'

We all slowly looked back towards Angel's room. The tiny clusters of the little red seed-like jewellery were scattered all over the floorboards.

An image of his bangle-clad arm drifted in my thoughts. A paint palette of mismatched colours and chains. This one consisted of hundreds of tiny red beads strung together on what looked like quite flimsy string. I remembered the woman, Nell, on the ship falling into the seat next to Angel and smiling up at him. He had been showing her the bracelet.

The sea-green eyes floated there for a moment in my memories. She was looking back at me, before the hand began to push her under again. I looked down at Spear's thick hands.

'Nell spoke to Angel about it, didn't she, Spear? On the boat?'

He looked at me and then quickly away. His face pulled into a frown. 'How would I know?'

'Come, come, Mr Spear.' Bridget leaned towards him. 'It's no time to be coy. I heard her talking to Angel on the boat all about the poisonous jewellery he was wearing and I think you did too. Like Ursula, I thought she was talking about the mercury but I've been going over and over it and looking here at this room. She wasn't talking about that at all, was she? It was these beads. The bracelet.'

Spear stepped forward and bent towards the floor. He looked closely. I saw the realization travel across his face, that or he was a very good actor. He stood up and began quietly. 'Yes, I do recognize them,' he said. 'She got a load of these when she was down in Cornwall at some festival down near the Eden Project. She did a little talk there on foraging and edible plants. She knew a lot about that kind of thing.'

I noted again his use of the past tense for his wife.

'She was clever, knew exactly what you could eat and what would kill you, just by looking at it. She picked up a load of the bracelets then. She liked to do that, gather little tokens of where she'd been. She'd give them as gifts, especially if they had some sort of meaning. These ones were some sort of spiritual peace and love token, you know. She used to hand them out to people she wanted to "*spread the love to*", at least that's what she used to say.'

'That's right. I heard them talking about that on the boat.' Bridget nodded in confirmation.

I bent down to pick them up, but Spear grabbed my arm.

'No! Don't touch them!'

I looked up at him.

'They're lethal. They were recalled. She had to send them back and she wasn't too pleased that she had to go round all her hippy friends and tell them all. You know, it didn't look great when she prided herself on her knowledge of nature and foraging to have to say, "*Hey, you know that bracelet I gave you, well it's highly toxic so maybe give it back.*" It's a bad look.'

'Well, is that what she was saying to Angel on the boat, Bridget?' Mother said.

'I didn't really hear her say that. I couldn't hear all of it for the waves and the noise of the boat. They were sitting opposite me and it wasn't that close. I saw them going through all the friendship bracelets and jewellery, but they were talking about that one for a while. I'm sure of it.'

'Oh, I remember,' Aunt Charlotte cut in. 'I was thinking how incredibly ugly it was.'

'But you usually like nasty plastic jewellery, Charlotte.' It was Mirabelle. She'd walked up the stairs, keen not to miss out as usual.

Charlotte closed her eyes and turned her head away.

'Mirabelle,' Mother's face lit up. 'Where have you been?'

'Downstairs with Miserable Jess and Brendan the Brave. It's been fabulous.'

Mother snorted and Mirabelle pushed past me to nestle herself in next to her.

'We think we've found what it was that killed Angel. Spear's wife gave out poisonous bracelets.'

'Woah!' Spear looked around us. 'She didn't know they were when she gave them out. She bought them in good faith. The Eden Project had to recall them. They were some sort of seed. She called them . . . Oh Christ, what did she call them?' He still had hold of my arm and I could feel his grip growing tighter. It did seem genuine that this was only now occurring to him but part of me still doubted him. A man had died and these beads were on the floor. I didn't say anything. Spear looked guilty enough already without my help.

His face suddenly became animated. 'It's a rosary pea. She got an email about it, thanking her for the talk and apologizing about the recall of the bracelets. It's got abrin in it. They said they were recalling all of them and they'd got a record of her organizing to have a significant quantity delivered to her after she came to do the talk. She was furious, said she'd look like a fool, especially given what the talk was about. Turned out, the seeds can kill you. They said it's like ricin, you know, from the castor bean. It's in the seed and it's just as lethal. They're usually indigestible and it should have all been OK but because their casings were pierced to thread them onto the bracelet, it released the seeds. There was a possibility that the seeds could come out. You wouldn't need to chew it if it's threaded on the bracelet because the casing has already been pierced.

'They couldn't take that risk. They said it would only take a few seeds to kill someone. She'd traced all of them that she gave out, or she thought she had, until she saw Angel. She hadn't seen him since the Isle of Wight. He got in touch recently about the *botánica* he was running, he wanted advice for more foraged items, and she suggested he come out with us on this trip. At least, that's what she told me. Nell saw the bracelet and was trying to explain about it to him but then the boat got into trouble.'

I stared at the broken bracelet on the floor. They looked like such innocuous little beans, their shiny red coatings threaded together.

'Well, I for one prefer plain old-fashioned diamonds,' Mother sniffed. 'I don't understand all this poisonous jewellery nonsense. Mercury round his neck, ap . . . ab . . .'

'Abrin, it's from the . . . rosary pea.'

'I don't care if it's from Bird's Eye frozen peas, why didn't you say something before now?'

He sighed. 'About a bracelet my wife gave away years ago?'

'Well, how long ago was this?'

'God, I don't know. Wait, we went down there the year before the Olympics. I remember them talking about it. So, that would have been . . .'

'2011.' Bridget stroked her dog firmly as if confirming it.

'Yeah, that'd be about right. They said it was from the jequirity bean plant, but it's also known as the rosary pea. She liked that, rosary, you know — gave it an extra religious, spiritual flavour.'

'Or poisonous flavour.' Mother raised her eyebrows.

'Wait a minute, so Nell knew Angel for that long?' Aunt Charlotte said.

He shrugged. 'She knew a lot of people. They flitted in and out of the same circles. She often asked them along on trips. I didn't exactly like all of them, but she said it was good for business. She'd not seen Angel in years.' His voice started to break but whether it was with the upset of her being lost or the kind of people she got too close to, it was hard to tell.

'But you knew all this, about the pea thing.' Mother analyzed him.

'The boat was going down! My wife's just been lost in the sea and people are dying. Surely you're not expecting I'd remember one bracelet she handed out a decade ago! She handed out a lot of shit. Let's just say it slipped my mind.'

'Slipped your mind?' Bridget raised her eyebrows. 'That's not really very convincing now is it, Mr Spear? You're the only one on this island who knew that he was wearing a deadly bracelet — a bracelet your wife gave him as a gift, the man she'd clearly had a relationship with, the man you tried to beat to a pulp.'

'Wait a minute! I wasn't the only one who knew. You heard too.' He pointed at Bridget.

'Oh, only enough to tweak my interest and get me thinking. You would have been able to hear everything though, Mr Spear, from where you stood and so would Bottlenose.' Bridget smiled. 'Is that why you killed him?'

'That's right,' Mother nodded. 'He heard and now he's dead.'

I was trying not to look at Spear. The threads of my thoughts were so tangled. Bottlenose? Could Spear have killed him? Or did someone else realize the drunk captain must have heard the conversation about the bracelet and had to silence him? Everything was swimming in confusion. Spear was starting to be cast in a very bad light. There was no escaping that.

'How many people knew about this bracelet?' I asked. 'Nell, obviously, Angel, Spear and Bottlenose, right?'

'Yes.' He finally let go of my arm. The anger was fading and his voice was very quiet. 'I suppose that makes me the biggest suspect again.'

'Well . . .'

'Especially since your knife is sticking out of that captain's back right now.' Mother folded her arms defiantly.

'I didn't have my knife. Jess did! And why would I tell you about it all?' Spear said, gathering his defence again. 'Why would I tell you all about the bracelet now I've realized?'

'True.'

'Mr Spear,' Bridget said with slow consideration. She was beginning to sound like the prosecutor in a witch trial. 'The conversation about the bracelet that took place on the boat, was that before or after you got angry and started throwing bags over the side?'

'What?'

'Is that what made you angry, Nell talking so *closely* to him about these love tokens?'

'What? No. Well, yes.' He screwed up his face as if he was in pain. 'Of course I didn't kill him over that. If I killed everyone my wife got friendly with, I'd be a serial killer.'

We all paused on those words.

'Well, she knew that's what they were talking about.' He pointed at Bridget. 'It wasn't a big secret.'

Bridget put Mr Bojingles down for a moment and the dog instantly headed towards Spear and started barking as if he'd sniffed out the murderer.

I looked at Spear. Was that the stone-cold face of a killer? Were they the hands that had pushed those green eyes under? Had he run back here to kill Bottlenose because he knew too much about the bracelet?

'I didn't kill him.' His words had a quiet resignation to them, as if he thought we'd never believe him.

'We should leave everything as it is,' Mother said solemnly.

I nodded. 'Everything.'

We walked in a slow procession down the stairs. No one spoke.

CHAPTER 26: TRUTH OR DIE

We sat in the sparse sitting room, a sickly light pooled in the centre of the room. Mother and Mirabelle had checked all the kitchen cupboards and found as many candles as possible. Aunt Charlotte had lit them in the centre of the room. A séance-like feel had descended on us and a distinct air of distrust was forming. We sat on the floor and listened to the broken voice of the wind at the windows. I felt that same cold hand stroke down my back, the sickness rising up in my belly. Our eyes were wide, watchful.

'So, what do we know?' Bridget began. 'Because I have the strong feeling some people may know more than others and I think if some of us don't start telling the truth, there may be more deaths.'

Mother looked decidedly disturbed. She doesn't like other people knowing more than her.

Jess was there, in the corner. I don't know how much she'd heard of our conversation. She'd definitely been in the hallway for some of it. She spoke without looking at us. 'All I know is my fiancé is dead and I'm trapped here with a bunch of lunatics.'

'That's not helpful,' Spear said.

'Oh really.' She laughed dismissively. 'Well, leading us into this hell by your utter lack of management and disorganization wasn't that *helpful*. Whether you've murdered anyone or not, I've a good mind to sue you when we get off here. You should be done for manslaughter at least. You didn't even know who was meant to be on the trip!'

'That is true, mate,' Kemp added. 'You did steal my guests.'

'I don't want your bloody guests.' Spear was sounding increasingly agitated.

'Oh,' Jess continued, 'and let's not forget you threw our rucksacks over the side, our only source of food.'

'You threw their rucksacks overboard?' Kemp shifted uncomfortably.

All eyes were on Spear.

Spear looked at Jess and took a long breath. 'I haven't killed anyone.'

A sharp draught meandered its way through the cluster of candles on the floor, tugging at the flames.

We all looked at Spear. He was still. His eyes were set on one point. The amber lights flickered on the surface of his eyes. One tear fell but he made no effort to wipe it away. It landed on the grey wooden floor, leaving a small dark circle just in front of his legs.

'I think she's gone.' His voice barely touched the air. 'I can feel it. I can feel the hole where she should be. I know she isn't there anymore.' His head fell and the light played on the tiny threads of grey in his hair. He held his hands to his face and let out a great long note, flat and pained. 'She's gone.'

As much as I wanted to feel sorrow for him, something about this sounded too cynical. Just at the moment when he was cornered, the grief had come pouring out. I clearly wasn't the only one who felt this way.

'Mr Spear,' Aunt Charlotte began carefully, 'how much do you know about your wife's death?'

There was silence. The wind milled round the house. I could hear the deep, quiet breathing of Mr Bojingles mirroring the distant drone of those waves.

Spear looked at me. 'You saw it. What did you see? You must have seen who killed my wife.'

I shook my head and I saw that anger flash across his face again.

'You didn't tell me!' This time he spat the words out and moved towards me.

Aunt Charlotte and Mother came in from both sides around me in a pincer movement.

'I'm afraid you'll have to go through us first, Mr Spear,' Aunt Charlotte's face glowed fierce in the candle flame.

No one moved until finally Spear fell back onto his knees. 'I wouldn't hurt her. I wouldn't hurt anyone. Nell was all I'd got. She was my everything.' He let out a low, guttural sound and sobbed in great pitiful waves. 'Christ, she was all I'd got.'

'Oh please, Spear.' Jess's face was tight with anger. 'I think we'd all worked out how much she liked to play away. Angel even referred to it. They made it clear what they'd been up to. That's why they'd got back in touch and that's why you lost it. You even said it yourself, that you loved her "*no matter what she did*". You *knew* what she did. She slept around. For Christ's sake, man, she was wearing his bloody love charm. He was wearing hers. And you killed him with it.'

Bridget turned to Jess. 'So were you,' she said bluntly.

Spear and Jess glared intently at each other as if they might make the other disappear.

Mother, Aunt Charlotte and Mirabelle leaned closer over the candlelight. Their faces were keen and sharp, a little bit like on the opening day of the John Lewis sale.

'Well, whatever their marital state of affairs was, Nell is dead and so are Angel and Bottlenose.' Aunt Charlotte sat back and folded her arms. We took a moment to process the statement. 'Which does then seem to leave you, doesn't it, Mr Spear?'

Spear sighed and closed his eyes. 'I . . . did . . . not . . . kill anyone.' It was becoming something of a mantra for him. 'Why would I drag them all out here to kill them? How could I know the boat would capsize and we'd be marooned here?'

Jess spoke viciously. 'Who said it was planned? It didn't need to be. Your wife was sleeping with Angel, you saw your chance. Bottlenose got wise so he got killed. If Bottlenose knew about the beads, if he overheard, then he would be aware that you knew about the beads too, Spear. You were standing right with him on the boat.'

Mirabelle held up her hands. 'I think we should just take this a little bit slower.'

'Well, I didn't hit myself over the head.' Spear put his hand to the wound.

'That is right,' I murmured. 'I've been thinking a lot about that.'

Eyes shifted to me.

'Remember the room?' I continued. 'Birds everywhere. Spear lying on the hearth. Blood seeping *down* his face from the cut at the top. He didn't hit his head on the hearth and make it bleed. Something or someone else hit him first, then he fell.'

'Well, it couldn't have been me,' Mother said quickly, 'or Mirabelle or Charlotte because we were all together and came up the stairs to find Spear on the floor in the bird room.'

'Not forgetting me as well, Mother.'

'Oh yes, you, of course.'

'Thanks, *Mother*.'

'So, it was someone else,' Mother carried on. 'Someone in the other group who wasn't with us. Who was in that group? Angel — he's dead. Bottlenose — he's dead. Now, we have Bridget and the dog. She was back here when Bottlenose was killed too.'

'Typical.' Bridget held her head high. 'Blame the vulnerable one.'

'You've never been *vulnerable* in your life,' Mirabelle sighed. 'You'd survive a nuclear bomb.'

'Why would I hit Mr Spear and kill Bottlenose? Motive, dear. I have no motive. Next you'll be blaming Mr Bojingles.'

All eyes settled on the dog.

'And then there's you — Jess,' Mother added.

The eyes shifted again. Even the candle flames seemed to be moving in concert now.

'You're the only one who had the opportunity to kill both Angel and Bottlenose,' Mirabelle said.

'You did have a bust-up with Angel and you pulled a knife on him,' Aunt Charlotte added.

'And you've been in the chapel without us,' I said.

Everyone paused.

'How do you know that?' Mother stared at me as if I'd been keeping secrets again.

'Because, Mother dearest, Jess said she wouldn't go into that chapel to lay out Angel's body, especially not since he hadn't even bothered to put her fiancé's boots back on. When we got there, her fiancé did indeed have bare feet and the boots had just been thrown to one side. Angel hadn't bothered to put them back on her fiancé's feet. But how would Jess have known that unless she'd been back in the chapel on her own since we put her fiancé in there?'

Everyone's attention travelled back to Jess. She sat, motionless, and closed her eyes. 'I loved Ryan with every single part of me and now he is gone. He won't come back. He'll stay here, lost on this island for ever, floating around this horrible old house with the rest of the ghosts.'

'I knew it!' Aunt Charlotte said. 'I knew it was haunted.'

Bridget leaned forward and placed her hand on Jess's leg. 'He won't. We will be rescued very soon. We're not far from the mainland and when they see all the candles we've lit and the fires, they will realize where we are and come, I'm sure. You can take Ryan back for a proper burial then. They know Mr Brown is out here looking.'

Bridget's words were uncharacteristically calming. My mind began to settle. I started to put the pictures together. I could hear their voices at the edge of my thoughts.

'I don't mean that,' Jess was saying in the background. 'His spirit will be here. He will be here, wandering around lost in these cold hills when I have gone. I had to be with him, see him again and hold him. That's why I went to the chapel, if you must know. Yes, I went to the chapel. Yes, I wanted to be with him.' She sobbed quietly, her eyes clenched tight as if she never wanted to see anything ever again.

The distant breaking waves were almost soothing now, out beyond the hills. The drifting lights were pricking the skyline. Witch lights, I'd imagined them. But those lights had been no more than a small bothy, its chimney smoking, a long-set fire inside. My mind wandered out there in the dusk again.

'And what about you, Brown? How long have you really been here?' Spear said. 'Because, you see, I'm not sure you haven't been trotting around this island all along, bashing me over the head and murdering people.'

'Wait a minute!' Kemp protested. 'I was with you lot when Bottlenose was killed. I wasn't even on your boat when it sank. I definitely was not even here when the other bloke, Angel, was killed and I've got absolutely no reason to kill any of you.' He looked around, appealing to all of us. A line of sweat travelled down his temple.

I watched Jess, weeping her broken tears. No other feeling on earth can compare to overwhelming grief. Nothing. In this state, she could have been capable of anything. Nothing could have broken the tears or the heart-wrenching feeling that I would never see my dad again when he was gone. Grief takes hold of you deep inside and fills you up like a sickness. Everything is skewed by it, every moment tinted. It's a toxic little friend who is always there humming away in the background, waiting for any weak, stolen moment to reinfect you. And part of you welcomes it. It brings the sense of the person back to you in that moment of pain. But it's an imitation. The black figure that stalks me is not the real man, not my dad, but a mark that his passing has left behind — just like the smoke left on the walls is not the fire that was lit there before. It is a reminder, but it isn't the real, living flame at all, just what remains. There is no warmth left to it. It is cold, barren. Only smoke.

What Jess had said sounded suspicious but I could understand her stealing out to that chapel to hold her fiancé one more time, or what was left of him, imagining that he was just sleeping. Imagining that he would wake up and give a slow smile of recognition. She would feel his warmth and then it would be over. The grief would die. But it doesn't. Grief is not just a jacket you can take off. It becomes part of you.

I pictured the poor man lying in a strange, abandoned tomb with strangers for company. What awful, cold places we condemn our loved ones to haunt. Jess would have seen his marble face, as perfect as it had always been, wearing his same clothes as if he could just stand up on those bare feet. They had been an affront to her, his boots so precious that she'd held a knife to a man to make sure they were returned to such useless feet.

I thought of her dead fiancé. He was showing me those boots again on the boat, so proudly, such care over their choice. What had he said? *'The Tecnica CAS are the best money can buy. CAS — Custom Adaptive Shape? Heat-formed custom mouldable hiking boots with a Vibram sole?'* I remembered him holding his foot up for inspection.

His words smouldered in my mind as the voices still bickered around me. They faded into the background.

'Give me the phone,' I said in a dream-like voice.

They stopped talking.

'The phone.' I held out my hand to Kemp.

He frowned and fumbled in his pocket. Slowly, he unlocked it and handed it to me. I went to the photographs, the macabre selfie with me and the watch and Bottlenose dead. The photograph showed it all just as it had been, just as I remembered it. Only, it wasn't. Something was different.

'Ursula?' Mother's hand was on my arm.

'Oh, what is it now?' Mirabelle sighed. 'These endless battles for attention are just so—'

'Be quiet, Mirabelle,' Aunt Charlotte said.

'It's different.' I studied the screen.

'Dear, give the phone to me,' Aunt Charlotte said softly. 'This fascination with dead bodies has clearly moved up a gear.' She held out her hand.

'For the millionth time, Aunt Charlotte, I don't have a fascination with dead bodies, they just keep cropping up in my life. I can't help it.' I looked into the screen and imagined the body upstairs on the floor. 'We need to go back upstairs. We need to see Bottlenose.'

'See! What did I say? Back to the bodies again.'

CHAPTER 27: A PICTURE
TELLS A THOUSAND LIES

I studied the small image on the screen in my palm and everything was just as it should be, in its right place. And yet it wasn't.

'Ursula?' Mother looked impatient. 'Well, are you going to let us in on this?' Mother can't bear secrets when they are other people's.

'How can I let you in on this, when I'm not sure what *this* is yet?'

'It's a phone, dear,' Aunt Charlotte offered.

I turned it over in my hand as though I'd never seen one before.

'It's not top-of-the-range,' Kemp said. 'I keep breaking them.'

'Whipping that belt around,' Mirabelle muttered.

I stood up and everyone's eyes stayed on me. 'I need to go upstairs and look at the body again.'

'Oh no, dear,' Aunt Charlotte sighed. 'We need to stop this.'

'Now, Aunt Charlotte! I need to see that room again *now*.'

They followed me up the stairs like I was some strange Pied Piper. Whether they were the rats or the children was unclear. Slowly, I opened the door to Bottlenose's death-room.

My eyes went straight to him, the giant knife still sticking straight up from his back. It was so tempting to run to him and pull out the knife, as if that might do any good. The iron smell hit us, like walking into an old butcher's shop on a hot day. The dull silver of the blade reflected our movement as we came in. His dead finger reached out to the word it had written in the dust.

Aunt Charlotte sounded it out again. 'Macdiv.'

'That's not what it says,' Mother corrected her.

I bent down in the exact same place as before. I looked at the phone and then back at Bottlenose. The picture I'd taken was exactly the same as what I saw now.

Bridget handed me her watch. 'Any difference?' She was genuinely intrigued.

I shook my head.

'Take the picture again,' Spear said. 'Maybe it will occur to you.'

'Can it occur quickly? It stinks in here.'

We all looked at Aunt Charlotte and she shrugged. 'I'm just saying what everyone else is thinking.'

I crouched down in the exact same position and held out the phone and the watch. I could see my own face, exhausted and pale, then the hair of the dead body and the blade in the corner. The phone jittered in my cold, shaking hand. The smell of the body breathed out in waves across my face. I held my thumb over the button on the phone and just as I was about to take the shot, it was there. My thumb hovered over the button. I didn't dare move. Barely opening my lips, I whispered, 'The picture is different.'

'In what way, Ursula? You've said it was different already. How?' Mother sounded irritated.

'Just take the shot,' Jess said drily.

'No, it's not the shot that's different.'

'You're making no sense, dear,' Aunt Charlotte said.

'Shhh,' Bridget hissed. 'Let her speak!'

My thighs were beginning to shake from the crouching position. 'Come closer, everyone. Get behind me,' I whispered as if the dead body could hear me.

They paused.

'Quickly,' I hissed.

They gathered behind me, trying not to nudge or touch me.

'Now, crouch low and look at the screen.'

They did and I could feel them all clustered round me. It began to look a little like the celebrity selfies that do the rounds after award ceremonies, only this time there was a dead body in the foreground.

'Look, it's different to the eventual picture. The selfie image I can see before I take the shot is backwards. It's a mirror image. The camera then normalizes the picture so it no longer appears backwards when the shot is taken. But I saw it like a mirror image when I was holding up the phone for the selfie before I pressed the button to take the picture.'

They all stared at the screen and there it was, an exact mirror image of what we were seeing.

'Look at the word as it appears on the screen before I take the shot,' I whispered.

I felt them all move slightly.

'Vibram,' Spear whispered.

'Oh Christ,' Jess breathed.

'Now, if I take the shot—' which I then did — 'the word is now normalized and appears as we are seeing it on the floor with our eyes. It is no longer the mirror image that was there when I was readying to take the selfie.'

We all stared at the shot I'd taken on the screen, which had the letters as we were seeing them on the floor now.

To prove it, I moved around the body and held out the phone in front of the word ready as if to take a selfie but without taking the shot. The word appeared filling the screen, the phone's screen acting as a mirror before I took the picture — *Vibram*.

'What the hell is *Vibram*?' Mirabelle sighed.

'The make of a fancy shoe,' Kemp said as he took the phone back. 'Technical walking shoe, high-end. Very expensive. They have the name *Vibram* on the sole in raised-up letters.'

'So if you had *Vibram* stamped on the bottom of your shoe and you stood in a pile of dust, the letters would make their marks in the dust but they would be backwards,' Bridget stated as if this was in some way her discovery. 'Like this.' She pointed to the markings on the floor. 'But the phone acts as a mirror *before* a selfie is taken. So, when she holds up the phone for the selfie, it shows her the mirror image of the letters. Exactly how they would appear if we looked straight at the sole of the boot. But only the person taking the shot would see that momentarily.'

'All right, we get it,' Mirabelle said sourly.

'Do we?' Aunt Charlotte was utterly mystified by all of it. She's only had a mobile phone for a couple of years and I'm yet to see her indulge in taking selfies.

'It's important to clarify matters for the cheap seats.' Bridget looked pointedly at Aunt Charlotte, who then looked behind her as if Bridget must mean someone else.

Aunt Charlotte began, 'I'm afraid I don't . . .'

'Understand? I know.' Bridget cleared her throat. 'The footprint has left the word the wrong way round but in a mirror it would look exactly how it does on the sole of the shoe. Only Ursula, who was holding the phone up to take the selfie, would have seen how the word really appears on the boot rather than the print it leaves behind. If we were to see the boot now, we would see the word "Vibram" on the sole.'

'The make of shoe I believe you wear, Jess.' Spear looked at her defiantly. 'If you wouldn't mind showing us all.'

Jess stared at us and sighed. 'Lots of people wear them.' She held up her foot and there on the sole of her shoe in raised letters was the emblem '*Vibram*'.

'Dear God, girl.' Aunt Charlotte held up her hands. 'But why? What had Bottlenose ever done to you?'

'Wait!' Bridget said. 'What did you just say, Jess?'

'What? When?' She lowered her foot.

234

'"*Lots of people wear them*",' I repeated for her.

Mother looked around quickly. 'Is anyone else in this room wearing boots with that on the sole?'

No one moved.

'Come on,' Mother ordered. 'Feet up!'

Slowly, we all raised a foot.

'Right, let's see.' She ran down the line of us, careful not to trip over the dead body in the middle of the room. It didn't seem like the most respectful pose for us all to be lifting a leg over the corpse with a massive knife in its back but sometimes, in a survival situation, you have to do what's necessary.

Mother grabbed each trouser leg as she passed and pulled the foot up. Every foot got a thorough examination and the conclusion was no one else had that raised lettering on their shoe.

'Right, missy, put your foot in the dust next to that lettering,' Aunt Charlotte directed Jess.

'And if I won't?' Jess folded her arms.

'That's not really going to make you look any less guilty is it?' Mirabelle grabbed hold of the girl's elbow.

'Hey!' Jess pulled free. 'OK, OK!' She walked over to the markings in the dust and placed her foot down next to the word. She left it for a moment then lifted her foot. There in the dust was the exact same backwards impression.

'I believe you are looking at your murderer!' Spear said with a triumphant smile, as if that was a good thing. 'No wonder you were so quick to point the finger at me. Did you kill my wife as well?' He stepped towards her.

'No, we're not looking at the killer,' Bridget said.

'Well, we're looking at the shoe-print of the murderer and she's wearing the shoe.' Kemp was still looking between his phone and the print in the pile of dust. It didn't look as though he was entirely clear about what had just happened.

'No, we're not looking at that either.' Bridget spoke in that irritating sanctimonious way she has when we all know she's right.

235

'The lettering is too small,' I said slowly. 'It's not her shoe.'
Everyone turned to look at me now.

'But someone else had Vibram soles. Your fiancé's boots had that on them as well, didn't they, Jess? You both showed them to me on the boat.'

'Oh, I see what she did,' Aunt Charlotte began. 'She told us she went to the chapel on her own. She changed into the other boots there!'

'And why exactly would I do that?'

'To disguise yourself, dear.'

'Oh, so I changed into a pair of boots that had exactly the same name on the sole so I could purposefully leave a footprint next to the body I'd just murdered.' She leaned closer to Aunt Charlotte. 'Wouldn't it have been easier for me just to leave no footprint or rub it away?'

'Yes,' I said. 'The footprint has to be a mistake on the part of the killer. But they were wearing your fiancé's boots, that's for sure.'

Bridget spoke carefully and slowly. 'Jess, when your fiancé was washed ashore and you lay across his body, *you* told us he was dead. No one else could take his pulse or check him because you were sprawled across him spreadeagled, preventing us from doing so. You were the only one who confirmed he was dead.'

'And by your own admission, you have been visiting the chapel without us,' Mother added.

'Was there a reason you objected so strongly to Angel taking your boyfriend's boots, Jess?' Mirabelle asked.

'Was your boyfriend really dead, Jess?' Mother was on the same track.

We all looked at one another in the awful silence.

'Oh my God, are you in league with your dead boyfriend?' It sounded slightly crazy when Aunt Charlotte said it, but there was no denying we were all thinking the same thing.

Jess started laughing. 'You people are utterly insane. No one will ever believe you!'

We paused and looked at one another.

'They're his boot marks, Jess,' Bridget said matter-of-factly, 'and you've been visiting him out there. None of us ever checked to see if he was dead because you *told* us he was.'

'Yes, I *told* you he was. I suppose I could've told you he was Tutankhamun and you'd have believed me.'

'Tutankhamun, as in the mummy?' Aunt Charlotte was lost again.

One by one, we started to move gradually towards the door. We kept our eyes on Jess. Then we started to move quicker, until we were basically jostling our way out of the room.

As I looked at the floor on our way out, I noticed something else I hadn't seen before, near the bottom of Bottlenose's shoe. I bent down to look at it. It was a small cream-coloured splash on the floor. I reached out and touched it. It was candle wax.

'Ursula, come on.' Mother was growing impatient. 'What are you doing?'

'There's candle wax on the floor.'

'That's because there's no electricity,' she sighed. 'Did you think we lit all those candles for a romantic atmosphere?'

'No, I . . .' I shrugged. 'I just didn't think anyone had brought one up here.'

I looked at Jess, the strange grin still on her face, her green eyes glaring at me.

CHAPTER 28: THE BAREFOOTED MAN

A sullen sky watched us as we scrambled out of the door and across the grass. For a moment, I felt strangely separate, as if I was no longer part of any of this. I was just a bystander. Not an unfamiliar feeling for me.

I paused at the threshold. Did we all really believe this new theory? As the cold air hit me and I stood outside the grim confines of that house, it seemed much more likely someone who was among the living had perpetrated these crimes. Perhaps it had just been a lot easier to make it someone outside our group.

I watched them: all arrayed in a line, stomping out to the chapel. One of them was perhaps a murderer. They stumbled through the long scrub grass. Towards what? Discovery? What did they hope to find? It suddenly seemed so ridiculous. It made no sense. There was no *reason* to it. Why would Jess and her fiancé hide his death so he could sneak out to kill people? Why would they even want to kill Angel and Bottlenose? Angel and Bottlenose had no obvious connection beyond being on this trip together, and neither had had any previous knowledge of Jess and Ryan. Not that we knew of, anyway. They'd hidden it well if they did. But Angel or Bottlenose were not the kind of men to have let that go unmentioned. If they'd known them in some way they'd have said, wouldn't they?

I turned to see Jess slowly walking down the stairs. I moved out of the door. She didn't seem to be racing to stop them, to stop some crazed discovery about her undead boyfriend. She wasn't scared of what they would find in that chapel. She had no fear left. The worst thing that could have happened to her had happened and she had cried those bitter tears of grief. That couldn't possibly have been an act — her desperate loss, her new-found desolation. Surely she hadn't been faking it all this time? Had I been taken in by her grief?

And what of Spear and Kemp running out in front as if this was some assault course training exercise? They really were racing as if there was something there to find, as if they had to get there first. It could just have been competition but both of them had attracted enough reasons for suspicion to fall on them. Spear knew those beads were poisonous. He must have known all along.

I watched him now scrambling over the dunes. He'd run back so quickly after we'd found Kemp's boat. Spear had made sure he was the *first* back. Then Bottlenose was killed with his knife. He'd certainly shown enough aggression to be capable of it — on the boat hurling the rucksacks over because Angel and Nell were close. Had Angel paid for his indiscretion? Angel had made no secret that he'd spread his love charms around. And it was certainly no secret that Nell had a past that drove Spear to jealous rage. He'd admitted as much and that they were separating, getting a divorce. He'd even physically fought with Angel.

As they ran, Spear elbowed Kemp out of the way. There'd definitely been a tension between those two from the very beginning. And what about Kemp? His washed-up commando routine was wearing as thin as his hair. Just how long had he been here on the island? I'd seen those witch lights out there since our first night. Something was making them. And then there was the candle wax near Bottlenose. Perhaps the same candle wax I'd seen in the bothy. Had Kemp visited the house first before we found him, killed Bottlenose, then doubled back to the bothy and claimed he'd only just arrived? But why would he smash up his own boat?

Mother, Aunt Charlotte and Mirabelle were stumbling along behind the two men as if this was no more than a charity fun run that had reached the point where they were regretting it. In reality, when they'd reached that point, their solution had been to stop at a wine bar and stay there.

Only Bridget held back from the rest. She walked along primly, just behind, with Mr Bojingles at her feet as if this was a little country walk. She was irritating even when she was only walking. Like Jess, she'd been back in the house when Bottlenose had been killed. She'd shared a room with him the night Angel was killed. Had Bottlenose seen her sneak out to kill Angel? Had Bridget returned and noticed his eyes follow her back in and realized she and Mr Bojingles had to murder again? I watched them shuffling along.

I paused and looked back towards the house. The figure of Jess was still ambling behind as if nothing mattered.

Dad's bent figure was there, near the door over in the corner, turning away — his face bleak, anxious this time. He was almost part of the shadows but at certain times, certain moments when the light fell just right or I turned my head slowly to the side, I caught him there in the periphery. He didn't appear if I looked straight at him. I had to really make myself aware of the edges of the world. But he was there now. He was watching me. He nodded once towards the others as if I should follow.

Jess was getting closer and I didn't want the awkward walk with her. There was that same disconnected look on her face. I turned and looked out at the silver film of mist. The others suddenly seemed quite distant. I started to walk a little faster.

My mind was so disjointed. The line between the dead and the living seemed to be growing increasingly blurred. This island held us in such a constant state of strange chaos. It was a disorientating world that should have been an oasis

240

of beauty and calm but was instead confusion and fear. I looked across the sea and there were those green eyes again, lingering below the surface of the waves. Nell's eyes. Did those eyes still look out from the seabed or did she watch us from somewhere else now — somewhere much closer on this island?

All along, the most overwhelming feeling on this island had been that of being watched by someone or something, a presence that hung at the edges of what we could see, that had dipped in and out of our lives, taking one of us when it could. Picking us off one by one. Perhaps Bottlenose had been right, there was more to the heaven and earth of this place than we could dream of.

We didn't belong here. That much was clear. This was a place for the dead, like those that rested under its Druid stones, like the bones that littered the abandoned cemetery on the beach, the skulls lining that cupboard, the shod witch galloping over the hills and the memory of those two old women with their rocking horse.

The low gleam of dusk touched the edges of the water giving them a yellow-green light. The thin breath of the wind had haunted every step since our arrival and it sang out across the sands now. The vast wilderness was all around me but with no sense of freedom. It gripped me like a straitjacket, crushing me.

The dark, moss-covered stones of the chapel caught the last of the faint light. Its mournful eyes watched our approach again.

They were all waiting at the door. No one had dared to open it.

'Hurry up, Ursula.' Mother was exasperated, as if I was the reason they had all stalled instead of their own fear.

'This is ridiculous.' Jess was close behind me now. 'I don't know what it is you're expecting to find. Don't you think I've suffered enough without you bursting into my fiancé's tomb?' She looked from one to the other of us. 'Please, just leave him alone.'

'When you put it like that,' Kemp said awkwardly, 'it does sound a little . . . a little disrespectful.'

'And your suggestion would be?' Bridget put her hands on her hips. The dog watched him as if he was about to do the same. They both widened their eyes in expectation.

Spear stepped forward. 'Brown here may have—'

'A point?' Bridget interrupted. 'Don't forget, Mr Spear, that at this moment you are our number one suspect, with motive and opportunity to kill all of the victims. So, I would have thought any exit strategy was better than none for you.'

He shook his head. 'You women are unbelievable.'

'Thank you.'

'Let's just get in there and settle this.' Aunt Charlotte started towards the door.

'Wait!' Jess said. 'Don't hurt him.'

Everyone paused and stared at her. Aunt Charlotte shoved the door hard and it fell open.

In the dim hollow of the chapel, it was hard to make out the silent shapes. Our eyes began to adjust. The troublesome boots with their distinctive tread were thrown in the corner, mud and candle wax on their soles. The *Vibram* symbol was clear to see.

Aunt Charlotte took a breath and stepped inside the dark cave. She turned to us. 'Right, let's get this over with.'

CHAPTER 29: THE CHAPEL OF UNREST

The rest of us clustered in the doorway. The remains of the light filtered round our outlines, sending our long shadows out into the chapel.

'Charlotte? What the hell are you doing?' Mother frowned.

'Seeing if he's alive.' She was already crouching down by the side of Ryan's cold shape.

Mother raised her eyebrows. 'And how exactly were you hoping to do that, given that in fifty-eight years on this planet, you are yet to master tying your shoelaces or taking a pulse?'

Aunt Charlotte gave Mother a tart look. 'There's more than one way to skin a rabbit, Pandora.'

'Yes, I think that's already been adequately illustrated.' I waited at the door.

Spear looked towards Kemp. 'So, you *are* still skinning your pet rabbits!'

Kemp looked away and muttered 'murderer' under his breath.

'What's that?' The smile fell quickly from Spear.

'Nothing.'

'Listen, if you've got something to say . . .'

'Come on, man, get up!' We all looked into the chapel to see that Aunt Charlotte had Ryan by the lapels of his expensive outdoor jacket, his body suspended beneath her like a rag. She pulled him closer towards her. 'We know you're alive. The game is up. Speak!' She lifted him further, then slammed him back down again into the wet stone, his head lolling to the side. 'We know you're not dead!' She lifted him up and cracked his unmoving head back down with a deep thud. Our theory was unravelling before us in a painfully obvious fashion.

'Jesus! Aunt Charlotte!' I pushed past the bickering Kemp and Spear who had now started to square up to each other. 'Aunt Charlotte, please, stop, for God's sake!'

'We need answers, Ursula.' She lifted the body again.

'Right, I see.' Spear stepped towards Kemp and looked down on the top of his head. 'You're too much of a coward to say it to my face.'

'I'm not the coward here.'

'And what exactly is that supposed to mean?'

There was only the smallest gap between their faces, close enough that they would be able to feel the angry spray of each other's words. Aunt Charlotte banged Ryan's head back onto the stone again.

'Aunt Charlotte, please!' I tried to push myself further forward between everyone. Mirabelle and Mother were not moving. They'd become spectators and were caught looking between Aunt Charlotte and the Kemp/Spear contest.

'Oh, you know exactly what I mean!' Kemp leaned in.

'Oh, oh, do I?' They were chest-to-chest now. 'I know you've been hiding out on this island for longer than you'll admit, you creepy bastard.'

'Creepy bastard? Who are you calling a creepy—'

'You!' Spear pushed Kemp in the chest and Kemp stumbled into the chapel, banging into Mother and Mirabelle. In one move, the situation had escalated. Kemp fell backwards. 'Nell saw you.' Spear stormed in. 'Looking at her, spying on her. This was the one trip she hated because she had to come back near you.'

Bang.

Aunt Charlotte sent Ryan's head back down onto the stone again. We all looked into the chapel.

'Woah there! You already told us she was leaving you. It was you she didn't want to be with anymore.' Kemp pushed Spear in the chest this time. 'Is that why you killed her?'

Aunt Charlotte paused with Ryan's dead body in her hands.

I stepped further into the chapel and felt something clip beneath my foot. Before I had chance to look down, Spear was lunging towards Kemp.

'You little fucker.' Spear sent a fist out and it glanced across Kemp's cheek.

'Mr Spear, no more violence, please.' Bridget grabbed Mr Bojingles and held him close. She shuffled into the small chapel. It was getting crowded now.

Mirabelle held out her hands too. 'I don't think—'

'Hitting me won't solve it,' Kemp said. 'I was the first man Nell truly loved and you couldn't deal with that.'

Everyone paused. It seemed improbable. We stood still, watching Kemp.

'You delusional little prick.' Spear's face twisted into a sneer. I hadn't seen him look like that before. It was disturbing.

'I'm delusional, am I? Before she ever met you, she loved me and you know she did. You know what she gave up because you made her.'

It was becoming slightly less improbable.

'I didn't make her give up anything! She wanted to leave this shithole. She always complained when we came back. It was her who came to find me. Remember?'

Kemp gave a malicious smile. 'Oh, you didn't know either, did you?' He gave a joyless laugh.

Spear took a step back as if he was afraid of the words.

This time it was Kemp who threw himself towards Spear. 'You took her away from me and now you've killed her. You bastard.'

'I didn't kill her!' Spear shouted.

There was so much noise echoing round the small chapel. I was shoved as Kemp and Spear rolled forward, locked together and punching. My head smacked into the door frame and suddenly everything was a confused sea. I could feel the nausea rising again. Sweat prickled its way down my back. It seemed as though the air was being squeezed out of this tiny room. Spear and Kemp were reeling all over, battering into the wall like frightened birds. I watched them flailing, their arms and feet clattering into the walls.

'They're just like birds,' I whispered. The sweat trickled down my temple. I was finding it harder to breathe. The chapel was becoming more claustrophobic with every turn and punch they made.

'Ursula?' Mother was moving closer towards me, but she seemed so far away.

'Someone hit Spear over the head in the room with the birds.'

'No prizes for guessing who.' Mother nodded towards Kemp scuffling into Spear's chest with his fists rounding.

'Mother, where did Jess get the knife?'

'What?'

I stumbled. 'The knife.'

'Spear's knife?'

Spear paused and turned to us, Kemp nestled into his shoulder as if they were almost embracing each other. 'So it's your turn, is it? I didn't kill anyone! Least of all Nell and I didn't use a knife on Bottlenose. If I was going to kill anyone I wouldn't wait until I was marooned on an island with you clowns. I'm with . . . *was* with Nell every day.'

'Yes, but where did Jess get the knife from?' I breathed. I could hear the distant whistling start in my head again, passing over the sands that Bottlenose had said sang out. The old sea shanty notes mingled with the tide as if something was coming out of the sea. I leaned back onto the smooth stone wall. I could feel the boots behind the back of my legs.

'Boots.' My voice broke as if the feel of them was a sudden relief, a welcome comfort.

'What's that, Ursula?' Mother came closer and the whistling grew louder in my head. She looked into my eyes.

Aunt Charlotte dropped the dead man to the stone with a resounding thud.

'The boots, Aunt Charlotte.'

'Yes, dear.' Aunt Charlotte stepped towards me and gripped me hard under the arms. I felt my legs scoop from under me.

'Look at the boots . . .'

They all looked down at Ryan's boots behind my legs. The Vibram sole was clearly visible — the sole that had made the print in the dust.

'Angel said . . .'

'I can tell you, dear, he's very much dead.' Aunt Charlotte held me in what felt like an attempt at a wrestling hold.

'Jess said the knife was his. It fell—'

Mother sighed. 'Yes, we know it's Spear's knife. We've been through this. He's admitted that. You're very confused. We need to get you—'

'No, Mother. Listen,' I panted. 'The whistling.'

Aunt Charlotte began to drag me across the stones towards the door.

'I don't know what the hell is wrong with you all,' Spear began, 'beating up dead guys. It's like he said, you're all mad as hatters if you ask me.'

'We've covered that,' Bridget said dismissively. 'It can't be the mercury. Had to be the beads.'

'The knife, Spear's knife—'

'Christ! This is ridiculous. We're going round in circles.' Spear sighed. 'I'm not staying in this morgue.' He started to walk away. A winded Kemp crouched on the floor.

'The knife fell—'

'I did not murder my wife!' he shouted.

My mouth was so dry I could barely speak, my legs were weak and strange images flashed through my raging thoughts.

'Well, let's get you out of here,' Aunt Charlotte said tenderly. 'No more staring at dead people today.'

247

I saw a shadow travel across the window outside. 'Dad?' I whispered.

The dog ground down low and started snarling at his shadow.

'The dog can see him?' I trembled. 'His ghost? Mr Bojingles can see him too?'

Bridget picked up the dog. Mother moved quickly towards me. 'OK. Time to get her out of here. That's enough, Ursula. Come on. You need to rest.'

'Bottlenose's story on the ship.' I glanced over to the passing outline of my dad on the other side of the window. He paused, then drifted away.

'Make sense!' Mirabelle snapped.

Aunt Charlotte dragged me, and my feet slid across the stones with a strange, sharp sound. I tried to lift my foot. 'Look underneath my boot.' I was losing consciousness.

'Stop, everybody!' Bridget said firmly. 'Stop dragging her and shouting at her. Let her speak before she faints again. We need to hear this.'

Somehow, Bridget's sudden faith in me stalled everything.

I hung precariously from Aunt Charlotte's hands wedged tightly under my arms. I pivoted my foot to the side. Mother bent down towards it.

'Jess said . . .' I began, but the words wouldn't form.

'Yes, where is Jess?' Mirabelle looked around as if there was anywhere to hide in this tiny space.

Mother held something small in her fingers and stood up slowly.

'What is it, Pandora? What's wrong with her now?' Mirabelle leaned closer, frowning.

'Jess said . . .' I whispered.

Aunt Charlotte looked into my face. 'Said what?'

'Jess said the knife fell from his pocket.' I dropped to the floor, just managing to keep my eyes open.

'I'm surprised at you, Spear—' Kemp raised his eyebrows — 'I always keep my knife safely secured in my Beaver belt.'

'Oh, so you have a knife too!' Mother frowned. 'This is all making a lot more sense now.'

'No.' My voice cracked. 'It didn't fall from his pocket.'

Mother closed her eyes. 'You just said it did.'

'No, the boots . . .'

'We need to get her out of here.' Mother sounded so stern.

'Warm, Angel said the boots were warm. They shouldn't have been. They were the boots he wore after Jess made him come and change them. It wasn't Spear's pocket. When Jess said it fell from "*his pocket*", she meant the boy's pocket. It was the boy's boots that were warm.'

Mother was slowly holding out her hand. 'A coin,' she whispered.

'That coin was on the boy's eye. His eyes were open when we left him here. But they were shut when Bottlenose put the coin back on later.' I looked at Mother. 'He's coffin boy.' My head began to fall into my chest. 'He's Bottlenose's wicked coffin boy who should never have been on the ship.'

Slowly, everyone turned to look towards the outline lying on the other side of the chapel. A dark, unmoving mass of clothes.

Mr Bojingles struggled free from Bridget's arms and bounced towards the bundle. He bit into a sleeve and dragged it, shaking his head. The body made no attempt to resist. The dead arm didn't flinch. The coat unravelled and pulled away to reveal that it was no more than an empty pile of clothes. The boy had gone.

We stood, frozen in silence, looking at the space where the body should have been.

'Nate,' Spear said.

CHAPTER 30: DEAD MEN DON'T WEAR SHOES

'What the hell is going on?' Spear's voice was angry confusion. He held up the empty clothes tentatively as if they were evidence. It was looking increasingly like they *were* evidence. 'Where's the body?'

'We need to find him.' I sounded hoarse. 'He has to be out there. He's still alive. His boots were warm. The coin keeps falling from his face when he stands up. When Angel came out with the boy's boots on, he said they were warm. If he was dead, they wouldn't have been, especially when he'd been in the sea so long.'

'She's right,' Bridget said. 'I knew it all along.'

'Angel's room is empty,' I continued. 'He would have had Nate's boots in his room. I think the boy took his boots back when he came in the house, when he murdered Bottlenose. He came into the house in Ryan's Vibram-soled boots and took the knife from Jess.'

'Wait, how did he know she had my knife?' Spear said.

I was getting into my stride now. 'He would have heard the argument about the boots. He was right here in the chapel — alive. She pulled the knife and threatened Angel. He would have heard everything. He comes into the house through one of the many windows he keeps opening. Takes the knife. Kills Bottlenose, and on his way out, took his own boots back. He runs back to the chapel and flings in the Vibram boots, knowing full well we'll be taking Bottlenose's body in there soon and that will alleviate suspicion. He fixes up a bundle of clothes that in the darkness might fool us.'

'But where is he now?' Mother said slowly.

'The bothy.'

No one spoke.

'That's who's been coming and going making noises at the house. It's not a ghost.' I paused for a moment, aware of what I'd just said. 'Listen to me, they're not witch lights. It's him up at the bothy. I'm sure of it. It wouldn't just have been Bottlenose and Spear who heard the conversation between Nell and Angel on the boat about the poisonous bracelet. Nate was crouched on the floor below them. He would have heard too. It's him! He's our killer. He's the coffin boy who got on the ship at the last minute.'

'OK. Take it slowly, Ursula,' Mother said.

I nodded. 'Not only was he in a perfect place on the boat to hear their conversation, he was in the perfect spot inside the chapel to hear Jess had the knife. But also the boy would have been able to hear that Angel realized the boots were warm. Angel could quite easily start thinking about that in a calmer moment when no one was waving a knife at him. He could easily start to get suspicious. So Angel had to die. All the way through, that boy has been in that perfect spot, right next to us, hearing everything. He's been stalking us, hiding, letting us lay out everything we knew, piece by piece. Basically, we've been telling him who he needed to kill next.'

'Ursula, isn't this just a bit . . .'

'No, Aunt Charlotte. Think about it! If he's just destroyed the boat he was out near there, he would have heard us saying Bottlenose had the passenger list — the list that would have shown he shouldn't even have been here. And remember, it was Bottlenose who placed the coin back on the boy's face — his eyes now closed and his skin still warm. Even though he was a sad old drunk, he'd have worked it out sooner or later. So Bottlenose had to die too.'

'Wait! What are you all talking about? This is ridiculous.' Mother frowned. 'The boy was dead. He can't have suddenly risen up. I refuse to believe that this is ghosts or spirits, faeries, witches or any other form of the undead. The killer must be a living human being who has killed three people and then stolen the boy's body.'

Aunt Charlotte bent over me and began trying to lift me. It was starting to become quite disturbing given what I'd seen her do with Ryan's body. I looked into her anxious face. 'Aunt Charlotte . . .'

'Yes, dear.'

'You checked if he was dead, the boy, didn't you? You said he was dead. You were the only one who checked to see if he was dead.'

She paused and looked around the silent group. Then she looked towards Mother.

'Really?' Mother looked stunned, then her face fell. She closed her eyes.

'I just . . .'

Everyone looked at Aunt Charlotte in expectation.

Mirabelle began to laugh viciously. 'Oh, hang on, you genuinely *can't* take a pulse. That's not just a joke. He was alive, you bloody idiot.'

'No.' Aunt Charlotte looked panicked. 'That's not possible. He was stone cold, and I did feel his wrist and there was nothing. The coin has dropped off every time we've come in here and knocked it. The knife could have fallen from a dead man's pocket. The boots would have been warmer to Angel than wearing nothing. Seriously? Come on.'

I pictured the slim-framed body rolling in the waves. Alongside him, twisting in the waves like a water snake was . . . 'His belt,' I said quietly.

'An old trick,' Bridget confirmed. 'He didn't know Charlotte would be such an incredibly inept idiot—'

'Hey!'

252

'Now is no time for feelings, Charlotte. We need the truth.' Bridget looked at her firmly. 'Say if he'd already tied the belt around his wrist tight enough to sedate the flow. He was freezing cold from being in the water. He knew if he slipped off the belt and played dead there was a chance we might not think he was alive. A chance he could get away with it.'

'Away with it?' Mother stared at her. 'You're speaking in code. Is anyone actually going to explain?'

'Get away with the murder he'd already committed, of course,' Bridget said stony-faced.

We all seemed to instinctively pull our heads back as one.

'Oh dear, Mr Bojingles, yet again the *Smart* Women is an utter misnomer.'

'Miss who?'

'Charlotte,' Mother said sharply, 'you've done enough. Be quiet.'

'Ursula saw someone pushed under in the water,' Bridget continued. 'Someone with green eyes, who really could only have been Nell.'

I glanced quickly over at Spear. His hands squeezed tight into a ball. He was staring ahead of him.

Bridget continued. 'It couldn't be Kemp who pushed her down as he wasn't on the boat. It had to have been one of us. It could have been Ryan before he died in the water, but then who killed Angel and Bottlenose?'

Aunt Charlotte shrugged.

'From what Ursula described, it was a man's hands that pushed the woman under. It could possibly have been Angel, but then who killed him? That just left Spear and one other — the boy, Nate. We eliminated the boy from the very beginning because we thought he was dead but we never considered the idea that we'd been mistaken. He may have been half-drowned, but half-drowned is still half-alive.'

We all looked open-mouthed at the dishevelled collection of clothes, dragged out by the dog across the stone.

Mother held out her hand with the tarnished coin in it and I remembered how I'd found it on the floor before, when we'd delivered Angel's body to the chapel.

'It was me who made Bottlenose put the coin back on the boy's face.'

'Oh, very possibly you might then have signed Bottlenose's death warrant.'

'Thanks, Bridget. I feel a whole lot better now.' I looked again at the pile of clothes.

Bridget continued. 'Perhaps that's why Bottlenose told the story on the boat. Remember, Nate was crouched below him and as he told the tale of the coffin boy, Bottlenose looked down at the boy. He was telling him, telling Nate — he knew he shouldn't have been on board the ship.' Bridget stroked the dog methodically as if ordering her thoughts. 'He kills Bottlenose, with the knife, the one he'd slipped from Spear on the boat.'

'One thing—' Aunt Charlotte leaned in — 'Why did the lad steal Spear's knife in the first place? He couldn't have known he'd need it for Bottlenose later, that it would be Bottlenose who'd put the coin back on his face.'

I thought for a moment. 'He was planning on killing someone else.'

'Correct!' Bridget was becoming insufferable. 'I think the knife was for someone else who isn't even dead yet.'

Bridget was enjoying this. 'Bottlenose and Angel were accidentals who needed to be silenced before they let anything slip. Before they spoiled his chances of killing whoever it was he really wanted to stab. He was hunting someone.'

We all fell silent, listening to the tortured wind circling the walls of the chapel. The sea fell with a great noise across the sands as if an audience had suddenly broken into applause, the strange fluting sound still travelled in the lull of the sea over the dunes. And then the whistling began to drift behind it, that soulful sea-song I'd heard before.

'The whistling,' I said. 'It's back.'

Mother twitched. 'Wh—'

'Quiet, Mother!'

She looked stunned.

The dog began its low guttural noise again.

I held out my arms and spread my fingers wide as if to stop them all speaking. The whistling wove in and out of the sound of the foam drawing back across the beach. It was moving further away. But the air was so full of noise that I couldn't unpick each sound very easily.

'We need to go outside.'

'With the murderer. Of course we do.' Mirabelle turned away.

'Oh, Ursula, why must you always seek out danger, dear?' Aunt Charlotte was shaking her head slowly.

'Because, dear Aunt, we have left a woman out there with a killer.'

Their eyes widened.

'Oh shit!' Spear whispered. 'Jess.'

Bridget let out a great sigh. 'Well, it would appear that you have left another of your travelling companions to die, Mr Spear.' She shook her head at the dog who gave Spear a very disappointed look.

'Unless, of course, Jess is involved in some way.' Bridget looked as though she was speaking to the dog.

We watched one another. We had to go out there but we had no idea what was waiting for us. Was the boy really alive? Was Jess working with him or was she the killer? Were they both standing out there waiting, knowing what we'd said, knowing what they now had to do?

We slowly edged towards the door, eyeing one another. I looked out at the beating rain. I couldn't see anyone out there. The sky was the colour of wet flint now and sheets of rain came blowing down over the hills. A sudden crack of white light split the dark clouds, momentarily lighting up the surface of the sea. We looked at one another as if needing confirmation that we should go out there.

A bird screamed above us and wheeled out on the wind. The thick green waves reached up as if to grab its thin legs.

The bird's cry was enough to shake us from our doubts. We stepped outside.

The rain fell like small pebbles, dappling the scrub and sand around us. Mother and Aunt Charlotte turned their faces from the full force of it, closing their eyes and hunching their shoulders as soon as they stepped out. Bridget picked up the dog and buried it into her coat, her eyes round with fear. I turned to look out at the hills and my hair snaked round my face, instantly covering my eyes. I wiped it back, my face already running with rainwater. I held my arm up uselessly over my head and scanned the fields above us.

There was so much noise. The wind rushed over the grass, rippling waves through it as it ran down over the beach. The sea churned in great thick lines as though it was being ploughed by the wind. Sea and sky seemed to be merging, sealing us in to this dark world. The weather changed so fast here, it was as if it was an entirely different land from one moment to the next. My eyes squinted against the salty air. I knew already what I was looking for. I watched the open fields, waiting for them to appear. And there they were, floating against the dark sky as if they were stars on the sea. Just as they had been from the very start. The witch lights.

CHAPTER 31: A BLASTED HEATH

I pointed over towards the distant lights. 'That's where we need to be. I'm sure of it.'

We peered out through the dark air flecked with silvery lines of rain. Kemp clicked on his torch and highlighted the rain as if a thousand insects had suddenly swum into the white circle of light. We looked out in the direction of the bothy. Spear nodded. 'She's right. Someone's out there.'

The simple use of the word 'someone' created a nervous tension. No matter what our theories, no matter that the body was clearly missing and so was Jess, we had no real idea what we were heading towards. No one suggested splitting up. Not this time. There was too much fear among us.

Black clouds swam low across the hills, opening only for a moment. The marble moon cut through the gap and some weak light slipped over the waters. The waves rose high, rioting noisily against the shore.

We headed out, slowly at first, through the thick grass. I could feel the incline in the ground as the backs of my calves pulled tight. My legs were stippled with cold, weary with exhaustion already.

Every step grew more difficult as if the weather was beating us back towards the sea, away from the hills. Away from the witch lights that dotted the hillside.

'Are you sure Jess came out of the house with us?' Aunt Charlotte was panting and wiping the rain from her face with her sleeve.

'Of course, Charlotte.'

'How can you be so sure, Pandora? What if she's back at the house safe and sound? We're out here dying.'

'Don't worry, it takes longer than that to die from exposure,' Kemp attempted to reassure her.

'Young man, *I* shall not be exposing myself under any circumstances. No matter how dire the situation.' Aunt Charlotte struck out in front as if she'd found some new motivation.

The rain fell in fast lines, irregular, short white streaks in the air, intermittently broken like lines of Morse code. The wind drove it at strange angles to the land, dousing my face from every direction, rolling down my cheeks in cold beads that slipped under my collar.

I looked over at Mother's flushed face, raw with the cold. Determination ran through every feature. She glanced at me then frowned. Was she worried? She looked ahead and my eyes followed hers. She was looking at Spear, distrustfully. Surely we'd moved away from being suspicious of him.

'Mother,' I said in a low voice. 'You OK there?'

'No, clearly not.' She didn't look at me but continued to stare at Spear's back.

'You know that he can't see you giving him *The Look*, don't you?'

She switched *The Look* to me.

'He's trouble.'

I took a deep breath. 'Aren't they always, Mother?'

'Yes. Always.' She looked away.

The cold air was sharp in my throat. The wind savage. 'I don't even pretend to understand anymore. There's a boy out here with us somewhere who faked his death, who is very likely a killer. But you're worried about the one guy who might be able to lead us out of this just because you think . . .'

258

'Think what, Ursula? That he's just lost his wife? That he might be a terrifically desperate man? We still don't know for sure he isn't a killer and now a bodysnatcher!'

'Desperate? Thanks. You always do this and I just don't—'

'Now is not the time, Ursula.'

'Oh, it's never the time, is it?'

'Leave her alone.' Mirabelle had pulled alongside Mother as usual. 'You don't know anything about it.'

'And what the hell would you know?'

Kemp turned round to look at us. 'All right back there?'

We nodded. Spear turned and looked without slowing down. 'They do nothing but argue. I've never heard anything like it.'

'You need to leave your mother alone about this. Just trust that she knows what she's talking about. She knows when a man's trouble. She's got the scars to prove it.'

Mother glanced over in warning at Mirabelle.

'What?' I snapped. 'If you've got something to say, just say it. You've been dancing around this.'

Mother turned to Mirabelle and shook her head. Mirabelle looked frustrated. As usual they were having one of their guarded non-conversations that excluded me.

'Come on, dear.' Aunt Charlotte had fallen back a little and looked at me with concern. She hooked her arm through mine and gripped me tight to her. 'Give an old auntie a hand here.' She guided me away purposefully and I watched Mother and Mirabelle give each other those same deep looks.

'I wish she'd just come out and say it. She's been like this for months.'

'Oh, ignore her, dear. It's just Mirabelle. You know what she's like. She's scared like the rest of us. She just shows it differently. They both do.'

'Still bickering are we, ladies?' Bridget was alongside us, holding Mr Bojingles tight as if he was the only life jacket.

'Bugger off, Bridget,' I snapped.

She laughed, then started muttering something to the dog and looking sharply at Kemp and Spear. It was like she was putting some sort of hex on him. She turned to us eagerly. 'Let's go catch a killer!' She strode off with renewed vigour.

As we headed further out into the darkness, I could see the outline of the Druid stones jagged against the sky. Battered by sea spray and rain, this was an ancient scene, the sea its constant breath. I thought of Bottlenose's tales of men buried beneath them and wondered if they were there now, looking up at us from their time-worn graves. The bitter clouds hung low above these old, great monoliths as they had for centuries, pushing them further down into the earth. What did this place care if there were a few more deaths? We were nothing in the history of this place. Perhaps Mother had been right, this was the Isle of the Dead. We were chasing a dead man, after all.

The light flickered in and out of the horizon as if it was a low star reflecting in the sea. But it was too close for that and with every step, the light grew closer. The outline of the rough-stone bothy grew more distinct at the end of the field and snippets of that same whistled tune sailed on the wind. Fear squeezed tight on my stomach until it was a physical pain, a lump just below my ribs. I gripped Aunt Charlotte's arm and she looked at me.

'It'll be all right, girl,' she said firmly. 'We just go in, get the girl and wallop the lad. We can throw him back to the devil in the sea too if you want.' Aunt Charlotte was a strange kind of hero but somehow I was glad she was there.

The rain wasn't stopping, and we were close enough now that I could hear it drumming on the slate roof of the bothy. The light prickled through the shadows inside, moving as if guided by someone.

Spear stopped us all when we were still quite far down the field, but it was hard to place anything with accuracy in such darkness. He beckoned for us all to gather round him and held his finger to his lips. His eyes were set wide in warning.

When we'd formed a small group, he pointed towards the bothy, then to himself. His finger swept round the rest of the group then pointed firmly at the floor in a very clear signal that we should stay put.

Aunt Charlotte looked confused so I leaned over and whispered. 'He wants us to stay here. He's going in.'

She nodded. 'Righto. Ten-four, Big Budgie.'

Spear frowned.

'She means "Big Buddy",' Kemp clarified.

Spear filled his chest with air and looked decidedly irritated. He turned to set off.

'Be careful.' I don't know why I said that. It just came out. The rain dripped down my face unchecked.

He looked back and turned the sides of his mouth down, then started jogging towards the small building, his body scrunched tight and his head bent low. Kemp followed, which I'm not sure was really part of the plan.

Now we'd stopped, I started to feel the cold sinking further into my skin. My bottom lip began to shake and I moved from one foot to the other holding my arms around me. We were so exposed just standing there in the dark field. But there was nowhere else to go except the small grey bothy that watched us silently.

'Don't start with the dramatics,' Mirabelle warned me.

I closed my eyes.

'Mr Bojingles will freeze out here.' Bridget pulled her coat further round the dog. 'I vote we just go and knock on the door and see who's in there and then talk it all through like civilized people.'

We stared at her. Mirabelle shook her head. 'You're kidding, right? This is not some drawing-room denouement at cocktail hour.'

I caught Mother looking wistfully towards the bothy as if part of her had thought the tiny stone house might actually have a sneaky espresso martini hiding in there.

'There's a bloody knife-wielding maniac on the loose who pretended he was dead so he could kill people.'

'Now, we don't know that for sure, Mirabelle.' Aunt Charlotte tried to look reassuring which made it worse.

'The young lady, Jess, might have become truly unhinged and stolen the body of the boy to dress him up as her dead boyfriend.'

No one spoke.

'Wouldn't she just take her boyfriend's body for that?' Bridget asked.

'Maybe she wanted a younger model.'

'Aunt Charlotte, please!' I held my hands to my head. 'This is utterly inappropriate.'

'When has that ever bothered her?' Mirabelle sighed.

'Why don't you just go back to stalking my mother?'

Mirabelle paused and then leaned closer. 'Don't you dare.'

'Mirabelle, leave her!' Aunt Charlotte stepped forward.

'Why? You tell me why we're all tiptoeing around Little Miss Fragile again? We're all in danger.' Mirabelle spoke in a hushed voice that hissed constantly. She glanced across at Mother, who seemed very distracted. 'There's people being murdered and all anyone is worried about is whether *she* discovers that her father was an alcoholic philanderer.'

The world slowed around me. I couldn't feel the cold wind battering my face, I could barely see the two men running towards the bothy or the light flickering in its window. All I could think about was the dark shadow at the corner of my eyes, his head hung low and shoulders bent. He didn't need to speak to let me know the answer, but I still asked the question.

'*Is it true?*'

'What?' I could hear Mirabelle out there, outside my head, still talking. 'Why is everyone looking like that at me? She needed to know. I couldn't stand the martyred-saint nonsense anymore. We could die out here and all we're thinking about is her again and her bloody cheating father.'

I could feel Mother by the side of me. Her hand reached out and I instinctively pulled back. 'Ursula?'

'Is it true, Mother?' I looked into her face, daring her to answer.

Aunt Charlotte tried to link her arm through mine, but I pulled away. 'Look, we are outside a killer's house. Why don't we just focus on that. We need to—'

'No, there is no *we*,' I snapped. 'We're just a sad group of people thrown together.'

'That's most families, dear.' Aunt Charlotte tried again with holding my arm.

'*She's* not my family.' I stared at Mirabelle.

Mother looked at her too but didn't speak.

'Pandora . . .' Mirabelle looked weaker. 'I'm sorry. I'm stressed, I'm tired and all I hear is how wonderful *he* was.' She looked at me. 'He was no saint. There was someone else and you might as well know it now before we all die!'

Aunt Charlotte squeezed my arm. 'Don't listen to Mirabelle. She's just trying to—'

'Trying to what? Lie?'

I felt Mother's sigh. She closed her eyes and when she opened them to look at me again, I felt sure I could see the shadow of Dad reflected on the black beads of her pupils. 'Mirabelle has gone too far.'

'What?'

'Be quiet, Mirabelle. You've said enough.'

The rain poured down my face in fast-trailing rivulets. I could tell the shadow was looking at the side of my head, but I didn't look back at him.

Mother bowed her head. 'You didn't need to know.'

As I closed my eyes, it dislodged one lone, warm tear that fell much heavier than the rain along the turn of my face. 'Go away,' I whispered. 'Go away.'

'This is ridiculous,' Bridget began. 'We are hunting a killer out here in the wilderness, in a storm and we're doing your family meltdown again. For goodness' sake, really! Now is not the time.'

'I agree.'

'Oh, Mirabelle, you are the cause of all this!' Aunt Charlotte jabbed her finger at her. 'You always are . . . You just . . .'

Her voice drifted away and all I could hear was my own voice whispering, 'Go away.'

It was Mother who answered. 'We need to focus. Look at me. Ursula, Spear and Brendan have nearly reached the bothy. We need to be ready. We can deal with this later.'

'Go away.'

'We can't. We—'

'Not you! Him!' I shouted into her face.

I turned to look at his shadow. I looked straight at him and he looked back. 'Go away,' I whispered. He stood, watching me. Everyone watched me and then looked to the space in the air that I was staring at.

'Ursula?' Mother said softly.

I closed my eyes and turned my head to the side. When I looked back, his shape had gone. There was nothing but wind-whipped fields. A fierce darkness looked back at me.

'We need to move,' I said looking at the ground.

'Stop. Ursula.' Mother grabbed my arm.

'So we just wait here do we, in the middle of this nowhere, waiting to be picked off because we can't save ourselves? Because some man we don't know told us to?'

Mother stared at me.

'She's right.' Bridget sounded resolute. She picked up Mr Bojingles. He looked determined too. 'We should move. There is no point standing in the middle of a field listening to your family catastrophizing. I'd sooner die any other way.'

'OK. We go. Come on.' Aunt Charlotte nodded and began to walk. 'Come on!'

'I—'

'You've said enough, Mirabelle. Just move.' Aunt Charlotte turned to me and Mother. 'You too.'

Mother watched me and then nodded. 'OK.' She was quiet.

I took a long breath and felt the cold air linger in my chest. I nodded once but didn't look at any of them. I started to walk.

The rain was driving like grit into my face. The relentless tapping of it on my head was grinding. I bent low, staring at the ground, suddenly very aware of how exposed we were — out in a field with no cover from the rain. Or random killers.

I watched Spear turn to look back at our group moving towards him and saw his disappointment as Kemp approached. At the last moment, Kemp seemed to fall and do some sort of sudden army roll into the wall of the bothy. It was unclear whether this was an attempt at a military manoeuvre or he'd just fallen and was trying to style it out. Whatever it was, Spear looked furious.

The lights had stopped moving in the bothy as if someone had been alerted to us. As we drew closer, I felt sure I heard a small sob that was quickly silenced. All there was now was the constant rush of the rain and the sea. Another splash of light flared across the sky.

'What if Jess went willingly with him?' Aunt Charlotte was saying to Mother. Mother didn't answer. 'What if they've been acting together?'

'Let's just wait and see, all right.' Mother's frustration was growing.

'What if Spear's luring us out here to kill us?' No one answered Aunt Charlotte.

As we approached, I watched Spear inch towards the door. Kemp followed, copying him.

The light in the bothy started to move, quicker now and towards the door.

It disappeared for a moment.

'Spear!' I shouted. He glanced over and ducked down. 'He's at the—'

The door was wrenched back and a thin, dark shape hurled out. He fell over Kemp's back where he was now crouching low on the ground and landed on top of Spear. The shape reared up and the blade was high in the air before cutting down through the rain. Kemp's torchlight caught on the metal for a moment. It sunk down into Spear. We had discovered who Spear's blade was meant for. Spear.

'Shit!' Kemp was up and dragging the boy over onto his side. The slight frame fell easily into the mud and I saw his face, pale against the ground. I barely recognized him. His eyes shone and he breathed heavily through a wide, dark mouth. Then he started to smile. It was definitely the boy from the boat, his face smeared with mud and his hair spiked with rain. And, we'd been right. He was very much alive.

'Spear!' I ran the last few metres. The blade was still visible, standing up proud from his chest. Kemp was grappling with the boy.

Aunt Charlotte was running, the puddles splashing up around her, the tweed jacket flaring out behind as she dove through the air and crashed down on top of the strip of boy.

The sound of the sea washed in the background. 'Spear!' I shouted again.

The rain fell on Spear, sluicing the blood down into the mud. He didn't respond.

CHAPTER 32: THE SINS OF THE FATHER AND THE MOTHER

Aunt Charlotte was spreadeagled on top of the squirming lad. His legs stuck out into the mud behind her, his own boots, the boots Angel had worn for so short a time, were on his feet. The thin, white face was to the side, looking out into the darkness. And he was laughing. Great gales of laughter came out of him and spluttered into the mud pooling round his face.

I knelt down next to Spear.

Mother and Mirabelle ran towards us. Bridget walked with a rigid speed behind them, holding the dog close. I could hear her chuntering away. 'Mr Bojingles, stay vigilant.'

'Come on, Spear,' I shouted. I held him by the shoulders and looked down at the knife. The pool of blood was spreading across his camo jacket as if it was a new part of the pattern.

There was a groan. He was alive.

His eyes flickered open. He coughed and his face wrinkled in pain. He looked confused for a moment. His head fell to the side and he looked over at Aunt Charlotte holding the boy down. There was a flash of recognition on Spear's face and then another spike of pain took him.

He held his hand to his injured chest and seemed surprised to feel the knife there.

'Hey, you were right,' the boy shouted over at me. 'You pointed me in the right direction every time. So thank you.'

Aunt Charlotte frowned and pushed her hands into his chest.

He laughed. 'I did steal the knife to kill someone, and how poetic that it should be the knife's owner.'

'You little bugger.' Aunt Charlotte pushed with more determination. 'And it's not poetic if it doesn't rhyme.' She drew her knee into his abdomen. Kemp was in front of her and held the boy's shoulders down.

'Sins of the father, eh?' Nate clipped his head towards Spear.

Kemp looked down into his face. 'What are you talking about, boy?'

Nate looked up. 'I heard you, with her, the night before we sailed. You were in the Anchorage with that whore, Nell. My mother.'

Spear's breathing suddenly grew more stuttered.

'It's OK. It's going to be OK,' I said. Spear glanced at me and then back at Nate.

'This is where you die, Spear.' The lad smiled.

Aunt Charlotte ground her knee further down.

'Don't hurt him,' Kemp muttered.

'What the hell are you talking about — "Don't hurt him" — he's nearly killed Spear. And he would have done if I wasn't such a fan of WWF.'

'The World Wildlife Fund?' Bridget asked.

'No, she means the wrestling.' Mother was beside me now, but I didn't look at her.

The dog leaped from Bridget's arms and eagerly headed over to us, sniffed round the blade and started licking.

'Christ, get the dog away!' Spear tried to push the dog.

'Don't push Mr Bojingles,' Bridget scurried over and picked up the dog. 'How dare you!'

'We have a man down here, severely injured! You need to control your animal!' Mother had once more adopted a very military tone.

Spear groaned again and this time it sounded as though he was gargling on something. He closed his eyes.

'Stay with me, Spear!' It's strange how we borrow unreal phrases when unreal events unfold. I'd never imagined myself using these words, but then I'd never imagined being on an isolated island watching a man die.

Nate was moving frantically now, desperate to escape from under Aunt Charlotte. 'Not sure how long I can hold him,' she murmured.

Mother ran over and Mirabelle followed. They each took an arm and pinned him, while Aunt Charlotte remained with her knee on his chest. Kemp held tight to his shoulders.

The gale lashed round us. The boy laughed manically as he was held down.

At the bothy door, I could see Jess stagger and fall to the floor.

'Jess!' I shouted.

She nodded, her face pale in the darkness.

I looked down at Spear. Sweat was blistering on his forehead. I held his hand and felt him weakly squeeze my fingers.

'It's OK. Just don't move,' I whispered.

Spear coughed and the sound rattled in his throat. He looked at the knife sticking from the side of his chest and closed his eyes. 'We can't take that out.' He raised his hand to the knife, his fingers circling the area where it had punctured his clothes and skin. The cough bubbled up again. 'You met with Nell?' he said quietly but Kemp heard him. He squeezed his lips together and his face gathered as if he was in some way conflicted. His head dropped over to the side and he looked straight at Kemp.

Pain was etched deep in Spear's eyes now. The breath ruckled in his throat as if his chest was filling with the sea.

'Mate, mate, she only told me the night before you sailed.' There was a strange desperation in Kemp's voice now, a guilt. 'She said she knew this was her last trip. She wouldn't be coming back here again so she had something she wanted to tell me.'

Spear coughed again. His breathing was becoming more difficult.

'Spear, when she left here, eighteen years ago, when she left me for you, she was . . .' He paused and a conflicted look came over him. 'Spear, all those years ago, when she left here . . . Mate, Nell was pregnant.'

The space between Spear's eyebrows bunched tight.

'I didn't know. I swear,' Kemp said. 'It's why she didn't come to find you for nine months after she left. When we met in the Anchorage the other night, she told me that she had had the child quietly, with relatives and left him there in their care on a small island.'

'Grimsay.'

Slowly, we all looked at the boy. He'd stopped laughing and was lying very still, Kemp holding his shoulders, Aunt Charlotte still with her knee to him. His black hair was plastered against his head.

'Quite a fitting name for that place. There was nowhere more grim.' The boy's face twisted into a sneer. His low, soft voice had a strong Scottish accent. But there was menace in it. A deep bitterness.

'You knew.' Spear mouthed.

'What?' Kemp's mouth fell open. 'I . . . I knew nothing about him — this lad. Nell said nothing else, I swear. I've never seen him in my life before.'

'Oh,' Nate smirked, 'but that's not true, is it?'

Kemp paused for a moment and then realization seemed to spread across his face. 'Oh God, I remember you.'

Kemp turned to look at Spear and then round all of us. He sighed. 'I only know that this lad came up to me that night after I'd finished talking to Nell in the Anchorage. He asked if I sailed with Nell and I told him no. He seemed quite friendly. A little nervy but nothing else.' Kemp's head dropped. 'I told him *The Terror* was the boat he wanted and to go see Bottlenose and you, Spear. I had no idea he'd overheard our conversation.'

Nate laughed. 'I heard more than enough, you foolish man. So had Bottlenose, which was sad for him.' He laughed again. 'He was in that night and I went back in the bar and asked him if I could come aboard. The drunk old bastard, he'd heard your conversation, I'm sure of it. When he told the coffin boy story, I knew he was onto me and then when he put the bloody coin on me . . . well. It wouldn't have taken him long to work it all out. Should have kept his mouth shut. The pissed old bastard deserved to die.

'And so do you—' He nodded towards Spear — 'I tried in the house but the birds got in the way. Mummy dearest had been easy to kill. I thought I'd need your knife, stole it on the ship but it dropped out of my pocket on the beach and Crazy Woman over there picked it up.'

Nate's tongue passed over his teeth. 'I couldn't believe it! Mummy was so easy to push under, gasping and flailing.' He smiled. Mother glanced at me. 'But then I realized I could kill two parents with one stone if I was a dead man. I would have the freedom of a ghost to roam around, in and out of the house, through the windows. I used the bothy as a base then haunted you bastards whenever I could.' The lad squirmed, trying to escape.

'You're the witch lights aren't you?' I said slowly.

He sneered at me.

'You're the whistling man too?'

He nodded once and began whistling the sea shanty I'd heard so many times. Then he stopped. 'It was quite fun watching you clowns stumbling around, imagining witches and ghosts jumping out every minute. I'd gone to the house first but then you lot turned up. I had to make a run for it, but Spear came in the room disturbing all them birds. I enjoyed smacking you one over the head. After all, if it weren't for you I'd have had a chance at a decent life.'

'I heard you,' I said softly. 'Whistling.'

He laughed. 'I had to think fast if I was going to kill Daddy-o as well as Mummy. I tied my belt really tight around my wrist and rolled around, dead like in the sea. I almost froze to death! I slipped off the belt before you got to me but there'd been no need, you didn't even check properly that I was dead!'

Aunt Charlotte pushed her knee harder into him. 'You little bastard.'

'Then I was truly free! I could come and go as I pleased, getting rid of the people who stood in my way.' His face turned bitter. 'Angel knew I was alive, I could tell. He looked at me so strangely. I even heard him saying my boots were warm. So he had to go. And it felt good to kill some dick who'd been banging my mother. Silly Mummy had even told me just how to do it with one of her own so-called love tokens. She didn't know anything about love. I heard them cooing over each other on the boat talking about the bracelet. I just had to drop a few of those beads into his mouth and—' he clicked his fingers — 'dead,' he said.

Aunt Charlotte frowned. 'Mr Spear, I don't—'

Spear coughed again. 'Let him speak.'

Nate continued, slowly, savouring every word. 'I want you to know it all before you die, Spear, you bastard.

'Not a chance!' Aunt Charlotte pushed down.

'It's OK. Let him,' Spear spluttered. 'I need to know who she was.'

'Bottlenose was easier . . .' Nate said it wistfully as if he was enjoying the memory. 'I knew Crazy over there—' he glanced towards Jess — 'had the knife. I'd heard all that little display about the boots, which caused Angel's death. I climbed in through a window, stole into Jess's room and got the knife. Bottlenose was pissed and so in goes my sweet knife without any trouble or struggling. Even got my own boots back on the way out! I could chuck that sad man's massively uncomfortable ones back into the chapel and no one would be any the wiser.'

Spear groaned again and gripped my hand.

'And now you're on your way too. I'm done. So, there you are. She dumped me in hell, abandoned me so she could go round the world having fun — with him. They got what they deserved.'

'You're evil,' Bridget said firmly and pulled Mr Bojingles closer.

'Oh, am I? Have you any idea what it's like to live in these islands in the middle of nowhere, with no one but a pair of old bastards who don't even want you? Minute they were gone . . .' He paused to smile again. 'I went through their stuff. Searching their dirty little house. I knew what I needed. And I found it — a birth certificate, my birth certificate. And her name glaring back at me was right there, under the roof I'd slept beneath all of my life.

'She was easy to find online — a woman like that — all Insta-pretty and social-media-obsessed. "Here's me looking wistfully into a sunset while my baby rots." "This one is me being beautiful and ignorant of the life I abandoned." And then I saw it. "Here's me about to revisit the town of my past." *Coming home*, she posted. I didn't comment "*for some home truths*". I just set off. Back to Leverburgh. It was the only place I knew to go. Imagine my thrill when I heard that woman from Instagram, slightly older, slightly less filtered, telling her tale of dumping a baby on Grimsay eighteen years ago. There I was staring at Mummy and she didn't even know me.

'She was a cold beast flirting with Angel on that boat. She disgusted me.' He flicked his head to the side and looked straight at Spear. 'And now, Daddy, your death completes it.'

'You're not mine. You can't be. I . . .'

'What are you talking about?' Kemp cut in. He looked down into Nate's face. 'You're not his son. You're mine!'

We all watched Kemp in silence. 'Why else would she want to see me in the Anchorage?'

The boy lifted his head and stared into Kemp's eyes. 'What the hell— are you? I . . . couldn't hear all of it . . . but . . . but you can't be.' His face tightened resolutely. 'Well, that bitch left me, to grow up with old bastards who didn't

273

care if I lived or died. It was her who died for what she'd done. Though you will too.' He stared at Kemp. 'I swear it.'

Kemp shook his head slowly. 'I didn't know. I had no idea you even existed until she told me the night before you sailed when we met in the pub.'

The boy laughed. 'Well, she's at the bottom of the briny now. You should have seen her face. Last thing she heard was "Hello, Mum."' He shook with excitement.

'You bastard,' Spear breathed. His voice was so weak and he was losing consciousness.

'Spear, mate.' Kemp looked over earnestly at him. 'It was eighteen years ago, Spear. I promise you, I had no idea. It was just before she came after you.' Kemp leaned closer. 'She met you and everything changed. She told me that night she'd wanted nothing more than to sail off into the sunset. She loved you, not me.' He paused. 'But she couldn't sail away with her pirate captain and go on all these adventures if she was pregnant with another man's child. My child.'

'I'll kill you too!' Nate shouted, rearing up into Kemp's face.

Aunt Charlotte pushed him back down.

'I didn't know.' Kemp shook his head. 'She just left one night. I didn't hear from her for months. Next I heard, she was sailing on adventure tours with you and I was left here. I had no idea she'd even been pregnant. She'd just gone.'

Spear closed his eyes. 'She came to find me, nine months after I left Leverburgh. Said she couldn't stop thinking about me and that we were meant to be. I had no idea she'd . . .'

'It was all because of you!' Nate shouted. 'You bastard. Die!'

A white light was growing in the dark sky. The rain still thundered into our faces but a steady thudding beat was rising above the sound of the wind. The beam of light drew closer and the noise filled the air. It was the rhythmic pulse of rotor blades. As the helicopter drew into view, a voice shouted from the skies.

'This is Hebrides Mountain Rescue — we are about to land.'

274

CHAPTER 33: WE ALL NEED SAVING

Mother was wrong, I did need saving. We all did. There are moments, such as being marooned on an Outer Hebridean island with a killer, when we do need to be saved. And, thankfully, the Hebrides Mountain Rescue people proved to be very good at this. The local harbour master had noticed Kemp hadn't come back. He couldn't get in touch with him, Nate having smashed the radio to pieces, so he'd alerted the rescue team. Their drone had picked up the sign of fires and a broken boat on Orlon. It was pretty hard to explain why Aunt Charlotte was sitting on someone, but Nate didn't put up any fight with the rescue team. He just kept smiling and laughing and whistling.

* * *

We landed in Stornoway into a sea of flashing blue lights. The pilot had radioed ahead that not only did we have a critically ill man, but his attacker as well. Nate was escorted into a waiting police car, his strange, cruel smile still firmly in place. There were no relatives to inform of his arrest. Only Kemp.

Nate nodded to him as he was loaded into the waiting car. 'See you again someday, Daddy.'

Kemp made no response.

And did Spear survive?

Of course he did. He's a survivalist, after all, as he reminded us when the danger had passed. The wound was deep and he'd lost a lot of blood but he was rushed straight into the Western Isles Hospital in Stornoway, where they operated immediately.

The rest of us were taken into a private room to be checked over by doctors. Jess was treated for shock and dehydration. We waited eagerly for news of Spear's operation. Various police officers took our statements, their eyes widening and eyebrows rising with each new revelation and death.

When the full story emerged, the small community was swamped with media. Some of the locals relished it and gave interviews about survival courses and people coming in from out of town. But when the first member of the press realized just who the people on the island were, the Smart Women from the Slaughter House, our world was thrown under the intense glare of the spotlight again. How had we managed to find ourselves in another murderous situation? How did it feel to be stalked by death? I was tempted to say, 'No different to usual.' But I didn't.

There didn't seem to be a minute to talk to the others, especially not Mother. It was days before Mother and I were alone, sitting in the small hotel room. The grey net curtains only let in a weak light. And we talked.

We faced each other as if it was an interview. 'He was a good father to you,' Mother began with, 'and I could not shatter your illusions. He liked a drink though.'

I nodded, thinking of the only thing I took away from that island — Dad's hollowed-out Bible.

Mother said she didn't know the other woman's name but she'd heard her on the phone when she rang the house. 'Your dad always denied it, but I saw her at the funeral. She smiled at me, but she never spoke. Mirabelle took her away.'

We talked all afternoon. Mother said the things I knew she would, and I didn't even care if they were true. She just wanted to protect me, she didn't want me to get hurt — the predictable phrases. But all it really came down to was that

Mother had never really found a way to forgive Dad. The question was, could I?

Dad didn't appear for a few weeks. Not until we were back in London —only then did I see his dark shape in corners, his head bent in shame. It's still like that now. I don't know if it will ever go back to normal. Bob the Therapist says it's a good thing to let go of Dad's ghost but then he also advised that I should continue to live with Mother for my recovery. So he doesn't get everything right. I suppose it's familiar at least.

We went to Ryan's funeral first. Jess didn't speak to us. She didn't speak to anyone. Her recovery looked like it hadn't really started and wouldn't do for some time.

Angel's was next and his mother was there, as were a number of other women wearing the silver charms he'd given them.

And finally there was Nell's funeral back on Harris, where she grew up. It was a small affair in Scarista with a wake at the Anchorage in Leverburgh. It was a joint send-off for her and Bottlenose as he had nobody else. Nell's body hadn't been found. It's still out there somewhere.

It seemed strange to go back. The town was exactly the same, the air still fresh with the smell of seawater. Kemp was right where we'd first met him. He'd not been to see Nate yet, but he said he would one day, when everything settled. Nate had been transferred to the State Hospital in Carstairs, for high-security psychiatric patients. Kemp wanted to stay here in Leverburgh and try and salvage his survival business, which, although quite infamous, wasn't attracting many bookings now.

And then there was Spear. He'd recovered enough to organize the funerals for Nell and Bottlenose. I hadn't seen him since we'd left Scotland although we'd texted a couple of times, but it had been awkward. The nature of his relationship with Nell had been dragged through the press along with his wife's character.

When I saw him, standing there by the harbour, he looked like a man hollowed-out by life. He stood outside the Anchorage looking towards the sea, staring out into the waves as if he was still searching them for her.

'All right?' He gave me a weak smile and pulled at his tie until it loosened.

I walked towards him and held the glass of warm white wine close to my chest. 'It was a nice service. I mean, this is all nice too. You know. You did a good job.'

'Thanks. I didn't know what else she'd want.' He looked down at his feet. 'Turns out I didn't know her very well at all.'

Anything I said would sound fake and contrived. 'Well, I thought I'd come and say hi.' I started to walk back inside.

'Listen,' he said hurriedly, 'I'm thinking of going on a bit of a trip, down to the West Country. Get far away from all this. I've got a mate down there and I'm going to get a boat and—'

'Mr Spear, you wouldn't be trying to take my daughter back out on the water, would you?' Mother stood at the door to the bar.

He took a deep breath. 'Not at all, Mrs Smart. It was just an idea.'

'Well, I'd be grateful if you didn't have any more of those around my daughter, thank you.' She stared at him then flicked her eyes towards me. 'Ursula, come inside soon. Bridget's fed all the cocktail sausages to Mr Bojingles and he's been ill in Mirabelle's bag. Your aunt's found the rum and an old sailor. I'll need your help.' She gave me a knowing look. 'After you've said goodbye to Mr Spear.' She made it have an air of finality.

I started to walk back towards the door but paused and turned to Spear. 'Listen, when this is all over, when it all dies down, call me. I think I can talk her round. We'd all love a little holiday, I'm sure.' I walked back inside.

'We?' I heard him say.

I smiled to myself.

THE END

278

ACKNOWLEDGEMENTS

I've never really felt worthy of doing this before, but if I miss anyone, I'll make sure you're in Book 3 (cunningly slipped in a mention of third book there!).

First of all, a massive thank you to Joffe Books, which is like a great big, warm family, and not at all like the Smarts! Jasper, I will never be able to thank you enough, for taking a chance on me. You have not only given me my dream, but you've made it the best job in the world! Thank you. And thank you to lovely Emma, who has been so inspiring and constantly supportive. And is a very wonderful person! To Nina, Annie and Laura for being utterly wonderful, kind and always having the answer! You guys are amazing. Also, to Cat and Laurel and all the editorial team for so much care and attention. To all the lovely people in promotions. Jill, Bev and Alyson especially have taken me under their wing from that very first sausage roll and a drink. Your parties are the best online! And to all the other Joffe authors, Janice, Joy, Helen, Charley, Judi, Charlie, Jeanette and all of you who have been so warm and welcoming. Especially Margaret Murphy who has always been ready to help and give advice. Thank you so much, Margaret. You are fabulous!

Thanks also to everyone at EAA and for the opportunity to do the wonderful Story sessions. Thank you to the D20s for all your help, inspiration and Friday zooms. To Venetia and everyone at the Barnes Bookshop for your support over the years. And to all the fabulous Smart Women readers who send me such lovely gifts and messages, and post wonderful reviews! It's nothing without you!

To my amazing family, who have supported me all the way. Thank you for putting up with all the talk about the book and the endless Agatha Christie films. Delilah and James, I love you beyond any words I can put in a book. Thank you. You are the best kids a mother could wish for. Thank you to my darling Delilah for your incredible brilliance, ideas and love. And to James for always being ready to talk about a plot or Lego or, as we discovered, both combined. And for all the hugs and love. Especial thanks to Sarah, you have always been there with love, support, reading and advice. Thank you. Catherine, thanks for all the reading and for being there to help whenever I've asked. Thanks to my mother for maintaining a full library of my work and to Amanda for getting me my celeb shots!

And finally, to Kev for all the years of love and support. For the wonderful days. For quietly lifting me up whenever I fall and for taking such good care of all my dreams. I love you.

ALSO BY VICTORIA DOWD

SMART WOMAN'S MYSTERY SERIES
Book 1: THE SMART WOMAN'S GUIDE TO MURDER
Book 2: BODY ON THE ISLAND

Thank you for reading this book. If you enjoyed it please leave a review on Amazon or Goodreads.

We love to hear from our readers. If there is anything we missed or you have a question about then please get in touch: feedback@joffebooks.com

Join our mailing list to get new releases and great deals every week from one of the UK's leading independent publishers.

www.joffebooks.com